KT-371-426

What NOT to Do if you turn INVISIBLE

What **NOT** *to Do* if you turn INVISIBLE

ROSS WELFORD

schwartz & wade books • new york

 Published in the United States by Schwartz & Wade Books, an imprint of Random House Children's Books, a division of Penguin Random House LLC, New York. Originally published in paperback by HarperCollins Children's Books, London, in 2016.

Schwartz & Wade Books and the colophon are trademarks of Penguin Random House LLC.

Visit us on the Web! rhcbooks.com
Educators and librarians, for a variety of teaching tools, visit us at RHTeachersLibrarians.com

Library of Congress Cataloging-in-Publication Data
Name: Welford, Ross, author.
Title: What not to do if you turn invisible / Ross Welford.
Description: First U.S. edition. | New York : Schwartz & Wade Books, [2018] | "Originally published in paperback by HarperCollins Children's Books, London, in 2016"—Title page verso.
Summary: When thirteen-year-old Ethel Leatherhead becomes invisible, her best friend, Boydy, helps keep her secret while she seeks a way to become visible again, keep herself safe, and solve the mystery of her birth.
Identifiers: LCCN 2017037018 (print) | LCCN 2017049585 (ebook) | ISBN 978-0-399-55152-9 (trade) | ISBN 978-0-399-55153-6 (glb) | ISBN 978-0-399-55154-3 (eBook)
Subjects: | CYAC: Invisibility—Fiction. | Secrets—Fiction. | Acne—Fiction. | Grandmothers—Fiction. | Identity—Fiction. | Adventure and adventurers—Fiction.
Classification: LCC PZ7.1.W4355 (ebook) | LCC PZ7.1.W4355 Wh 2018 (print) | DDC [Fic]—dc23

The text of this book is set in 12.25-point Whitman.
Book design by Rachael Cole

Printed in the United States of America
10 9 8 7 6 5 4 3 2 1
First U.S. Edition

To Mum, with love

Part One

Just before I fell asleep, I could see myself. I was visible, and I knew who I was. That was before.

I'm not sure what actually wakes me: the brightness of the tanning bed's UV tubes, or Lady nudging her food bowl past the door between the hallway and the garage.

The purplish lights are so bright that even when I screw my eyes up they're still blinding me.

Have I been asleep?

Why didn't the timer go off?

How long have I been here?

Crowding out those questions, though, is one main thing, and that is how thirsty I am. My tongue's not even sticking to my mouth, but scratching around inside it. I summon up enough spit to at least get my mouth working.

I lift the lid of the tanning bed and swing my legs over the side. There's a little pool of sweat—"perspiration," Gram would say—left where I've been lying. I'm still blinded by the lights and I'm blinking hard, but—and this is strange—blinking doesn't seem to make anything go dark, although there are spots and flashes behind my eyes.

With one hand, I grope for the switch on the side of the tanning bed, and off go the lights.

That's better, but only a bit. I still feel awful. I have a splitting headache and I sit for a while.

I should have tested the timer first. As I watch it, the old digital clock on the garage wall flips over the final digit to 11:05 a.m.

Oh. My. God.

I've been under those lights for, like, an hour and a half. Hello, sunburn! Pale skin, red hair (well, auburn), galloping acne, and severe sunburn: what a combination.

I stare ahead, letting my eyes become accustomed to the dusty gloom of the garage. There's the old rolled-up hallway carpet, my kiddie bike that somehow we haven't chucked away yet, some cardboard boxes of clothes for the church, and raindrops spattering the single narrow window in the door that leads to the backyard.

Probably twenty, even thirty seconds have gone by since I woke up.

Then my phone rings. I look down at it lying on the garage floor and see that it is Elliot freakin' Boyd—which is not his full name, obviously. I'm not in the mood to talk to him, so I reach down to switch my phone to silent and let it go to voice mail.

It is a moment that will stay with me forever.

A moment so strange and terrifying that it's quite hard to describe, but I'll give it my best shot.

You see, at first I don't notice that I have become completely invisible.

And then I do.

CHAPTER ONE

The actions of reaching down, picking up my ringing phone, finding the SILENT button, pressing it, and staring at the screen while the phone vibrates in my hand and then stops . . . all those things are so absolutely *normal* and everyday that I think my brain just fills in the missing stuff.

Missing stuff like my hand, and fingers.

It must be a bit like watching a cartoon. Everyone knows that a cartoon, or any sort of film, for that matter, is really a sequence of still pictures. When you watch them quickly, one after the other, your brain fills in the gaps so that it doesn't look all jerky.

I think that's what my brain and eyes do in those two or three seconds that it takes to switch off my ringer. They just "see" my hand because they *expect* to see it there.

But not for long.

I blink, and look down at my phone on the floor. Then I look at my hand. I actually hold my hand in front of my face and turn it around.

It is not there.

OK, stop for a minute. Actually hold your hand in front of your face. I'll wait.

It is there, isn't it? Your hand? Of course it is.

Now turn it round and examine the other side. This is exactly what I was doing a few seconds ago, only my hand wasn't—isn't—there.

At this stage, I'm not scared or anything. More confused.

I think, *That's weird. Has the tanning bed affected my mind?* Like, am I still half asleep, or dreaming, or having a hallucination or something?

I look down at my legs. They're not there either, although I can touch them. I can touch my face. I can touch every bit of me, and feel it, but I just cannot see it.

I don't know how long I'm sitting there, just looking again and again at where I should be. It's several seconds, but probably not as long as a minute. I'm going through things in my mind, like: *Has this happened before? Is this in any way normal? Is it my eyes—have I been temporarily blinded by the strong UV light?* Except I can see other things—just not me.

Now I'm scared, and my breathing has become a bit rapid. I stand up and go to the sink in the corner of the garage, where there's a mirror.

That's when I scream. Just a little one—more a gasp, really.

Imagine, if you can, standing in front of a mirror and seeing nothing at all. Your face does not look back at you. All you can see is the room behind you. Or the garage, in this case.

After gasping, I realize what's going on. I shake my head, smile, and even give a little chuckle. I tell myself, *OK, so you must be dreaming.* And—wow!—this is a vivid one! It really feels real. You know how some dreams are obviously dreams, even as you're dreaming them? Not this one! This one is as real a dream as I have ever had, and I start to think it's quite good fun. Nonetheless, I run through the Am I Dreaming? checklist, blinking, pinching myself, telling myself, *Wake up, Ethel, it's just a dream.*

Except, when I'm done, I'm still there, in the garage. This is one stubborn dream! So I do it all again, and again.

Nope, not a dream.

Definitely not a dream. I stop smiling right there.

I close my eyes tight and nothing happens. That is, I *feel* my eyelids tightening, *but I can still see.* I can see around the garage, even though I *know* I have my eyes shut tight—screwed up, in fact.

I put my hands over my eyes, and I can *still* see everything.

In my stomach there's a lurch of fear, dread, and terror, which is a horrible combination when they all come together.

Without warning, I throw up into the sink, but I can't see anything coming out. I hear it splatter. I taste the hot puke in my mouth. Then, in a second or two, it materializes as I watch: my half-digested cornflakes.

I run the tap to wash it away. I put my hand into the stream of water and the water takes its shape. I stare, awe-struck, as I lift a palmful of water to my thirsty mouth and this bubble-like *piece* of water rises up before me. I suck it up, then look in the mirror again: for a second my lips are almost visible where the water has touched them. I can just make out the water as it starts to go down my throat, and then it's gone.

I am consumed with a horror that is more intense than anything I have ever felt before.

Standing in front of the mirror, gripping the sides of the sink with my invisible hands, with my brain practically throbbing with the effort of processing this . . . this . . . *strangeness,* I do what anyone would do.

What you would do.

I scream for help.

"Gram! GRAM! *GRAM!*"

A WARNING

I'm going to tell you how I got to be invisible, and discovered a whole load of other stuff as well.

But if I'm going to do that, you need a bit of what my teacher Mr. Parker calls "backstory." The stuff that led up to me being invisible.

Stick around for a couple of chapters. I'll keep it brief, and then we'll be back in the garage, with me being invisible.

However, the first thing I'd better do before I continue is to warn you: I am not a "rebel."

I only say this in case you're hoping I'm going to be one of those daredevil kids who are always getting into trouble and being "sassy" to grown-ups.

That is, unless you count becoming invisible as getting into trouble.

As for the time I swore at Mrs. Abercrombie: that was an accident, as I have said a thousand times. I meant to call her a "witch"—which, I admit, is rude enough in itself, but not as rude as the word I used by mistake, which rhymes with it. It got me into a *lot* of trouble with Gram. To this day, Mrs. Abercrombie thinks I'm a very rude girl, even though it was more than three years ago and I wrote her a letter of apology on Gram's best notepaper.

(I know she's still angry, because her dog, Geoffrey, snarls at me. Geoffrey snarls at everyone, but Mrs. Abercrombie always says, "Stop it, Geoffrey"—except when he snarls at me.)

Anyway, usually I just sit quietly at the back of the room at school, minding my own business, getting on with my stuff—la-la-la, don't-bother-me-and-I-won't-bother-you kind of thing.

But you know what grown-ups say, in that way they have that's designed to make them seem clever: "Ah, you see—it's always the quiet ones, isn't it?"

That's me. A "quiet one." So quiet that I'm almost invisible.

Which, come to think of it, is quite funny.

CHAPTER TWO

How far back do you want to go?

If you ask me, it all started with the pizza thing. That was what got me so upset that I kind of lost a bit of my mind, and then ended up losing a lot more.

This is how it happened.

Jarrow Knight—who else?—shouted, "Pizza delivery!" when I walked into the class, and pretty much everyone laughed. Not an LOL sort of laugh, more a spluttering cackle. Most people in the class are not *actually* cruel.

I didn't get it at first. I had no idea it had anything to do with me. In fact, I thought it was some joke that I had walked in on, and so I smiled and laughed a bit as well, like you do when you don't want to feel left out.

That must have looked odd, I realize in hindsight.

Then, a couple of days later, Jarrow, her brother, and some others were walking past me when I was talking to the girls outside the chemistry labs, and Jarrow said in a loud-ish voice, "Did you order the American Hot, Jez?" and they high-fived, while Kirsten and Katie looked at their feet.

Do you get it? It still hurts to remember. (There's going to be quite a lot of hurting and remembering, so we may as well get used to it.)

"Pizza delivery" was a reference to my face.

"Pizza face" = acne. That is, spots and zits and boils and the whole pimply shebang. You get it, yeah? The reference, not acne.

My face supposedly resembles the surface of a pizza. Hilarious. It doesn't, anyway. It's not as bad as that.

Acne on a twelve-year-old? I know, it's kind of early. Even Dr. Kemp says I'm "at the earlier end of the spectrum," but it's not freakish. No, "freakish" we'll reserve for the acne itself, which is "towards the more severe end of the spectrum." That's nice family-doctor-speak for "Jeez, you've got it *bad*."

I'll spare you the details. You might be eating while you're reading this, and the details are not very nice.

So that was about three months ago. I realized a couple of things with those words, "pizza face":

1. My policy of keeping a low profile at school had met with only limited success. Everyone knows

Acne Girl. Up till that point, most of the mean stuff had been directed at Elliot Boyd, which was fine by me. Now *I* was a target too.

2. I honestly think some people reckon you can *catch* acne. I mean, I'm not some saddo who spends the entire day alone, surrounded by people taunting her. It's just that the whole "best friends" thing is taking longer than I expected and I wonder if the acne is the cause. Gram says, "Just be yourself," which sounds like good advice. I guess it *is* good advice if you have a reasonable idea of who you are—and I do. Or at least, I did, until everything started to go wrong. Gram also says, "If you want a good friend, then be a good friend." She's full of stuff like that. I sometimes think she collects it. Problem with that one is that there is a distinct lack of people around to be a friend to.
3. Jarrow Knight is a total nightmare. That's not exactly a revelation, but she and her twin brother together are pure poison.
4. I have got got *got* to do *something* about my skin.

My acne started about a year ago with a single tiny pimple on my forehead. That pimple, I like to think, was sent as an advance scout by the Acne Army. It reported back to Pimple HQ, and within weeks a full regiment of spots and blackheads had encamped on my face. Nothing I did could beat them back.

And then the Acne Army started colonizing other parts of me. My neck hosted a small platoon of boils, which are large, shiny, and painful. My chest had a company of tiny blackheads, which occasionally grew into whiteheads with pus in them, and within two months there was an expeditionary force annexing my legs.

Worst of all, though, Gram doesn't really take me seriously, and that is driving me nuts.

"Spots, darling? You poor thing. I had spots too, and so did your mum. It's just a phase. You'll grow out of it."

Even before the pizza incident, school had become *much* less fun than it had been in elementary school. It was just a coincidence, but at the same time all this was happening, Flora McStay—who was probably my best friend—moved to Singapore, and Kirsten Olen was moved to a different class and started hanging out with the Knight twins.

Of whom more later.

The point is, I needed a plan to get rid of the acne, and that's how the tanning bed and the Chinese medicine entered my life.

And, no, becoming invisible wasn't part of the plan. That would definitely be "at the extreme end of the spectrum."

Nor—in case it needs to be said—was getting any closer than strictly necessary to Elliot Boyd.

CHAPTER THREE

So, we're still on backstory and you're still around, which is good.

Elliot Boyd, eh? "Smelliot" Boyd, as he's known, because someone once made the joke and it kind of hangs around him like his smell is supposed to.

The kid no one likes.

Is it his height? His weight? His hair? His accent?

Or, in fact, his smell?

It could be any of them, and all of them. He's a big bear of a boy, as tall as a couple of the teachers, with a large stomach, and a chin with a fuzz of blond hair on it that I imagine he thinks disguises the fact that there's another chin beneath it.

As for his smell, to be honest, he doesn't seem to smell *that* bad, though I go to some lengths not to test the widely held belief that he is a stranger to soap and deodorant by simply avoiding him.

I think it's his manner that grates on people. Overconfident, pushy, cocky, loud, and—my favorite, this one—"bumptious." That was Mr. Parker's word, and he's very good with words.

You know what, though? I think it's just because he's from London. Honestly. People were against him from day one because he started bad-mouthing Newcastle United (he's an Arsenal fan, or so he claims). Round here, unless you've got a very good excuse, you follow Newcastle. Possibly Sunderland or Middlesbrough. But definitely not a London football team—not even, it turns out, if you're actually from London.

Boyd came into our class on the first day of Year Eight. No one knew him, so you'd think he would have kept his head down a bit, but no. I *think* he thought it was funny, what he did on his first day—you know, bold and a bit cheeky, but it didn't come across like that.

As well as teaching physics, Mr. Parker's our form teacher. He does the attendance and stuff. He clapped his hands and cleared his throat.

"Welcome back, you lucky people, to the northeast's finest *edifice* of *erudition*. I trust you all had a restful break? Splendid."

He talks like that a lot, does Mr. Parker. He used to be an actor and he wears a cravat, which—incredibly—looks quite cool on him.

"We have a new addition to our class! All the way from sunny London . . . Thank you, Mr. Knight, booing is for *boors*. . . . Please give it up for Mr. Elliot Boyd!"

Now, at this point, the class—who had done this routine a couple of times before with new kids—would usually applaud on Mr. Parker's cue, and the new kid would look all shy and smile a bit and go red and that would be that.

Elliot Boyd, though, immediately stood up and raised both hands in the air in a triumphal gesture and said loudly, "Ar-sen-al! Ar-sen-al!"—which killed the applause dead. To make matters worse, he added, in his best London accent, "Wot? You lot ain't never 'eard of a propah footbaw team?"

Wow, I thought at the time, *way to become instantly unpopular, Elliot Boyd!*

At that moment, at least half the class decided they hated him.

Yet it didn't seem to put him off, or make him any less pushy. Elliot Boyd was like one of those large, shaggy dogs that lollop up to other, smaller dogs in the park and freak them out.

Worse, he then started to hang around *my* locker after school, as if—just because we shared part of the route home—we should automatically be friends.

Fat. Chance.

I would have carried on ignoring him, except he was about to become part of what happened, and how I ended up turning invisible.

<u>THINGS I HAVE TRIED FOR ACNE</u>

1. **Good Old Soap and Water. This was Gram's first suggestion. "It worked for me," she said. And I had to stop myself from saying, "Yeah, but that was back in the Dark Ages of the twentieth century." Besides, the Good Old Soap and Water treatment comes from the idea that people get spots because they don't clean their faces, and that's not true.**
2. **Cleansers and Wipes. They just mean that my spots are shining out like beacons from a *really clean* face. I sometimes wonder if these products actually make the spots worse.**
3. **Cutting Out Fats. That was a horrible month. This theory is based on the fact that my skin is sometimes quite oily (and *there's* an understatement to frame and hang on your wall). So if I didn't eat butter, or cheese, or milk, or fried stuff, or salad dressings, or—as it turned out—**

anything delicious at all, then my face wouldn't be greasy. Didn't work. *And* I was hungry.

4. Garlic and Honey. Every morning, I would chop up three cloves of garlic and eat them with a large spoonful of runny honey. Gross. And ineffective.
5. Spot Cream. This involved rubbing a cream into my face at night. Oddly, it's quite an oily cream, which you'd think would make the acne worse, but it didn't. Nor did it make it any better.
6. Good Old Fresh Air. Another one of Gram's suggestions. Goes with Good Old Soap and Water. The only one to benefit from this was Lady, who for about a month got extra walks, until I noticed that my face was no different. Sorry, Lady.
7. Homeopathy. There are about five homeopathic medicines that are supposed to work for acne. None of them worked for me.
8. Nettle Tea. Tastes as bad as it sounds. Worse, actually.
9. Vitamin B_5. All over the Internet as the "miracle cure." Next.
10. Antibiotics. This was what Dr. Kemp finally

recommended on my second visit, after I showed him the list above. One Septrin tablet daily for a grand result of . . . no difference at all.

11. The latest one: Dr. Chang His Skin So Clear. An Internet purchase. Gram said it looked dodgy and refused to buy it for me, so I had to resort to subterfuge. Dr. Chang, like Elliot Boyd, plays a big role in how I came to turn invisible.

CHAPTER FOUR

Gram tells me that Mum had acne when she was my age, yet she grew up to be "such a beautiful young lady."

She was. In the picture in my room she has shortish reddy-blond hair and these massive, slightly sad eyes. It sometimes makes me think she knew she would die young, but then I look at other pictures where she's laughing and I think she wasn't really sad at all. Just—I don't know—a bit . . . manic?

I hardly remember her, in case you're wondering if I'm upset about it. She died when I was three. Cancer.

My dad had already left by then. Gone, disappeared. "And jolly good riddance too" was Gram's verdict. She can hardly bear to say his name (which is Richard, though to me he looks more like a Rick), and the only picture I have of him is a grainy snap taken shortly after I was born, with Mum holding me, and Dad next to her, smiling. He's skinny, with a beard, hair longer than Mum's, and dark glasses on, like some sort of rock star.

"He turned up at the hospital drunk," said Gram during

one of our (very) occasional conversations about it. "It was his usual state."

Mum and Dad were not married when I was born, but they got married later. I took Mum's last name, Leatherhead, which is Gram's too. It's there on my birth certificate:

Birthday: 14 August
Birthplace: St. Mary's Hospital, London
Mother's name: Lisa Anne Leatherhead
Occupation: teacher
Father's name: Richard Michael Malcolm
Occupation: student

And so on.

I'll give you the brief version. It's pretty much all I've ever had, anyway. Gram is not keen to talk about it, I think because it upsets her too much.

Gram moved to London when she was little, and she grew up there. She and Grampa split up sometime in the 1980s. He now lives in Scotland with his second wife (Morag? Can't remember). Mum was twenty-six when she had me. She and Dad weren't planning a family, Gram says; I just kind of happened.

My dad disappeared when I was little. It wasn't a disappearance that involved the police or anything. There was no mystery. He just "left the scene" and was most recently heard of in Australia, according to Gram.

The last time we talked about him was a few weeks ago.

We've always had tea, Gram and I, when I come in from school, ever since I was about seven. I know: most seven-year-olds drink juice or milk, but not me. Tea and cake, or biscuits. And none of your mugs: it's made in a proper teapot, with china cups and saucers, plus a sugar bowl, even though neither of us takes sugar. It's just for show. I didn't really like tea at first. It was too hot. I love it now.

In school, we had been talking about careers in Mr. Parker's health lesson. I was at the back, keeping quiet as usual, when the talk came round to what people's parents did and how people sometimes follow their parents' careers. All I knew about my dad was that he had been a student, according to my birth certificate.

I had been planning this for a day or two, how to bring it up. I asked Gram as she poured the tea why Dad had disappeared, as a lead-in to asking what he'd been studying.

Instead of answering me directly, she said, "Your father led a very wild life, Ethel."

I nodded without really understanding.

"He drank heavily. Took far too many risks. I believe he wanted to live without responsibility."

"Wh . . . why?"

"I really do not know, darling. I suppose it comes down to weakness of spirit. He was cowardly and irresponsible. Some men are not equipped to handle the demands of fatherhood," said Gram. Her glasses had slid down her nose and she looked at me over the top of them as she spoke. "I think perhaps your father was one of them."

It was the nearest she ever got to saying something kind about him. It was rare for her to mention him without also using the words "drunk" and "childish." Whenever she talks about him, her shoulders stiffen and her lips go tight, and you can tell she'd rather talk about anything other than my dad.

We never got as far as what he was studying, because Gram changed the subject by saying how she'd told off a young man that morning who had his feet up on the seats of the Metro.

So anyway, now it's just Gram and me, back where Gram was born, on the blustery northeast coast in a town called Whitley Bay. According to Gram, though, we don't live in Whitley Bay—we live in Monkseaton, which is a slightly posher bit that most people would say starts at least three or four streets further west. I still think of it as Whitley Bay. So now we happily live in the same house, but apparently in different towns.

Well, I *say* it's just Gram and me. There's Great-Gran too, who is Gram's mum. She's not exactly here very much. She's very nearly a hundred, and "away with the fairies," says Gram, but not in a mean way. She had a stroke years ago, which is when your brain bleeds; there were "complications," and she never properly recovered.

Great-Gran lives in an old people's home in Tynemouth, about two miles away. She doesn't ever say much. The last time I visited her, my spots were really bad, and she lifted up her tiny hand from under her shawl and stroked my face. Then she opened her mouth to say something, but nothing came out.

I sometimes wonder what would have happened if she *had* said something. Would it have changed what happened next?

CHAPTER FIVE

He was with me. Again. Making three times that week.

This was just a couple of days before I turned invisible, so we're nearly back to that.

"Awright, Effow?" he said. "You headin' home? I'll walk wif you, eh?"

It's not like he gave me any choice, appearing just as I was shutting my locker, as if he'd been lying in wait.

(I've looked up "bumptious," by the way. It means "full of yourself," and that's a good description of Elliot Boyd. There are plenty of other things about him that annoy me. "Effel" is one, or, as he says it, "Effow." I know it's just his accent, but, saddled as I am with a name from a hundred years ago, it would be nice to have it pronounced properly.)

So we walked home, Elliot Boyd keeping up a near-constant commentary on his current favorite topic: the Whitley Bay lighthouse. At least it was a change from him trying to show me card tricks, which was last month's obsession.

The lighthouse is there at the end of the beach. It doesn't

do anything, apart from appear on postcards. It doesn't even light up, which really bugs Elliot Boyd. (And only him, so far as I can tell.)

I have learned—without wanting to know:

1. This one was built in eighteen something-or-other, but there's been a lighthouse there forever, practically.
2. It was once the brightest lighthouse in Britain. I suppose that is *sort of* interesting.
3. You can get up to the top via a back door that's never locked.

There's something a bit touching about his enthusiasm. It's probably because he's not from around here. For everyone else, it's just the disused lighthouse at the end of the beach, you know? It's just kind of . . . there.

For Elliot Boyd, though, it's a way of getting people to like him. I have a feeling he pretends not to care what people think, and secretly cares a lot, and he hopes that taking an interest in something so local could be his way.

I may be wrong, of course.

He may be:

a) a tiresome nerd, or
b) trying to hide something behind his constant blabber-

ing. I have noticed that he never talks about himself or his parents; it's always about some *thing.* I could be wrong. It's just a hunch. I'm going to test it soon. I'm going to ask him something about his family and see how he reacts.

Anyway, I'd kind of switched off and I was letting him chatter on, because there was a shop coming up on the right that I'd had my eye on for a couple of weeks.

Whitley Road is a long strip of half-empty coffee shops, charity shops, nail salons ("rather common," according to Gram), and—next door to each other—two tanning salons, Geordie Bronze and the Whitley Bay Tanning Salon, which wins the prize for the least imaginative shop name on the street.

It was the window of Geordie Bronze that I was looking at. There was a huge handwritten sign saying *Closing Sale,* and if shops could wear a smile there would *definitely* have been a smug one all over the face of its next-door competitor.

I just didn't have the heart to tell Elliot Boyd to shut up/go away/stop bothering me about the lighthouse and some plan he'd got, but I was wishing he'd give it a rest.

Who. Cares?

"Honestly, Effow, it wouldn't be 'ard! Get a few of us

togevver, make a little campaign website, an' that. Call it 'Light the Light'—you know, like the song?"

He started singing. In the street, and not under his breath either.

"Light up the light, I need your love tonight! Dee dee something something . . . love tonight!"

People turned to look.

"It's a landmark, innit? It should be shinin' out—a beacon to the world. Otherwise what's the point of havin' it there?"

On and on he went. He'd done this "Lighthouse Facts" thing at school during homeroom a few days earlier. No one had paid much attention. The general opinion was that he is/was nuts.

Most of the lights were off inside Geordie Bronze, but there was a woman sitting at the reception desk reading a magazine.

"I'm going in here," I said, and I moved to enter. "You don't have to wait."

"Ah, I'm all right, fanks, Eff. I'll just wait here for you. It's . . . you know, it's a girl's place, you know?"

I knew what he meant. Tanning salons, like nail salons and hairdressers', are not the natural habitat of a teenage boy.

As for me, talking to strangers is one of the things that

Gram thinks is really important. She definitely thinks shyness is "not to be indulged."

"Anyone above the age of ten," she told me on my tenth birthday, "should have learned to hold her head up and speak clearly, and if you do that, you are equal to anyone."

So I straightened my back and pushed the door, which tinkled a bell as I walked in, making the girl at the desk look up from her magazine.

She had extra-blond hair extensions and she was chewing gum. She had on a white(ish) tunic that buttoned down one side, like dental hygienists wear, and its color made her tanned face seem even darker.

I smiled and approached her desk.

"Hello," I said.

(Incidentally, Gram always recommends "How do you do?" on first encounters, but she's in her sixties and I'm not.)

According to a badge on her tunic, she was called Linda. Linda nodded in acknowledgment and stopped chewing for a second.

"I see you're selling off your equipment," I continued.

She nodded. "Aye."

A short conversation followed, during which I managed to learn that three all-over, walk-in tanning cubicles were being sold off because Geordie Bronze had fought a "price war" with the salon next door and lost. Geordie Bronze had gone out of business, or something like that, anyway.

The cubicles could be mine for "two grand each." Two thousand pounds.

"I see," I said. "Thank you." I turned to leave.

"Hang on, pet," said Linda. "Is it for yourself, like?"

"Umm . . . yeah?"

"Is it for the . . . ?" And she made a sort of circular motion with her hand around her face, meaning, "Is it for your spots?"

I nodded while thinking, *What a nerve!*

She gave a little half smile, and it was only then that I noticed that, beneath her thick makeup and tan, her cheeks were pitted like the skin of a grapefruit.

Acne scars.

"Aw, pet. You've gorrit bad, haven't you? I had that when I was about your age." She paused, then looked again, head cocked on one side, and added, "Mind you . . . not quite as bad as that."

Gee, thanks. She beckoned me to follow her to the back of the shop, where she pulled a sheet off a long white tanning bed and lifted the lid.

I'm guessing you've seen a tanning bed before? You lie on it, and then pull the lid down, and you're sort of encased in this giant sandwich toaster. Brilliant UV tubes come on above you and below you and, well, that's about it.

"It's old," said Linda, rubbing at a scratch on the lid. "But it still works. We're just norrallowed to use it commercially anymore. New regulations. We cannit sell it neither. It's gonna go to the dump tomorrow."

Long story short, she let me have it for free (I know, right?), and five minutes later, me and Elliot Boyd were carrying it up Whitley Road, one end each.

Halfway home, we stopped for a rest. He was panting much more than me.

"I've never had a suntan," he said. "Never even been abroad."

If he was hinting that he'd like to come and use it, then I was going to pretend that I hadn't understood. Even he wouldn't be crass enough to ask directly.

"I was just wonderin', seeing as I'm helping you home with it, if I could come and use it sometime?"

Hmm. Subtle. I found myself totally unable to say no. It would have been kind of rude, and he was so pleased, he babbled on—suggesting when he could come round, and saying how tanned he'd be—and I just switched off, heaving the thing along the pavement.

Fifteen sweaty minutes after that, I'd cleared a space in

the garage. I propped the tanning bed upright and covered it with the sheet; it kind of blended in with the old wardrobe, a pile of boxes, and other garage junk destined for a church bazaar.

Gram and Lady were out. And it's not like we ever use the garage for anything other than storing stuff.

In fact, given that Gram hardly even goes in the garage, I thought I might be able to get away with not telling her at all. The very last thing I wanted was her forbidding me to use the tanning bed, because it was "common" or unsafe or it used too much electricity or . . . I dunno. Gram's odd sometimes. You can never tell.

Boyd was red-faced and sweating.

"You'll get a nice tan," he said.

He was kind of making conversation and it was kind of him to help me carry it, so I said, "Yes. Erm . . . thanks for the, you know . . ."

There was one of those awkward silences before I said, "Soooo, erm . . . I'd better, you know . . . erm . . ."

And he said, "OK, erm . . . I'll be . . . you know . . . erm . . . See you."

That was it. He was off.

By the time Gram let herself in the front door, I was trying not to gag as I forced down my daily dose of Dr. Chang His Skin So Clear (three weeks with no sign of improvement).

"Hi, Gram!" I said when she came into the kitchen.

Gram looked at me with an expression that could easily have been suspicion. Was I a bit too enthusiastic?

But perhaps I was overthinking stuff.

Later, I remembered Elliot Boyd's round, sweaty face and it occurred to me that I'd been very close to him and he didn't smell.

CHAPTER SIX

The next day, Saturday, I was dying to try out the tanning bed, naturally, but I couldn't because it was Great-Gran's one hundredth birthday and there was a bit of a party in her home.

I say "party" like it was a wild affair, but of course it wasn't, seeing as Gram and I are about the only family Great-Gran has. There was a cake, and there were a few people from church and the other residents and the staff of Priory View, and that's about it.

Great-Gran has been in this house as long as I can remember. Apparently, when Gram first moved back to the northeast, Great-Gran was still living in a big old house in Culvercot on her own. Great-Grandad had died years before, and then Great-Gran fell over in her kitchen. (Gram always says she "*had a fall*," which I think is odd. I never "have a fall." If I ever fall over, I just "fall over.")

The house was sold and turned into flats, and Great-Gran moved here. The home overlooks a little beach and the ruined old monastery on the clifftop.

It's very quiet, and *very* warm. As soon as you go in the big front door, the cold seafront breeze outside is swapped for a hot, stuffy blanket of air that manages to smell both super-clean and a bit dirty at the same time. The clean smells are disinfectant and wood polish and air freshener; the less-clean smells are school dinners and other stuff that I can't identify and probably don't want to.

Along the thickly carpeted corridor is Great-Gran's room. The door was half open. From inside I could hear the cheery nurse talking loudly to Great-Gran in a heavy Geordie accent, which is how they talk around here.

"There you are, Lizzie, sweetheart. You're gerrin' some visitors, you lucky birthday girl. No misbehavin', now, eh? Ah've got me eye on yuh!"

The nurse winked at us as she left the room, and once again I found myself baffled as to why they talk to her like that. I wanted to follow the nurse and say, "She's a hundred years old! Why are you talking to her like she's six?"

But of course I never do.

Great-Gran's name is Mrs. Elizabeth C. Freeman. Gram told the staff she was never called Lizzie and preferred to be called Mrs. Freeman, but I think they thought she was being snooty.

I know I shouldn't dislike going to see Great-Gran, but I do. It's not her. Great-Gran is a sweet, harmless old lady. No, what I dislike is *me*. I hate the fact that I find going to see her a chore, that I get bored, that I feel uncomfortable.

What's worse is that that day should have felt special. One hundred years old? That's pretty awesome. I was wishing I felt more stoked about it.

Then Gram started talking. It's nearly always a monologue, because Great-Gran so seldom responds, preferring instead to look out her window and nod, a little half smile often appearing. Sometimes she even falls asleep. She looked tiny in the big armchair, propped up with cushions, her little head with wispy white hair emerging from a woolen blanket.

"So, Mum, how have you been keeping? Have you been out for your walk today? It's blustery out there today, isn't it, Ethel?"

"Yes, very windy."

Usually I'm not required to say much, and I just sit in the chair by the window, looking at the waves and watching the minutes tick by on the clock next to Great-Gran's bed. I'll chime in with a comment now and then, and sometimes I'll sit next to Great-Gran and hold her thin hand, which I think she likes, because she responds with a weak squeeze.

That's basically how it went this time too, except at the end when something weird happened.

After a few minutes of talking, Gram said something about heating up the sausage rolls, and she left to go and talk to the kitchen staff.

That's when Great-Gran turned to me, and for a moment her watery gray eyes seemed to sharpen and she was really looking at me carefully. At first I thought she was looking at my spots and I shifted my position, ready to move away, but she gripped my hand a little tighter so that I stayed, and I realized she wasn't studying my skin. She was looking right into my eyes, and she startled me by coming out with a whole sentence.

"How old are you, hinny?"

(Hinny is Great-Gran's name for me. It's an ancient Geordie term of affection. I reckon Great-Gran is the only person left alive who uses it. She never calls me Ethel. Only hinny.)

The words came out as a very quiet croak—they were the first Great-Gran had spoken all morning.

"I'm nearly thirteen, Great-Gran."

She gave a tiny nod. Gram had come back into the room, but Great-Gran hadn't seen her.

Great-Gran said, "Tiger."

Just that: "Tiger."

And then, with a huge effort, she said, "Pss-kat."

I leaned in a bit and said, "What was that?"

Again, slightly more distinctly: "Tiger. Pussycat."

She pointed to me and gave a weak smile.

I looked up at Gram, and her face had gone *white.* I mean, really—the color had drained from her face. And then, as if she'd caught herself out, she went super-loud, super-energetic, and all "Right, the party is about to begin. Let's sort you out, shall we, Mum? I've told them we don't want the sausage rolls straightaway. . . ." And so on. A long monologue of busyness that was *obviously* meant to distract from what Great-Gran had just said.

I had no idea what it was all about. None at all. *Tiger?* And had she said "pussycat"? Or something else? Thing is, Great-Gran is one hundred, and not everything works like it should, but she's not actually *senile.*

She turned her head to Gram. Her eyes still hadn't lost their intensity, and for just a moment, it was like looking at a person half her age.

"Thirteen," she said. There was something about all this I wasn't getting, but I'd have let it go if Gram hadn't suddenly come over, all brisk and matter-of-fact.

"Yes, isn't she growing up fast, Mum?" said Gram with a little forced laugh. "How quickly it all happens, eh? Goodness, look at the time! We'd better get into the sitting room. People will be waiting."

AN ADMISSION

So there's another problem with visiting Great-Gran, even on a happy occasion like a birthday: old people make me sad.

It's like, I'm starting to grow up, but they finished all that ages ago and they're growing *down*. Everything is done for them, *to* them, and they don't really get to decide anything, just like children.

There's a man who's very old and very deaf, and the staff have to shout to make themselves heard. So much so that everyone else can hear as well, which is sort of funny and sort of not.

"EHH, STANLEY! I SEE YOU'VE HAD A BOWEL MOVEMENT THIS MORNING!" bellowed one of the nurses once. "THAT'S GOOD! YOU'VE BEEN WAITIN' ALL WEEK FOR THAT, HAVEN'T YOU?"

Poor old Stanley. He smiles at me when I go past his room; the door is always open. (Most of the doors are open, in fact, and you can't help looking in. It's a bit like being in an overheated zoo.) When he smiles, he suddenly looks about seventy years younger, and it makes me smile too, but then I feel sad and guilty all over again, because why should it make me happy that he looks young?

What's wrong with being old?

CHAPTER SEVEN

Great-Gran was wheeled out of her room by one of the staff, Gram scuttling behind her, and I was left alone, staring at the sea.

There was something missing. Some*one* missing.

My mum. She should have been there. Four generations of women in the family and one of them—my mum—was being forgotten.

How much do you remember from when you were very little? Like, before you were, say, four years old?

Gram says she hardly remembers anything.

I think of it like this: Your memory is like a big jug that gets gradually fuller and fuller. By the time you're Gram's age, your memory's pretty much full, so you have to start getting rid of stuff to create room, and the easiest stuff to get rid of is the oldest.

For me, though, the memories I have of when I was tiny are all I have left of my mum. Plus a little box of mementos, which is really just a shoebox with a lid.

The main thing in it is a T-shirt. That's what I always see when I open the box, because it's the biggest item. A plain black T-shirt. It was Mum's, and it smells of her still.

And when I open the box, which stays in my cupboard most of the time, I take out the T-shirt and hold it to my nose, and I close my eyes, I try to remember Mum, and I try not to be sad.

The smell, like the memory, is really faint now. It's a mixture of a musky perfume and laundry detergent and sweat, but *clean* sweat—not the sort of cheesy smell that people say Elliot Boyd has, but the sort that I've never smelled. It's just the smell of a person. My person, my mum. It's strongest under the arms of the T-shirt, which sounds gross but isn't. One day, the smell will be gone completely. That scares me a bit.

There's also a birthday card to me, and I know the rhyme by heart.

To a darling little person
This card has come to say
That I wish you joy and happiness
On your very first birthday.

And in neat, round letters is handwritten:

To my Boo, happy first birthday from Mummy XOXOX

Boo was Mum's pet name for me. Gram said she didn't want to use it herself because it was special to me and Mum, and that's cool. It's like we have a secret, me and Mum, a thing we share, only us.

The nice thing about the card is that it has picked up the tiniest bit of the T-shirt's smell, so besides smelling of paper, it smells of Mum.

I was thinking about this, sitting in Great-Gran's room, when Gram interrupted.

"Are you coming, Ethel, or are you going to daydream? And why the long face? It's a party!"

I'll skip through it quickly because it was about as exciting as you would expect . . . apart from another weird thing that happened towards the end.

GREAT-GRAN'S PARTY

Guests:

About twenty people. Apart from me and a care assistant called Chastity, everyone else was properly grown-up or ancient.

What I wore:

A lilac dress with flowers on it, with a matching hair band. Gram thought I looked lovely. I didn't. Girls who look like

me should just be allowed to wear jeans and T-shirts until the whole gawky-skinny-spotty thing runs itself out. As it is, I looked like a cartoon version of an ugly girl in a pretty dress.

What I said:
"Hello, thank you for coming. . . . Yes, I'm nearly thirteen now. . . . No, I haven't decided what I want to study yet. . . . No [shy, fake grin], no boyfriend yet. . . ." (Can I just say at this point: Why do old people think they can quiz you about boyfriends? Is it some right you acquire as soon as you hit seventy?)

What I did:
I handed round food. Gram had asked me what she should serve, but my suggestion of Jelly Bellys and Doritos had been ignored. Instead there were olives, bits of bacon wrapped around prunes (yuck—whose idea was that?), and teeny-tiny cucumber sandwiches. The chances of me sneaking much of this into my own mouth were slim to zero.

What Great-Gran did:
She sat in the center of the room, smiling a bit vacantly and nodding as people came up to her and congratulated her. I was thinking she was "not all there." As it turned out, I was wrong about that.

The photograph:
A photographer from the *Whitley Bay News Guardian* took a picture of me and Gram and Great-Gran next to a large cake. He had a tiny digital camera instead of a big camera with a flash that goes *whumph!* I was a bit disappointed: if you're going to be in the local newspaper, it should feel dramatic, like a special moment, you know? (Irony alert: as it happens, that photograph is going to turn out to have very dramatic consequences.)

CHAPTER EIGHT

Mrs. Abercrombie was at the party with Geoffrey, her three-legged Yorkshire terrier, who was doing his bad-tempered snarly-gnarly thing—and I have a new theory about this. I think the reason he's so snappy is that she never lets him run around. She is forever holding him in one arm. I'd be annoyed if I was forever pressed into Mrs. Abercrombie's enormous chest.

Gram looked nice. "A veritable picture," as Reverend Henry Robinson said.

She sipped from a glass of fizzy water and smiled gently whenever people spoke to her, which is about as far as Gram's displays of happiness go. She hardly ever laughs. "Ladies do not guffaw, Ethel. It's bad enough in a man. In a woman it is most unseemly."

(Personally, though, I have my own idea, and it has nothing to do with being "unseemly." I think, deep inside, Gram is sad about something. Not me, not Great-Gran, but something else. It could just be Mum, but I think it's more.)

The vicar was the last to leave. He played "Happy Birthday" on the piano, and then a classical piece off by heart, and everyone clapped. Old Stanley clapped *very* enthusiastically, and shouted "Bravo! Bravo!" until one of the nurses calmed him down like he was a naughty child, which I thought was a bit mean.

Gram seemed flustered as soon as Reverend Robinson had gone, and only me, Gram, and Great-Gran were left as the care assistants cleared up.

"Goodness me, look at the time, Mum! That was quite a shindig!" "Shindig" is a Gram sort of word, meaning "party," but it was only one in the afternoon. I think parties must happen earlier and earlier the older you get.

Honestly, if I hadn't already suspected something was up, then Gram's bad acting would have alerted me. She couldn't wait to get away.

Anyway, the "look at the time" remark seemed to have an effect on Great-Gran, like switching off a light. The distant gaze returned, along with the constant nodding, and that was that.

Well, pretty much.

As I leaned in to kiss Great-Gran's papery cheek, she whispered in my ear, "Come back, hinny."

"Oh yes," I said. "We'll be back soon."

Great-Gran's eyes darted to Gram, who was halfway to the door, and it was the way she did it: I knew instantly what she meant.

Come back without her is what she meant.

That's the weird thing that I told you about. That, and the whole tiger thing.

Just what was going on? And whatever it was, why was Gram so worried about it?

CHAPTER NINE

We drove home. Two miles in which I could ask Gram, "What did Great-Gran mean by saying 'tiger' and 'pussycat,' Gram?"

Except I couldn't because, from the moment we were alone in the car, Gram kept up a near-constant chatter that could almost have been a deliberate attempt to stop me from asking the question I was dying to ask.

The Reverend Henry Robinson this, Mrs. Abercrombie that, sausage rolls not heated through even though I asked them, the beautiful English spoken by "that nice girl" (Chastity), even the pattern in the carpet ("I do think swirls on a carpet are just a *little* common"), and so on . . . and on.

Honestly, I don't think she even paused for breath.

I would have no chance to use the tanning bed today, I knew that. I needed a time when Gram would be out for a good while, and that wouldn't happen till the next day, when Gram would be busy with church and one of her committees.

I'd have the morning to myself. So even though I was a bit confused by what was going on with Great-Gran and Gram, I was excited, because I was going to get to try my latest acne-fighting tactic very soon.

Tanning beds, by the way, very definitely fall into the category of things Gram would describe as "rather common." There are plenty of things Gram thinks are "rather common":

- Tanning beds, as I've already said. Any type of fake tan, really.
- Swirly carpets, apparently. But only "slightly."
- Tattoos, and piercings other than for ears.
- Ear piercings, if you're under sixteen.
- Naming children after places, and that definitely includes Jarrow and Jesmond Knight. Brooklyn Beckham is *not* included because Gram met David Beckham once at a charity do, and apparently he was a "real gentleman." And smelled nice.
- Designer dogs. Basically, anything prefixed with the word "designer," so: jeans, kitchens, handbags, and so on.
- Most people on television.
- Hanging baskets.

And if you're thinking of rolling your eyes at the ridiculousness of this list, then know this: rolling your eyes is common as well.

I tell you, I could carry on: this list could fill the book, and I haven't even started on things that are not "rather common" but are instead "frightfully common." Here are today's top three "frightfully common" things:

- Eating in the street.
- All daytime television, and people who watch daytime television, and most things that are not on public television.
- Football (although not David Beckham, for reasons stated above).

This "common," by the way, is not common as in "frequent." It's common as in "lacking refinement" and is not to be confused with "vulgar," which Gram is usually OK with, although the distinction can get blurry.

The Eurovision Song Contest is vulgar, says Gram, but she loves it. *The X Factor* is common, and she won't have it on.

Football, as I have said, is common. Rugby is vulgar.

Want another one? OK. Takeaway fish and chips = vulgar, and as such, acceptable, which is a huge relief because I love them. Takeaway hamburger and chips (or worse, *fries*) = common. And Burger King is *more* common than McDonald's.

I know: it's tricky to navigate.

"Eructating" is how Gram refers to burping. She says it is both vulgar *and* "frightfully common," so heaven knows what she'd make of what's to come. If you're like Gram and are completely horrified by burping, then you should skip the next chapter.

CHAPTER TEN

Sunday morning. Tanning bed–day morning.

Gram had gone off to church. Sometimes I go with her, but I told her I had a stomachache (which was true) and she didn't seem to mind at all. She was very keen to get to church, and left me at home with Lady.

Gram would be gone most of the day. This, by the way, is a big development in our little household. About a year ago, she started trusting me to be left alone in the house, sometimes in the evenings. I was nervous at first, but I soon got to quite like it.

After church she'd be going straight to a coffee morning for a Bible study group; then she'd have lunch at Mrs. Abercrombie's, and then she'd be on to the annual general meeting of yet another of her causes. I sometimes wonder where she gets the energy.

I had been guzzling Dr. Chang His Skin So Clear, and I had probably overdone it, which accounted for the slightly dodgy stomach. The drink—it comes in a powder that you mix with water to make a sort of cold tea—has a mushroomy smell and tastes exactly how I imagine worms taste. It's foul, but Dr. Xi Chang ("a highly noticed practicer of traditional Chinese Herbal Medicine" is how the website put it) claims that it's effective against severe acne and has some pretty impressive before-and-after pictures to prove it.

The effect had been that I woke up that morning with a bloated stomach. Really, my tummy was distended like a little balloon, and I flicked my middle finger against it and heard a noise like a tom-tom.

Now, embarrassing though this is, I'm just going to have to tell you, so "forgive my indelicacy," as Gram might say. I could use all sorts of words to get round it: words like "eructating" or "expelling gas," but nobody apart from adults and teachers and doctors *actually* says that, so here goes: Immediately after waking, I let go the most enormous burp, which—if you did not know otherwise—you would swear was the stench of a rotting animal. A skunk, probably, even though I've never smelled a skunk, what with them not being native to Britain. I just know they stink.

And the weirdest thing is, it didn't taste of anything (thank goodness).

Look, I know we all joke about bodily gases and so on.

(All apart from Gram, of course—do I need to keep saying this? Probably not. In the future, just assume it, OK? I'll mention it when relevant.) Anyway, *most* of us find it hilarious.

This wasn't.

It was so foul-smelling that it was kind of . . . scary, I suppose. Certainly totally unlike any, um . . . fart I have ever smelled, and much worse than the one Cory Muscroft let off one time in assembly that people *still* remember. Had I known what was to come, I might even have taken it for a warning. But of course we never know these things until after the event.

Anyway, after a couple of smaller burps, my tummy was a lot less swollen, and I was in the garage with its smell of dust and old carpets. I was shivering a little on the concrete floor because I was in my underwear, with bare feet, thinking, *This is so not the tanning salon/spa treatment experience,* so I went back inside the house to get my phone.

On Spotify, I found some slow, trancey nineties electronica tracks that sounded like the sort of stuff they put on in salons, and I plugged in my earbuds. Naked, I lay on the tanning bed, which was glowing purply white with the UV tubes. I set the timer on the side for ten minutes—better start gently. Then I pulled down the lid so that it was only a few inches from my nose.

My eyes were shut, the music was a soft *dum-dum-dum* in my ears, the UV tubes were warm, and I didn't mind drifting off a bit because the timer would wake me.

A bit later, though, I'm woken by the bright lights of the UV tubes shining through my invisible eyelids and Lady nudging her food bowl.

This is where we came in—remember?

CHAPTER ELEVEN

"Gram? Can you hear me? I'm *invisible*."

I'm on my phone in the garage, sitting on the edge of the tanning bed, and I was right. Before I had even tapped on Gram's number, I was wondering if calling someone up and saying I was invisible would sound ridiculous.

It does. Very.

But still I try.

"I've become invisible, Gram." Then I start sobbing again.

Long pause.

Really. Long. Pause.

There's a buzz of conversation in the background.

"I'm not sure I'm hearing you right. I can't really talk at the moment, but I can hear that you're upset. What's wrong, darling?"

I take a deep breath. "I'm invisible. I've disappeared. I was on a tanning bed and I fell asleep and now I've woken up and I can't see myself."

"All right, my darling. Very funny. Thing is, it's not a good time at the moment. Mrs. Abercrombie is about to read the minutes of the last meeting, so I have to go. There's some cold ham in the fridge, and Lady needs her walk. Got to go. See you later."

Click.

Gulping back more sobs, I quickly fling on my underwear, jeans, and a T-shirt. I'm mesmerized into silence as I can see the clothes filling out with my invisible body as I put them on. Somehow, the mundane action of getting dressed is a little bit calming (only a little bit—I'm still bubbling inside, like a pan of milk boiling over), and I can breathe better, and at least I've stopped crying.

On the way to the kitchen I catch a glimpse of myself in the long hallway mirror. Well, I say "myself." What I really see is a pair of jeans and my favorite red T-shirt walking all by themselves. It would be funny, like watching a special effect for real, if it wasn't me inside the clothes, and I catch my breath again and swallow hard to stop myself from restarting the crying.

In the kitchen, Lady lifts her head from her basket. She pads over to where I'm standing and sniffs at my feet, or at where my feet would be. I reach down and stroke her.

"Hello, girl," I say automatically, and she looks up.

I'm not sure anyone can really read the expressions on a dog's face, but I swear Lady looks scared and confused. I crouch down to reassure her, but it seems to have the opposite effect. I tickle her ears because I know she likes that, but instead of her licking me and making me laugh, which is what always happens, her tail goes between her legs and, with a little whine, she heads straight out the kitchen door into the backyard. I'm left looking at the door as it bangs shut behind her, and the corners of my mouth turn down.

I try Gram's number again.

It goes to voice mail.

I don't leave a message.

And now there's this kind of continuous monologue going on in my head, running through various courses of action.

I still haven't completely let go of the idea that I'm dreaming. Perhaps this is just some especially persistent dream state that the usual dream checks don't dislodge? I keep pinching myself, shaking my head—all that stuff.

None of it works, so I decide on something a bit more extreme. Standing there in the kitchen, I slap myself on the cheek. Gently at first, then a bit harder, then really quite hard, and finally—to finish off—a powerful wallop with my right palm against my left cheek that is both noisy and *very* sore, and more tears prick my eyes.

I do a sort of checklist.

This much I know:

1. I am alone, and I am invisible.
2. I am definitely, *definitely* not dreaming. (Pinch, slap, ow! Check again.)
3. Gram is not picking up her phone, presumably because she thinks I'm messing about, or—just as likely—she has put it on silent so that it doesn't ring during Mrs. Abercrombie's thing.
4. I could go round there. (Where? I'm not even sure where she is. The church hall, probably. Well, that's in Culvercot, for a start, and what am I going to do? Just wander into the church hall and announce I am invisible? No.)
5. Is there a friend I trust? Once it would have been Kirsten Olen, but more recently? No: I no longer trust her enough.
6. I am so thirsty my throat actually hurts.

First I will deal with the easiest thing to put right. Besides, it gives me something else to think about.

I start to make tea. Tea is Gram's response to pretty much everything. She told me once that the actual making of tea—waiting for the kettle to boil, putting the cups out, and so on—was just as effective as drinking it for calming the nerves.

Then my phone rings.

It's Gram. Yesss!

"I've come out of the meeting, Ethel. I see you've called me again. What is it now?" Her tone is brisk, no-nonsense, which doesn't bode well.

"I told you, Gram: I've become invisible."

And then I spill it all out: the acne, the "pizza face" jibes, the tanning bed, falling asleep, waking up ninety minutes later in a pool of my own sweat, looking in the mirror, screaming for help . . .

Everything up to now. Sitting here, drinking tea, telling Gram what happened.

It all comes out kind of garbled, I'm pretty sure, but not completely nonsensical.

I finish up by saying, "So that's why I called you. You've got to help me."

For a long time, Gram doesn't say anything.

CHAPTER TWELVE

That's when I know she doesn't believe me.

Why would she? It sounds completely demented. Gram doesn't believe me because she can't see me, and if she can't see that I actually am invisible, then why on earth *should* she believe me?

It's crazy. "Preposterous," even, to use one of Gram's favorite words.

I wait. I've told her everything. I've told her the whole truth and nothing but. All I can do is wait to hear what she says.

What Gram says is this:

"Ethel, my pet. It's hard growing up. You're at a very tricky crossroads in your life. . . ."

Oo-kaay, I think. *Don't like the sound of where this is going, but go on.*

"I think many of us feel invisible at some point in our lives, Ethel. As though everyone is just ignoring us. I know I did at your age. I did my best to fit in, but sometimes my best was not enough. . . ."

This is getting worse. Can there *be* anything worse than a sympathetic response that completely and utterly misses the point?

I'm struck dumb, sitting there listening to Gram drone on about "feeling like you're invisible" while I watch my teacup magically rise and fall to my lips and return to the saucer.

Then I look down and gasp in horror. There's the tea that I've just drunk, floating in a little misshapen blob where my stomach is.

My gasp causes Gram to pause.

"What is it, darling?"

"My . . . my t-tea! I can see it!" No sooner have I said this than I realize how silly it sounds.

"I beg your pardon, Ethel?"

"Oh, erm . . . nothing. Sorry. I, erm, I missed what you were saying."

"Listen, I'm sorry you're feeling this way, but we'll have to talk about it when I get back this afternoon. It's the treasurer's report next and Arthur Tudgey is sick, so I have to deliver it. I have to go back in."

And I've had enough. That's it.

"No, Gram. You're not listening. *I really have disappeared.*

I don't mean in an imaginary way. I mean really. *Really* really—not metaphorically. My body is not visible. My face, my hair, my hands, my feet—they are *actually* invisible. If you could see me, well . . . you wouldn't be able to see me."

Then it hits me.

"FaceTime! Gram, let's FaceTime and then you'll see!"

I'm not even sure Gram can do FaceTime, but I'm sounding hysterical.

I'm trying to put this the best way I can, but it's coming out all wrong, and the tone of her voice has gone from sympathetic and concerned to something a little bit harder, a bit stern.

"Ethel. I think you've gone far enough with this, darling. We'll talk later. Goodbye."

It's me who hangs up this time.

CHAPTER THIRTEEN

Think back to the last time you were on your own. How alone were you really?

Was there someone fairly close by? A parent? A teacher? A friend? If you were in trouble, could you have called someone to help?

OK, so I'm not exactly Miss Popularity at school, but it's not like people actually *dislike* me. Well, I don't think so, anyway.

"There is absolutely nothing wrong with being 'quiet and reserved,'" said Gram when she read this on a school report once (and until then I had never thought there was, actually, or that anyone would think there might be).

"Better to keep your mouth shut and be thought stupid than to open it and remove all doubt," she added in a typically Gram kind of way.

Gram has always been—to use a phrase she is fond of herself—"very proper."

She is fond of saying that a civilized, cultured Englishwoman should know how to behave in every situation.

Honestly, she has books on stuff like this. Books with titles like *Modern Manners in the Twentieth Century.* They're funny, usually, but most of them seem to have been written since Gram was born, so they're not that ancient. They include things like:

"What is the correct form of address when meeting a divorced duchess for the first time?"

And:

"How much does one leave as a tip for the staff after staying at a friend's country house?"

If you didn't know Gram, I daresay it could make her seem buttoned-up and straitlaced—the insistence on writing thank-you letters within three days, for example, or always asking permission before calling an adult by their first name. Actually, it's just about being polite to people, and that's quite sweet—only, Gram takes it further than anyone I've ever met.

She once gave me a lesson in shaking hands.

Yes, shaking hands.

"Eeugh, dead haddock, Ethel, dead haddock!" That was Gram's description of a limp handshake. "You must grip more. Ow! Not that much! And I'm here, Ethel! Over here: look me in the face when you shake hands. And are you pleased to see me? Well, tell your face. And . . . what do you say?"

"Hi?"

"'Hi'? *'Hi'*? Where on earth do you think you are? *California?* If one is meeting for the first time, it's 'How do you do?' Now show me: a firm brief handshake, eye contact, a smile, and 'How do you do?'"

(I actually tried this when I met Mr. Parker for the first time. I could tell he was pleased, but also a bit, well, *unnerved,* like it was the first time any student had greeted him that way—which it may well have been. Mr. Parker has been super-nice to me ever since, which Gram would say is proof that it works, and I think is probably just because Mr. Parker quite likes me.)

So Gram is not all that old but she *is* old-fashioned, at least in her clothes. She's proud of the fact that she has never owned a pair of jeans, even when she was much younger and good-looking. Her denim aversion is not a protest against the modern world, though. The reason she hates jeans, she says, is that they are unflattering.

"Wear them tight and they are indecent; wear them loose and you look like some gangster rapper."

Believe me: When my gram utters the words "gangster rapper," it's like she's practicing a foreign language. You can hear the quote marks around them.

Being able to talk to anyone, from any walk of life, is a great skill if you've got it, but even if I did, it would be no help to me right now. There is no one I can talk to about this whole invisibility thing.

Gram? Tried that.

I could go on Instagram and tell Flora McStay, my friend who moved to Singapore:

"Hey, guess what! I became invisible today! I'm in the picture next to the tree."

Funny.

I am completely on my own. It is not a good feeling.

SO what would YOU do? Come on, it's not a trick question—honest.

What would you do?

What *I* decide is that I need to get to the hospital, quick. Therefore, I need an ambulance. This is, after all, an emergency.

I dial 999.

CHAPTER FOURTEEN

"Emergency. Which service do you require?"

"Ambulance, please," I say with a trembling voice. I have never made an emergency call before. It's pretty nerve-racking, I can tell you.

"Putting you through now."

And I wait.

"North Tyneside Ambulance Service. Can I get your name and number, please?"

It's a young Geordie woman on the other end. She sounds nice and I relax a bit.

"It's Ethel Leatherhead. 07877 654 344."

"Thank you. What is the nature of your emergency, please?"

I should have learned my lesson from when I told Gram. It sounded ridiculous when I told her. It's not going to sound any less ridiculous when I tell an emergency services operator that I've become invisible.

"I . . . I can't really say. I just need an ambulance urgently."

"I'm sorry, erm . . . Ethel, is it? I do need to know the nature of the emergency before I can send an ambulance."

"I can't tell you. It's just . . . really urgent, OK? I'm in serious trouble."

The operator still sounds nice. She's being gentle.

"Listen, pet, I cannit help you unless you tell me what's wrong. Are you calling from home?"

"Yes."

"And are you injured?"

"Well . . . not exactly *injured.* It's just . . ."

"OK, flower. Calm down. Are you in pain?"

"No."

"And are you or anyone else in immediate danger of pain or injury?"

I give a little sigh. "No. Only—"

"And is there anyone else there with you? Are you bein' threatened in any way?"

"No." I know where this is going.

"Well, there is another number to call for nonemergency medical assistance, Ethel. Have you got a pen there, love?"

I am close to tears, and if I was thinking straight, I would foresee the consequences of blurting out to her as I do, but, well, I'm not exactly levelheaded right now.

"I've become invisible, and I'm really scared, and I *need an ambulance now*!"

That's when the operator's tone changes from reassuring and gentle to weary and tense.

"You've become invisible? I see. Listen, pet, I have had enough. You know these calls are recorded and traceable? I'm logging this as a nuisance call, so if you call back I'm informing the police. Now gerroff the line and make way for genuine emergencies. Invisible? You kids, honestly. You drive us up the wall!"

And with that, the call ends—along with my hopes for an easy resolution to my problem.

CHAPTER FIFTEEN

Two hours later, and I'm still invisible.

I've had a long, hot shower, wondering if perhaps the invisibility could be washed off—you know, like a coating or something? I scrubbed and scrubbed to the point that I was quite sore, but still the soap lathered up on what looked like nothing, and when I rinsed off there was still nothing, only wet footprints on the bathroom floor.

Since then, I've been wandering around the house, wondering what to do, how to deal with this, and I'm not making any progress.

The crying has stopped. That's not going to get me anywhere, and besides, I'm tired of it. I don't mind admitting, though, that I am completely, utterly, 100 percent

TERRIFIED.

Terrified squared. Cubed.

Roughly every five minutes I get up and check the mirror.

And then I go back to my laptop and search the Internet again for topics including the words "invisible" and "invisibility."

Most of the things I try to read are fantastically complicated, involving mathematics and physics and chemistry and biology that are way beyond what we do at school. All the same, it seems that people have been trying to achieve what has happened to me for decades.

On YouTube there's a clip of James Bond with an invisible car.

"Adapted camouflage, 007," says Q, walking around Bond's Aston Martin. "Tiny cameras on all sides project the image they see onto a light-emitting polymer skin on the opposite side. To the casual eye, it's as good as invisible."

Then he presses a button and the car becomes invisible.

You know what? Up to right now, I would have said that that was just silly. The clip itself was in an Internet list called "Top Ten Bond Baloney."

But now?

Now I'm not so sure.

If it can happen to me, why not to a car?

What I *have* managed to work out is that there are two ways something can be invisible.

Are you ready for this?

I'll keep it simple.

First you have to understand how we see stuff. Things are visible because light rays bounce off them and go into our eyes. So if there's a tree in front of you, the light hits the tree and is reflected onto the back of your eye, and after some nearly instant clever stuff in your brain, you see a tree.

So the first way to make something invisible is to cover it with a "cloaking device." This makes the light *bend around* the tree and keep on going, like sticking your finger in a stream of water from a tap: the water bends around your finger and carries on below as a single stream.

Lots of scientists say they are very close indeed to developing cloaking devices, especially for military purposes. I suppose they mean making invisible tanks, or ships or planes or even soldiers, which would be pretty cool, actually.

Are you still with me?

OK, the second way is to make the light pass straight *through* the object. This is how glass works, and if you've ever walked into a glass door like I did once at the Metrocentre, you'll know how effective it is.

If you look at it straight on, glass is invisible.

It's also how X-rays work. X-rays are a particular type of light, which can pass through some substances but not others. They'll pass through your flesh but not through your bones, so doctors can see inside you.

It must be the second one that's causing me to be invisible.

Light is passing through me, so even though I'm still here, it looks as though I'm not.

Not that knowing this helps me much.

I'm playing the sequence of events back in my mind: getting onto the tanning bed, setting the timer, falling asleep, being woken by Lady nudging her bowl, and . . .

Lady. Where is she?

I last saw her running off out the back door. Standing at the back door, I call for her, then whistle, then call again.

It's like: Have I not got enough to worry about at the moment without a lost dog to add to it?

I'm thinking of the rash of missing-pet posters on lampposts lately, and I feel sick. Everyone has been talking about them.

There used to be one or two a year taped to lampposts: Lost Dog, Lost Cat, Have You Seen It? That sort of thing.

Just recently there seems to have been about one a month. Gram mentioned it the other day, telling me to keep a close eye on Lady when I took her out.

"You never know, Ethel," she said. "There's some funny people around."

What if someone has taken Lady? Lady is so friendly she'd go with anyone.

I need to find her, and to do that I need to go outside:

probably to the beach, as that's where *I* would go if I was a dog.

It's a risk. It's a massive risk, in fact, but sometimes the only alternative to a risk is to do nothing at all, and that is not really an option right now.

I'm going to have to go outside, while invisible.

CHAPTER SIXTEEN

I add some clothes to those I already have on. Socks and sneakers, a turtleneck sweater that covers my invisible throat, a long-sleeved hoodie, and already I'm looking slightly less weird—kind of like one of those headless shop dummies, if that qualifies as "less weird."

In my bottom drawer is a pair of gloves, which leaves only my head to sort out.

There's a plastic crate in the garage with old dress-up gear. In it I find a sparkly wig from some school show I was in and a plastic mask with a clown's face. I hate clowns, but still: it does the job. With my hood up, I look like . . . what?

I look like some weird kid who's decided to go around wearing a clown mask. Odd, definitely, but not *totally* mad.

I'm halfway to the front door in this getup when my phone pings with an incoming text message.

From: Unknown Contact
Hi Ethel: Is now a good time 4 me to work on my beach bod? I'll stay out of ur way. With you in 2 mins. Elliot

And there you have it, in one single text message, why Elliot Boyd grates on you so much. Pushy, presumptuous, in-your-face, and a dozen other words that mean "total pain in the neck" that are all going through my head as my fingers compose a reply.

NO. Not a good time. Just on my way out. Try me later. Ethel

Why, why, why, instead of saying "just on my way out," did I not say "I have gone out"? If I had, I could have pretended not to be in when the doorbell rings.

Which it does—seconds after I press SEND.

I'm in the hallway. I can see his outline in the front-door glass. I can even *hear* his phone when he gets my text, and then he sticks his fingers through the mail slot and calls through into the hallway.

"All right, Eff! Good job I caught you! Open the door, eh?"

What choice do I have?

I open the door.

CHAPTER SEVENTEEN

We both gasp when we see what the other is wearing.

"Whoa!" he says. "You never told me I had to come in a costume. What's *that* all about?"

"What about *you*?" I say.

I may be in a bizarre outfit of sparkly wig and mask and gloves—but Boyd? He looks like he's heading to Florida: vast baggy shorts, a Hawaiian shirt decorated with sharks, sunglasses (unnecessary today), and a baseball cap sitting on top of his springy hair. He's carrying a beach bag, and I can see it contains a towel and various tanning lotions.

We stare at each other in the doorway for a good few seconds.

If I wasn't feeling so completely unnerved by what was going on inside my clothes, I could probably have said something smart, like "Sorry, I don't take clothes advice from someone ejected from Disneyland for fashion crimes." But I don't.

Instead I say, "It's a sponsored thing. I've got to stay dressed up for a whole day to raise money for, erm . . ."

Quick, Ethel. Think of something. He's waiting for you to finish the sentence.

". . . for your lighthouse thing."

Why? Why that? It's like there's another me inside my head, yelling: *What did you say that for, you complete* pinhead? *Now he thinks you care about his stupid lighthouse obsession.* You idiot! *Why didn't you just say "famine relief" or "cancer research" or "climate change"? Or anything else?*

And all I can do about the voice in my head is reply with another head voice saying, *I know! I'm sorry! I'm just not thinking straight. I've got quite a lot on my mind at the moment, in case you hadn't noticed.*

Boyd has been talking.

". . . Terrific! Fanks a lot! Sponsored fancy dress? Brilliant idea! The whole day? Sweet! 'Ow much money you raised? Tell you what—surprise me, eh?"

Oh, yes, I think. *You'll certainly be surprised.* He hasn't shut up, though.

"I just got your text. Sorry, should have checked earlier. Just on your way out, are you? When are you back? I could wait for you, or, you know—let myself out?"

No. Definitely not. Instead, I tell him about Lady.

"I saw her going down to the bottom of the backyard," I say to him. "I thought she was just going for a wee." That is less than entirely truthful. What I really thought was that Lady was utterly, totally freaked out by my invisibility and had legged it.

There's a gap in the fence at the bottom of the yard that a dog could squeeze through, no problem. In fact, Lady did it once when she was a puppy, and we intended to get it fixed but never got around to it because she's never tried to escape again.

Except . . . she's not in the backyard when we look.

So that's how I find myself down on the beach, me in my ridiculous clown-and-gloves costume, Elliot Boyd in his comedy beach gear, calling for Lady.

Whitley Sands is easily my favorite walk with Lady. We do it at least a couple of times a week. I throw her ball into the sea, and she leaps over the waves to retrieve it and then shakes herself, usually soaking me in the process, but I don't really mind.

It's hot under the mask. I check that Boyd is a little way ahead and I lift it up a bit to allow the sea air to cool my face. Then I call, for about the fiftieth time:

"La-dy!"

I am trying to sound normal and happy. Have you ever

lost a dog? It's important not to sound angry when you call for it, whatever you're feeling inside. What dog would return to an angry owner?

There are loads of dogs down here, but no Lady.

Soon we get to the end of the beach and we are by the causeway that links the mainland to the island where the lighthouse looms, white and enormous.

"Come on! Are you coming up?" Boyd shouts.

Going to the top of the lighthouse is the last thing I want to do.

"Come on," he repeats. "There's something I wanna show you, now that you're a proper part of it. It won't take long. Besides, from the top you can get a view of the whole beach and you'll be able to spot your dog."

Once we're over the causeway and on the island itself, we're pretty much the only ones there. It gets busier during the school holidays, but right now the café is closed and the only thing open is the little museum and gift shop where you buy your ticket to walk up to the top of the lighthouse.

There are some steps leading up to the entrance and a path that goes around the back, which is where Boyd is heading. Two big trash bins for the café are on either side of a rusty door, which he pries open with his fingers before beckoning me in.

Inside, we're in a cavernous chamber at the bottom of the lighthouse. There are one or two visitors looking at a big model of a lifeboat and some photographs on the wall, and our footsteps echo. One lady turns and raises her eyebrows, then nudges her friend, who looks at us too. I suppose that, dressed as we are, we're worth at least a glance, but that's all we get.

"Come on," says Boyd, grinning. I can tell he's really excited. "I've never shown anyone this!"

A narrow staircase hugs the circular walls and we climb up to the lantern room at the top, gripping the rusty rail all the way round.

Three hundred and twenty-eight steps later (I didn't count them—Boyd told me), I am panting like a racehorse. Boyd, for some reason, is not, in spite of the extra weight he carries. Perhaps it's just enthusiasm.

Being inside the circular lantern-room is like being in an enormous greenhouse: there are tall windows all around. In the center, imagine a huge, upside-down drinking glass, about a yard and a half high, made of glass lenses arranged in intricate concentric circles, its mouth about a meter from the floor—that's the lantern.

"See this?" says Boyd, indicating the glass contraption, his face glowing. "It's a Fresnel lens. With a light inside, it reflects the light and multiplies it so you don't need all that much power to make it visible for miles. Except there's no light in it now. Hasn't been for years and years."

I mean: OK. It is *sort of* interesting, but mainly I'm just being polite.

Then he takes me to a small hatch cut in the floor.

"Check the stairs, Eff. Anyone comin'?" He lifts the hatch lid. "Come an' look!"

Obediently I shuffle round the room between the giant lens and the windows and look down the hatch. There's a neatly coiled length of electrical cable—yards and yards of it—and a large lightbulb on the other end, about the size and shape of a two-liter bottle of Coke.

"I brought all this up a month ago," he says, pride seeming to ooze from every pore. "It's the brightest lightbulb you can buy—one thousand watts. When I'm ready, I'll put the light in here"—he indicates the "mouth" of the inverted glass tumbler—"and trail the cable out of this window here, down to the ground, where I'll plug it in and switch it on and . . . Light the Light!" He starts humming the song again.

I'm gazing at him through the eyeholes of my mask.

He is mad. Who would even *think* of such a thing? And why?

All I can say is: "I see."

His face falls. "You think I'm crazy, don't you?"

"Erm . . . no. It's just quite an . . . *ambitious* plan, Elliot."

"You won't tell anyone? It's going to be a sort of secret operation. Like a 'happening'—you know, announced shortly before it happens, then *boom!* The lights are on! A flash mob with a proper flash!"

Boyd stands up and replaces the hatch lid softly.

I can see that I've hurt him by not being more enthusiastic.

"Aren't you scared?" I ask.

He looks at me, puzzled. "Scared? What of? What crime will I have committed? Who will I have harmed? You could *possibly* charge me with trespass, but that's not even a crime; I won't have damaged anything, and I'll even use the money you raise by dressing like an idiot to leave some money for the electricity, so I can't be charged with theft!"

The grin on his face makes me smile too.

"Are you sure?"

"Course I'm sure! My dad's a lawyer."

This is the first time Boyd has ever mentioned his dad. Or his mum, for that matter. And as soon as the words are out of his mouth, it's as if he wants to take them back. He starts saying something else, but I cut him off.

"A lawyer? That's pretty cool. What sort of law?"

But he doesn't answer. Instead he stands up, and his voice loses a bit of its London accent, as if he's addressing a court.

"All right, then. 'Trespass' as defined in English common law—as opposed to *statutory* law—is an offense known as a 'tort,' which is a wrongful act, but is not subject to criminal proceedings and therefore—"

"OK, OK, I believe you."

"Promise you won't tell anyone?"

"What? That your dad's a lawyer? Is it a secret?"

"No, dummy. About the light—my plan. It has to be kept quiet till the time is right."

"I promise."

"Oh, and, erm . . . back in London my friends used to call me Boydy."

"Really?"

"Yeah, so . . . you know, if you, like . . . erm . . . wanted . . ."

He lets it hang in the warm air between us.

Boydy. A friend?

I hadn't realized I was quite that desperate.

<u>INTERESTING FACTS ABOUT LIGHTHOUSES</u>

By Elliot Boyd

With thanks to Ethel Leatherhead for allowing me space to say why lighthouses are awesome.

(I made this list for a talk I did at school in Mr. Parker's class. He said people really liked it, which makes me think lighthouses are not such a strange interest after all.)

Humans have been building lighthouses to warn ships about dangerous rocks ever since humans had ships. The first ones were basically just massive bonfires on cliffs!

Now there are 17,000 worldwide, and about 300 in the UK.

The lighthouse on the island of Pharos near Alexandria in Egypt was one of the wonders of the ancient world and was finished in 270 BCE. It stood for 1,500 years and then collapsed in an earthquake. In 1994, pieces of it were found at the bottom of the ocean!

In many languages, the word for "lighthouse" comes from "Pharos": *phare* (French), *faro* (Spanish and Italian), *farol* (Portuguese), *far* (Romanian), *fáros* (Greek)!

The brightness of a lighthouse is measured in candelas—that is, the brightness of a single candle. Most modern lighthouses have beams that are between 10,000 and 1 million candelas bright!

One of the brightest lighthouses in the world is Oak Island Lighthouse in the USA: 2.5 million candelas!!!

In 1820 a Frenchman physicist named Augustin-Jean Fresnel developed a lens that multiplied the brightness of the light, meaning it could be seen much further. Almost all lighthouses now use the Fresnel lens!

Long after the invention of electricity, most lighthouses continued to be powered by oil. St. Mary's Lighthouse in Whitley Bay did not convert to electricity until 1977. It has not been active since 1984, which I think is a real shame!

(*Mr. Parker wrote on my presentation*: "9/10. Well researched and confidently delivered. Well done. Easy on the exclamation marks.")

CHAPTER EIGHTEEN

One of the windows in the lantern room is really a little glass door that leads to an outside platform encircling the top of the lighthouse. An official-looking sign reads DANGER: NO ADMITTANCE.

"Come on," says Elliot Boyd, who I'm trying to get used to thinking of as "Boydy." "You gotta see this."

I follow him through the opening.

We stand on the narrow platform, gripping the iron handrail, and stare over the northeast coast, looking south towards another lighthouse that stands at the mouth of the Tyne River, about two miles away. A seagull, hanging motionless in the wind, is stretched out in front of us.

Boydy has removed his stupid baseball cap, and the breeze blowing his hair back from his forehead makes him look almost handsome. I smile inside my stupid clown mask. Boyd? Handsome? Ha!

I'm still boiling hot inside my two layers, gloves, hoodie,

and mask, and I decide to risk pushing the hood of my jacket back, exposing the glittery wig.

Bad move.

The wind changes for a few seconds from a breeze to a violent gust, whipping the wig from my head. I catch it just before it flies over the side of the iron barrier. I'm fumbling with the hood, desperately trying to pull it back over my head, when Boydy turns to me to say something and instead just yells.

"Wha . . . ah . . . ah . . . aaah! What? Oh my God. Ohhhh."

Oh well. I suppose *someone* had to find out *somehow.*

CHAPTER NINETEEN

Boydy has backed away and is just staring, blinking, opening and shutting his mouth like a fish, and he's making little moaning noises in his throat.

Poor lad, he really is terrified. The seagull squawks and swoops away.

"It's OK," I try to reassure him. "It's just me. I'm all right."

"But . . . but . . . you . . . the . . . Your head . . . Ethel?"

Where to start?

After ten minutes, I think I have convinced him that I am neither a ghost nor an alien from outer space. I have answered his questions, including:

1. Am I in pain? (No, apart from a slight tingling that could be sunburn from the tanning bed, but I cannot see my skin to tell.)
2. Does anyone else know? (No. He is the first. He's so massively flattered, that much I can tell.)

3. Is it permanent? (No idea yet.)
4. What am I going to do about it? (No idea again. My initial approach to the hospital didn't go as planned, and he agrees with me that an approach to the police might be equally unproductive.)

I say this as if it all happened like a sensible conversation anyone would have out on a lighthouse balcony. You know:

"Oh, so you're invisible? Cool. So tell me, are you experiencing any pain or discomfort due to this unusual condition, Ethel?"

No, it wasn't like that *at all*. Boydy was nervous, puzzled, stumbling over his words and reaching out again and again to touch my invisible head and hand, which I have shown him by removing a glove. At one point I removed my mask and he shut up for, like, a whole minute, just gawping and shaking his head, then looking away and turning back and starting the whole gawping, touching thing again.

I have to say, though: now that I've told him, the relief is immense. I've been lugging this secret around for hours, and it's exhausting. Even if there's nothing that Boydy can actually *do*, just sharing my problem with him makes me feel happier.

Slightly.

Why is it, then, that I start crying? Sorry, make that crying *again*. I am not much of a blubberer, to be honest. I think I leave blubbering to the more sensitive souls; but the hugeness of what I face would, I'm certain, bring tears from anyone, and that now makes it twice in a day that I've cried.

He hears me crying and he doesn't know what to do, poor Boydy.

"Hey, Eff. It'll be OK," he says, and he sort of awkwardly puts his arm around me, but I can tell he's not totally comfortable. He probably hasn't done it much. Then he looks at me.

"I can see your tears." He points at my cheeks. "That's one bit of you that's visible."

I wipe my cheek with my fingers and look down. Sure enough, my fingertips are glistening. I force a smile (why? No one can see me) and replace the mask and gloves and pull my hood up as far as it'll go. I sniff, and smile again weakly.

"How do I look?"

Boydy checks the angles. "So long as you don't look too closely, it's OK. There's a sort of invisible gap at the top there, but it's in shadow, so you don't really notice it that much. Just keep your head down."

I nod, and I'm turning to go back through the doorway when he says, "So, Effel, the clown outfit wasn't really to, you know . . ."

"What? Raise money? Ah, sorry, Boydy. No." I see his face and chest fall with a sigh, so I add, "But I do like lighthouses. Well, this one, anyway. And I'm sure the others are cool as well. I'll help you with Light the Light. Promise."

He smiles at that, but then his attention is caught by something on the ground. He's looking beyond me, towards the beach. I turn to follow his gaze. There, at the end of the causeway, on the beach, is a black Labrador, and I can tell from the way it walks that it's Lady.

She is not alone either. Walking with her are two identical figures.

We have trouble, and it's twins-shaped.

I haven't told you much about the twins, but now seems like a good time—if there is ever a good time to talk about the twins, that is.

Jesmond and Jarrow Knight are notorious at school, and they seem to revel in their sinister fame while managing—just—to avoid being suspended.

One or other of them is almost permanently on a written warning. It's Jesmond, the boy, at the moment. He swore at Miss Swan the music teacher when she smelled cigarette smoke on him. (I won't say exactly what he said, but imagine the worst thing you can say to a teacher, and then shout it at the top of your lungs. Actually, don't. But that's what he did in the foyer.)

I guarantee, after his written warning expires at the end of term, it'll be his sister Jarrow's turn to do something bad. Last year she was sent home for setting fire to Tara Lockhart's hair with a Bunsen burner, and then their dad had to come in to see Mrs. Khan and the head of the school administrators.

Most people steer well clear of the twins, which is easy enough if you spot them coming. They both have this shock of shoulder-length white-blond hair. From the back they're pretty much identical, and even from the front they're pretty alike, only Jarrow wears glasses and Jesmond doesn't.

Tommy Knight, their dad, looks exactly like them, except he's going bald. I've only met him once, when he bought something off a stall I was running at the school Christmas bazaar. He seemed shy and hardly ever looked up. It was a box of scented soaps he bought, with pictures of dogs on them, and when he took his change and said "Thank you," his voice was gentle and well-spoken, which was the opposite of what I'd expected.

I've never seen their mum. I don't even know if they have one.

Their house is around the corner at the end of our street, overlooking the wide sweep of grass, called the Links, that leads down to the promenade and the beach. It's large: a detached two-story villa, painted white, with pillars supporting the front porch and an overgrown front yard. I pass the house most days on the way to and from school.

So that's the Knights—my neighbors, more or less—and here they are: Jarrow and Jesmond at the end of the beach where the sand gives way to rocks and pools.

With Lady, my dog.

Which means I'm going to have to go down there and confront them, while wearing a clown mask and a sparkly wig.

I tell myself, *It'll be fine, Ethel.*

Sometimes I think the lies we tell ourselves are the biggest lies of all.

CHAPTER TWENTY

Three other people are in the lantern room when we step back inside, and one of them gives us a funny look, like *How come you've been out there when you're not allowed?* Or it could just be our outfits. Either way, we're off and down the stairs.

Running back over the causeway, I see that the tide has come in quickly, filling the rock pools and lapping the lower edges of the concrete path. It's a good job we left when we did. All the tide times are posted on notices at either end of the causeway, but still people get caught out, and kids in Whitley Bay have all grown up with scare stories of people who have risked a crossing and been swept away.

When we get to the beach, Lady bounds up to me; she's apparently less freaked-out by my clown mask than by the *total absence of a head* that she saw before—and who can blame her? I can't see the twins for the moment, but my vision is restricted by the mask—they could be right here, just behind a rock or something.

No time to worry about that now.

Lady sniffs around my feet, satisfies herself that it's me, and rolls on her back for a tickle of her tummy, which I'm happy to provide, although it feels weird through the gloves.

"You crazy thing, Lady. What happened to you?" I'm trying to be reassuring to Lady, but I'm scared that she might freak out again.

I go to grip her by her collar, but it isn't there. Instead, I make a loop with the spare leash I've brought and slip it round her neck. At the same time, I peer out the eyeholes of the clown mask to find out where the twins are, hoping of course that they've decided to walk away. I'm hoping too that Boydy is close by.

I'm out of luck on both counts.

The twins are standing in front of me.

Jarrow, the girl twin, speaks first, blinking hard behind her glasses.

"Is this your dog, like? We found it. We was bringin' it—What the hell?"

I've looked up from Lady, and Jarrow is staring at my clown mask.

"Oh, it's, erm . . . a charity thing," I say. "I've got to keep it on to raise money."

"Ha'd on. I know your voice," says Jesmond, the boy twin. "You're, erm . . . what's 'er name in our class, aren't you?"

I hesitate before replying, and it's enough space for Jarrow to chip in. "Yer right, Jez! It's Pizza Face! That's a canny mask ye've gorron there!"

The two of them chuckle. They both speak in broad Geordie. It's the accent of the northeast, and it's usually got an up-and-down musical sound that's funny and friendly. Except sometimes, in some people, it can sound harsh and aggressive—and that's how the twins speak, as if they're clenching their teeth and tensing their mouths.

Jarrow turns and says something I don't hear to her brother and they both cackle.

Now, if it was me on my own, I'd have turned around and walked away with Lady. That's the only thing you can do with people like that, in my experience. But by now, Boydy is next to us.

"You all right, Eff?" is all he says, but it's enough to change the twins' mood into something more challenging.

"Hey! It's Fat Lad! How are yuh, Smelliot?" says Jesmond.

Boydy ignores the insult as if he simply hasn't heard it. "All right, thanks, Jes. Just out looking for the dog. And now we've found her."

"Aye. Thanks to us. *We* found it. We was bringing it back, weren't we, Jarrow?"

I interrupt. "Where's her collar?"

Jarrow looks straight at me and blinks hard. "It didn't have one on. We thought it was a stray."

"But you said you were bringing her back," I say. "Where were you bringing her back to? You were walking in the other direction!"

"Wait on," says Jarrow. "Are wuz really having a discussion about this dog with Ronald freakin' McDonald here? Take yer mask off and we'll discuss this properly." She reaches forward toward my face and I flinch away quickly.

"No! It's . . . Like I say, it's a charity thing."

"Well, we're a charity too, aren't we, Jez?" In one swift movement, Jarrow has snatched Lady's leash from my hand and given it to her brother, who wraps the end around his fist.

Jesmond nods.

Jarrow continues, a note of true menace in her reedy voice. "Y'see, I don't know for certain that this is your dog, do I? We might just have to take it to the police as a stray, and you know what they do with strays, don't you?"

I feel a tiny bit victorious. Even though I am scared and vulnerable, I can still tell an empty threat when I hear one. I would probably have laughed in other circumstances.

"Go ahead, then," I say, and I probably even sound a bit cocky. "She's microchipped. You'll probably get charged for stealing a dog."

Do the Knight twins crumble in the face of this defiance? Not a chance.

"Microchipped?" says Jarrow, bending down to Lady. "You mean, like, just about here?" She puts her hand on the back of Lady's neck, exactly where dogs' microchips are implanted. "Just under the skin, like? I don't think that'll pose too much of a problem for us, do you, Jez?"

Jesmond shakes his head. "Last one healed up pretty quick."

They do an about-face and start marching away from us, pulling Lady along by her leash, which is looped around her neck, leaving me gawping with a sick feeling in my stomach.

Did I understand right? Surely not.

"Wait!" I say.

They stop and turn, smirking.

I decide to try to appeal to their better side, if they have one. "Just give us the dog back. Please."

"Your nan'll be dead happy to see it again, won't she?" says Jesmond, and I nod.

He goes on: "She'll probably think a reward is in order. You know—'reward for lost dog,' like you see on lampposts. It's usually at least fifty quid."

Jarrow steps closer to us. "We'll take it now, eh? Save yer nan the trouble. How much have you got? Ha'way, let's see."

Reluctantly, I go to retrieve from my jeans pocket the

ten-pound note that Gram makes me carry for emergencies. I wonder if this qualifies?

Problem: my gloved hand won't fit into my jeans pocket. Not at first, anyway. Under normal circumstances, you'd just take your glove off to get your hand in your pocket, but I can't do that without revealing my invisible hand. Awkwardly (and probably strangely, to look at), I work my hand and glove into the pocket where my money is. I grab the note and then tug hard to pull my hand out.

It comes out, all right—straight out of my glove, which is left trapped in my tight jeans pocket.

My apparently handless arm is left waving for a couple of seconds before I turn away. It looks exactly as if I have just pulled my hand off.

I hear a little gasp from Jarrow, and Jesmond whispers, "What the . . . ?"

But in just a moment I've fixed it, and I'm turning back to them, offering the money with a hand that has a glove on and looks perfectly normal.

Jarrow snatches the money from me. She's about to turn away when her brother stops her. He's still gawking at my hand.

"Did you see . . . ? What was . . . ?"

He just cannot put words to his thoughts, and who can

blame him? What I suppose he really wants to say is "Did you just see that her hand was suddenly not where it should be? Her sleeve just ended? Her glove was left in her pocket, but there was no hand?" But he is too confused to string the words together.

Besides, Jarrow is talking.

"Ha'd on," she says, turning to Boydy. "What've you got? Any cash on you?"

Boydy has been very quiet. Quiet? Silent. For a big guy he seems strangely powerless when it comes to resisting these two.

"Nothin'."

Recovering from his confusion, Jesmond takes over what is pretty much a mugging but without any violence. "Nothin' at all? You're out and about without even the money to buy a pie? I don't believe you. Shall I find out?"

Jesmond takes a threatening step towards Boydy, and that's all it takes. Boydy pulls a five-pound note and some change from his pocket.

"Thought so," says Jesmond. "And thank you both very much for the reward. Quite unnecessary, of course," he adds, with exaggerated politeness.

Then he throws Lady's leash down on the ground, and they both walk away in the direction they came from, back over the causeway.

But they're behaving strangely, heads together, talking earnestly. I see Jesmond hold up his right hand in front of his sister. They're about ten yards away when Jarrow turns back.

"Hey, Pizza Face! I'd keep the mask on if I was you. Big improvement!"

CHAPTER TWENTY-ONE

Boydy is red-faced with anger. His mouth is turned down in a perfect curve of unhappiness, and I can see straightaway that he's angry not only with the twins but also with himself for not having more courage to stand up to them. I don't exactly blame him, but it doesn't matter: he's doing enough blaming for both of us.

I'm about to tell him not to worry about it, but something feels different.

It starts in my fingertips—an aching sort of tingling—and spreads to my scalp. By the time Boydy and I are much further along the beach, I can feel rivulets of sweat trickling down my back and my whole skin is fizzing like a soluble aspirin.

"Hang on, Boydy! Stop," I call ahead to him. "I feel strange."

My stomach convulses, and I fall to my knees, retching and vomiting in the sand.

"You OK, Eff?" says Boydy—a bit pointlessly, because I'm obviously not. "Shall I call someone?"

Then the sensation stops almost as quickly as it started. I get to my feet, spitting the taste of puke from my mouth. I remove my glove because I want to feel the crawling skin on my face.

And there it is.

My hand.

I take off my other glove and look up my sleeve. My arms are there too!

"Boydy! Boydy! I'm back! Look!"

I take off the mask and wig.

Lady bounds up to me—relieved, I think, to see me again.

Boydy turns and looks, and grins slowly.

"Oh yeah," he says, nodding. "That's a *lot* less weird, Effow!"

CHAPTER TWENTY-TWO

An hour later, I'm back home with Lady and Boydy. Gram is still out, due back shortly. Boydy and I are in the garage, looking at the tanning bed.

Boydy shakes his head. "Why should a tanning bed make you invisible? People go on tanning beds all the time, and they're pretty harmless. What's special about this one?" He thinks for a moment. "We could ask the woman in the tanning shop?"

"I can imagine how that'll go," I say in a sarcastic tone. "'Oh, hi. That tanning bed you gave me? It's just made me invisible.' Besides, tell her, and by the afternoon half of Whitley Bay will know and then it'll be the whole world. Like, literally. Imagine: it'll be in the papers, on the telly, all over the Web."

"Assuming she doesn't just think you're nuts. You'll be famous!"

"Exactly, Boydy. Exactly. And I don't want to be."

"Really?" He sounds genuinely surprised.

"Yes, really! If I'm gonna be famous—and I can't see the appeal at all—I want to be famous for something that I've *done*, not for having an unfortunate accident on a tanning bed and being followed around by paparazzi. Besides, Gram would hate it. She'd probably think it was common."

But Boydy's not listening. He's wrinkled up his nose and he sniffs the air.

"Blimey, Eff. Was that you?"

I thought I'd sneaked the burp out unobtrusively, but evidently not.

"Sorry. Yup, guilty. It's a burp, by the way, not a . . . you know. I think it's a side effect."

His eyes widen and he sniffs again, almost gagging. "What *is* that? It's . . . it's inhuman!"

"I think it's my Chinese herbal medicine. I kind of overdid it, and it's playing with my guts, so—"

"Hang on. Your Chinese herbal medicine? Where did you get it?"

"Off the Internet. It's an acne treatm . . ." And then I trail off as it dawns on both of us simultaneously.

CHAPTER TWENTY-THREE

Back in the kitchen I have taken down the box of Dr. Chang His Skin So Clear. There's a picture of a smiling model on the front, and a tiny picture of some Chinese guy in a white lab coat on the back. Everything on the box is in Chinese, except for a white sticker in English that says 5 GRAMS IN WATER EVERY DAILY.

That's it.

"Did you weigh it out?" Boydy asks.

I shrug. I'm embarrassed.

"Kind of."

"So, five grams is about a teaspoon," he says.

"Ah. I thought it was a tablespoon."

"No, that's about fifteen grams. And you did this once a day?"

"Sometimes more." I'm mumbling like a kid found raiding the biscuit tin, only instead of there being guilty crumbs around my mouth, I'm blushing with shame.

"So . . . ," he says, "a massive overdose of some unlabeled, unlicensed, unidentifiable *stuff* might have combined with a massive overdose of sketchy UV rays from a secondhand tanning bed to make you invisible?"

"Um, yeah," I say.

Looks that way.

Boydy flips open my laptop, which is on the kitchen counter. "What's the website where you got this, anyway?" he asks, and I tell him.

He types in the URL.

Error 404. Sorry, the website you have asked for cannot be found.

He tries again in case he has made a typing error, but the same message comes up.

Next he types "Dr. Chang His Skin So Clear" in the search box. There are only three search results and they all lead to the same message saying that the website cannot be found.

I've got the beginnings of a horrible, cold fear, but then I hear a key in the front door, and Lady gets up to greet Gram.

Quickly, Boydy removes the paper bag of powder from the cardboard box and shoves the box in his pocket.

"I might be able to get the box translated," he says, just as Gram comes into the kitchen.

The second she sees Boydy, Gram straightens her shoulders and puts on a smile.

I think she's just relieved that I know someone. It's not often people come round these days. The last was Kirsten Olen and that was ages ago.

I do the introductions and Boydy doesn't mess up. That is, he stands up, shakes her hand, looks her in the eye, and smiles. He could almost have been taught by her.

"Will you stay for tea, Elliot?" she asks, beaming with delight that I have brought someone home who doesn't mumble and look at their shoes.

"Ah, no, thank you very much, Mrs. Leatherhead. I've got to be off. Very nice to meet you."

Wow, I think, *so he knows the rules as well. It's like being in a secret society.*

CHAPTER TWENTY-FOUR

Gram is making tea and I'm trying to behave as if this has not been the weirdest day of my whole life.

The radio is on. Gram always listens to Radio 3 or Classic FM. (She sometimes asks me if I know the composer, and if the music's on the organ I usually guess Bach and I'm right about half the time. She forgets the times I'm wrong, so she has this totally false idea that I know loads about classical music.)

Do you ever get that thing when someone's being nice to you, and chatty and everything, but you just can't be bothered? And you can't say anything because that would just be rude, so you have to pretend to be paying attention by making the right noises? You know, raising your eyebrows and going "Hmm!" and stuff.

That's what it's like with Gram right now.

She's blabbering on about . . . Well, that's the point. I'm not listening, so I don't know what she's blabbering on about. I pick up "Reverend Robinson" and something about his sermon that morning, then Mrs. Abercrombie and the Food Bank Committee, and something to do with something else, and . . .

"Are you all right, Ethel?"

"Hmm? Yes, Gram, thanks. Fine."

"Only, I have just told you about Mrs. Abercrombie's Geoffrey and you haven't said a thing."

It turns out—because Gram tells me again, and this time I make sure to pay proper attention—that Mrs. Abercrombie's Yorkshire terrier, Geoffrey, has joined the list of local missing dogs.

I pretend to be sorry, but:

a) I am too tired to be bothered.

b) Geoffrey, despite having only three legs, is detestable and seems to have grown an extra load of temper to compensate for his missing front right leg.

And . . .

c) There is—obviously—only one thing on my mind.

You know I said I was done with crying?

Turns out I was wrong.

All my bubbling emotions overflow and I start sniffling

at the kitchen table. I feel Gram's arms around me, and she doesn't even know what's the matter.

"It's all right," she says, though how can she know?

I hug her back; it feels good. I can smell her tea breath and her flowery, soapy scent. In that moment, in that hug, everything seems OK again, and I let myself forget that everything is very far from OK. Hugs are good like that.

It gives me the strength for one more try.

"Gram?" I start. "You know I said this morning that I had become invisible . . . ?"

I'm hoping she'll listen while I offload everything that's on my mind.

She doesn't, though. Instead she pulls up a chair next to me and carries on *exactly* where she left off before: feeling that the world sometimes ignores you, the sense that you have to shout to make yourself heard, that people look straight through you as if you are invisible.

And so on. She's being *nice* and everything, but it doesn't help.

My mouth is full of the words I want to say:

"No, Gram. I mean I was *really* invisible."

But I swallow them again.

"I'm a bit tired, Gram," I say. "I'm just going to go to bed, I think."

"All right, pet," says Gram. "I'll bring you up a cocoa."

I go upstairs and check myself over again and again in the big bathroom mirror. Everything seems to be back to normal—that is, there are no bits of me that are invisible.

What's more, I *think* my spots are getting a bit better. No—really, they are. It's not just my imagination.

I'm feeling very alone, and that makes me think of Mum.

I haven't opened my shoe box of Mum stuff for ages. It's there on the shelf, along with books and soft toys, and I get it down, open it up, and lay out the things.

WHAT IS IN THE BOX OF STUFF FROM MY MUM

- **The T-shirt I've already told you about. I give it a deep sniff, and it's like magic: a calming, comforting smell. I hold it in front of me, opened out, and try to imagine Mum filling out the black fabric. It's a lady's size 8, according to the label, so Mum wasn't all that big. (I lay it out on top of my bed.)**
- **The card is next. (I read the rhyme, although I know it by heart: I just like to imagine her hand holding the pen that wrote the words. She probably wore dark nail polish, and her hands will have been slim and pale.)**

- There are three little beanbag cats, all different. There's a black-and-white one, an orange stripey one, and a pink one. There should be four, actually, because I saw the full set in a toy shop once, and it's a blue one that's missing. But I've only got three and that's OK. I've never given them names, in case Mum did—I wouldn't want to choose different names. (I arrange them on top of the T-shirt in a neat line.)
- A little packet of Haribo sweets. A bit odd, I guess, but Gram says Mum loved Haribos, and at her funeral everyone who came was given a packet. I can't really remember, but I like the idea of people eating sweets at a funeral, although I didn't eat mine, obviously, which is why I've still got them. (I put the packet next to the cats.)
- Last, there's a pamphlet advertising a concert for a singer called Felina who was appearing at a music festival on Newcastle's Quayside. Except Mum died before the concert took place. I like to think she was looking forward to it in the way I look forward to stuff like Christmas.

CHAPTER TWENTY-FIVE

I've done it loads of times before, this laying out of the shoe box stuff. I do it the same every time, and I never get sad.

Only, this time, I do get sad, and that takes me by surprise, and makes me sadder still. I quickly put the stuff away in case I start to cry again, and I sit on my bed, listening to my breathing.

And that is where the whole invisible thing might have ended. Just some weird day that came and went, with nobody to say that I was telling the truth—apart from an unpopular kid at school who is well known for shooting his mouth off, so no one would have believed him.

I could have left it at that. That would have been fine.

But then I might never have discovered who I am.

Part Two

CHAPTER TWENTY-SIX

Once things start to happen, I find they happen pretty quickly.

The first thing, though, is not really a "thing."

It's Elliot Boyd. Well, Elliot Boyd and Kirsten Olen. And me.

Boydy first. He has decided that we are best friends, and for days now has been coming up to me, super-friendly, waiting for me at lunch and after school—and it has been noticed by other people.

I don't want to be mean to him, but he still gets on my nerves with his constant stream of one-sided conversation, always about himself and something *he* is interested in. The only thing he wants to talk about, apart from the lighthouse, is the invisibility thing—and we can't talk about that with other people, so it's just him and me. I'm forced to tolerate him because we share the secret, *and* he's taken the box of Dr. Chang His Skin So Clear, which I am furious with myself about.

The last couple of afternoons I've waited in the bathrooms along the corridor from the lockers to make sure he has gone before I walk home. Yesterday he was hanging around the lockers for half an hour, this slightly sad look on his round face, which almost made me change my mind.

So it's lunchtime, and the Knight twins are nowhere to be seen. I've spotted that Kirsten Olen is in line with Aramynta Fell and Katie Pelling, and I join them so that I am already partnered up if Boydy makes an appearance.

The girls are OK. It's not as if I dislike Kirsten Olen. We fell apart rather than fell out.

It's Aramynta I'm not so sure of. It starts as soon as we sit down (me being careful to make sure there are no spaces either side of me, just in case).

Aramynta smiles this warm smile that chills me, and half closes her eyes mysteriously.

Oh, God, this is not going to go well—I can tell from the smile. It's too friendly. *Why* did I sit here?

"The posse and I were talking . . ."

Oh, please. "The posse" is Aramynta Fell and some other girls at the table—presumably including Kirsten now, which is disappointing. Individually they're all right. Katie Pelling once let me copy her chemistry homework when I had forgotten to do mine, which is actually quite a nice thing to do. Together, though, they are so completely tiresome. It seems to be their mission in life to ignore the school's no-makeup/jewelry/short-skirts rules whenever they can, and they're forever getting into trouble for it.

Seriously: What is the point?

Anyway, Aramynta goes on:

"We were talking and we think your skin is, like, *so* much better than it was."

"Umm . . . thanks?"

Katie Pelling starts spluttering with laughter. When that happens, you know you are on the receiving end of *something* even if you don't know what it is. She tries to cover it up with a cough, but I can tell.

"Walk away," Gram would say. "Walk away and do not stoop to their level."

Good advice, but what if you want to find out what they were going to say?

"And we all kind of wondered: Is it, like, *official*—you know, you and your boyfriend?"

Katie Pelling gives up trying to hold back, and emits a snort of laughter—the sort that comes with an unwanted helping of snot, which makes the others laugh even more.

Aramynta is cross because they have ruined her straight-faced mockery, but she maintains an expression of pure innocence.

"Boyfriend?" I say, furrowing my brow and trying to

appear as baffled as I can even though I know *exactly* what she is referring to. "I don't have a boyfriend. You know that, Aramynta." *Good,* I tell myself. *Calm, but firm.*

"But you and Elliot Boyd—you look *soooo* cute together! Aren't they? Kirsten! Aren't they cute together? Elliot and Ethel. *Ethiot!*"

Kirsten nods, struggling to keep a straight face. "So cute! Together forever!" As she says this my heart sinks, as I realize I am losing my oldest friend.

"You'd better watch out, Ethel. The girls'll be after him."

"She needn't worry," says Katie Pelling. "There's plenty of him to go round!"

More spluttering and chortling.

I've had enough. Everything I have been bottling up for days rises in my chest, and I feel myself getting hot with anger.

"That . . . that *lump* is *not* my boyfriend! He's not any sort of friend. I don't even like him. Who does? He's a pain in the neck. I hate him. He hangs around me like a bad smell."

This last comment is a cheap shot. Irritating though Boydy is, I have been close enough to him to know that the "Smelliot" thing is untrue. Still, I think I have said it forcefully enough: opposite me, Aramynta and Kirsten are wide-eyed.

Except they're not looking at me, but a little beyond my

shoulder. Without turning, I mouth the words *"Is he there?"* to Kirsten, who nods almost imperceptibly.

I get up with my tray. Out of the corner of my eye, I see him, tray in hand, easily close enough to hear what I said.

Without even getting closer to look at his face, I know he's looking sad and puzzled, like he did at the lockers yesterday.

I hate myself.

CHAPTER TWENTY-SEVEN

There's a memory I have from when I was very little: it's about Mum's funeral.

Gram says Mum's funeral was quite a small affair, but in my memory it's not. I guess that's because we all like to think of our mums and dads as really important, and a small event wouldn't fit that image, would it?

Anyway, we're in a big church, but instead of organ music there's rock music. Loud, thrashing rock music, and lots of people, all eating Haribos.

(This is not a dream by the way—at least, I don't think so. It's definitely a memory, but maybe it's mixed up with other stuff because you wouldn't normally have loud rock music at a funeral, although there *were* Haribos, so I don't know for sure.)

Gram is with me, and I think Great-Gran as well, in a wheelchair. And Gram is angry, though not with me.

Not sad: just angry. Her face is cold and hard, like the sea on a Whitley Bay winter's day.

That's the memory. It's a weird one, eh?

It's not much, but bear with me.

Now, I don't want to freak you out or anything, but did you know that when we talk about a dead person's "ashes," they're not really ashes? They're ground-up bone. Bone is pretty much all that is left after a cremation, which is when you burn the body of a dead person rather than bury it, and you get given the ashes to bury on your own or to throw in the sea or something. It's what happens to most people nowadays, says Gram.

How did I get onto this? I know it sounds creepy, but I'll be done soon. The reason is this: my mum does not have a grave.

You see, I've watched films and read books that people die in, and the dead people always have graves. The living person—usually a husband or girlfriend or something—then goes to the grave and talks to the dead person and tells them about their life. Then they usually place some flowers there, or touch the headstone, and it's sweet and sad and I often cry in these bits.

But I can't do that—visit a grave—because Mum was cremated.

I don't even know what happened to Mum's ashes, now that I think about it. I'll have to ask Gram.

Why am I telling you this now?

I think I am punishing myself. The Boydy thing has upset me, and I deserve to feel bad by thinking of my mum.

Most people in my situation would try to be happy when they remember their mum. Not me.

At least, not unless I'm looking through my shoe box of Mum stuff.

(And even then, I don't feel exactly *happy.*)

It stays with me, though, that feeling of sadness and guilt, and is one of the reasons that I end up becoming invisible again.

Which is—to say the *very* least—inadvisable.

CHAPTER TWENTY-EIGHT

It's more than a week later, and I haven't yet been back to see Great-Gran.

To be honest, I'm beginning to think I imagined the whole thing. You know, Great-Gran secretly signaling to me that she wanted me to come back on my own. Why would she do that? I've replayed it again and again in my head, and all it was, really, was a look.

She's a hundred. It could easily be nothing.

But my instinct is that it's not. My instinct is that it's *something*—that Great-Gran is trying to tell me something I need to know.

On my way home (alone, obviously), I notice another Missing Pet poster has gone up on the Missing Pet lamppost. It's Geoffrey. There's a picture of him, and the text:

MISSING

Yorkshire terrier, front leg missing. Red collar.

Answers to Geoffrey.

Call Mrs. Q. Abercrombie
07974 377 337
REWARD

Back home, and tea with Gram is just strange.

She has gone *very* quiet. What with my guilt at hurting Boydy, and whatever it is that's going on with Gram, we sip our tea in virtual silence.

Shop-bought biscuits too. That *is* unusual.

I say nothing.

A little later, I text Boydy. It's probably the hardest thing I have ever had to write.

Hi. Sorry about the other day. It's not what I really think. Friends?

Thirteen words. I'm wondering if it will be enough when a text pings almost immediately.

Too late. Forget it. "Lump"? I thought some things were off-limits. Apparently not.

So he heard it all, including "lump." It's not *quite* calling him fat, but it's in the same territory. Why did I do that?

In the time we have known each other, Boydy has never *once* made a reference to my spots, or for that matter to my appearance at all, apart from once saying he thought my hair looked nice—and then he blushed so much that I think he must have regretted it.

Nor have I ever mentioned his size.

But some things are out of bounds, however upset you are. Making references to Boydy's weight, I now discover, is one of them. The hurt is written all over his text message.

He once told me he had been "large" all his life and that he hated it. I have just made it worse for him.

Hurting people's feelings would definitely merit a place on Gram's list of "rather common" things. Come to think of it, hurtful comments about someone's appearance are probably "frightfully common."

Ms. Hall said she would upload our homework to the school's website, but it's not there, or I can't find it, and I'm clicking around the website when I see the notice for the school's talent show, which is tomorrow, and there's Boydy's name as one of the contestants.

Inevitable, really. If there was anybody who would refuse to let an absence of talent hold them back from a talent show, it would be overconfident Elliot Boyd. He *has* told me about this, in one of his coming-home-from-school monologues, but it kind of got lost in the general Boyd-noise.

He has been learning the guitar for precisely one month. And I can see from the list who he's going up against and that he's already toast:

- A Year Ten thrash-metal group called Mother of Dragons, who played in assembly once and are really noisy and good.
- Savannah and Clem Roeber, who do ballroom dancing to modern music, like on TV. They're good too.
- Nilesh Patel, who's in Year Eleven and does *real* stand-up comedy and not just a long list of jokes from a book.

In fact, everyone's good. He's going to be slaughtered. Poor Boydy cannot play the guitar for anything and he will be booed off.

Actually, he won't be booed off, because that wouldn't be allowed. But he'll be watched in total silence, applauded insincerely, and mocked forever after.

And I realize that:

a) I don't want that to happen to him, and
b) if I somehow prevent it, then he will forgive me for insulting him to Aramynta Fell and Co.

That's when I decide I'm going to become invisible again.

To try to save Boydy. It's the least I can do, really, given how I've hurt his feelings.

It's odd, too, how quickly the decision forms in my

head. It's like I'm staring at the computer screen and then—*boom!*—it all becomes clear. That, I find, is reassuring: it *must* be a good plan if I've thought of it so quickly.

No?

See what you think: it is less harebrained than it sounds.

A bit less, anyway.

I will go onstage when he's performing. I will be invisible, having somehow got myself out of school for that day and spent the morning on the tanning bed. I will whisper directions in his ear and lift the guitar from his hands, thereby creating the most wonderful illusion:

The floating guitar!

I can actually play a bit. Better than Boydy, anyway, so as it floats I will strum some chords, and he will wave his hands like a magician and his act will be received with rapturous, elated, wondrous applause!

Sounds good, eh?

No. Now that I have outlined it, it sounds completely ridiculous: the fantasy of a mind that has been warped by herbal concoctions and overexposure to UV light.

You decide, but at least I've made *my* mind up. Yes, it's a risk. But any ill effects from the last time have been, well . . . nonexistent. My skin has improved. I can even convince myself that my hair is shinier, and I try tossing it like Aramynta

Fell but I can't really do it. I probably look like a demented horse being annoyed by flies.

So that's one decision made. But right now I have something else to do. This is the evening that I told myself I would visit Great-Gran alone and find out what on earth she meant—if anything—with that look she gave me on her birthday.

I hear Gram call from downstairs:

"I'm off! Bye, darling. I won't be late."

Tonight is Gram's "concert night." Once a month or so, Gram and some of her friends go to a concert. Classical or jazz: old people's music, basically.

It's an early one tonight. Six-ish at the Whitley Bay Playhouse. Some jazz quartet. It finishes at eight.

Which gives me a little over two hours to get to the rest home and find out why Great-Gran was being so odd on her birthday.

CHAPTER TWENTY-NINE

It's seven by the time I get to Priory View, and I'm soaking wet—on the outside from the rain that started the second I stepped out the door, and on the inside from sweating under my waterproof jacket.

I've come on the Metro and I've brought Lady with me. It's nice with Lady at Great-Gran's home, because if Great-Gran's in a not-saying-anything state (which is usual), then we can stroke Lady, who doesn't mind who says what so long as she has her tummy tickled. And Great-Gran always smiles when she sees Lady.

It's only three stops to Tynemouth. Then it's a five-minute walk down to the seafront, where fat needles of salty summer rain are coming off the North Sea.

So I'm going in the entrance of the Priory View Residential Care Home, Lady is on the leash, and a man is coming the other way, out of the door. Except he's not looking where he's going and we almost collide, but not quite. I notice straightaway, though, that he's a smoker: the smell of old tobacco lingers on him.

He looks up from his phone, which he's been texting on, and an exchange happens between us. It seems ordinary enough on the face of it, but it leaves me feeling uneasy and puzzled.

We almost collide, and we both say "Oh, sorry!" like you do; then he stops, kind of blocking my way, but not aggressively or anything, and the thing is, he's looking at me *really* intensely.

Then he looks down, as if he knows he was staring, and says:

"Nice dog!"

Do you have a dog? Whether you do or you don't, "Nice dog" is like the universal conversation starter among people when at least one of them has a dog. It's a bit like when people talk about the weather, but less boring.

It goes like this:

"Nice dog!"

"Is it a boy or a girl?"

"What breed is he/she?" (This is usually only used when the breed is not obvious. If it is, like in Lady's case, it goes: "Labrador, is it?")

"How old is he/she?"

"What's his/her name?"

That's it, more or less. After that, you're away and running with the conversation if you want, and if you don't want, then everyone goes their own way.

And that is pretty much exactly the way the exchange goes with this man, except it's a little awkward because:

a) We are both kind of stuck together in the lobby of a care home, and
b) he keeps *looking* at me.

Strangely, I don't feel creeped-out by it, which would be normal. An unknown man staring at you would usually be enough reason to feel creeped-out, but for some reason not this time. Every time I look up, he is gazing intently at me.

He's youngish—early thirties, I guess—and dressed like a teacher. Corduroy trousers, collared shirt open at the neck, shiny shoes. He has short sandy hair on top of a thin face and a set of perfectly even teeth that are far too white, and that he keeps flashing at me, and grinning—a bit too much for someone you've just met.

Lady is sniffing his shoes and wagging her tail while this is going on, and when the man puts his hand out to pat her head, I notice a thing that—to me—seems completely inconsistent with his sensible Head of Geography style, and that is that the first two fingers on his hand have got yellowish stains on them from cigarette smoke. (The only time I've ever seen that before is on a shabby old guy at church who Gram always stops to say hello to because, she says, no one else does.)

"Look, I'd better be, erm . . . ," I say, nodding my head towards the interior.

"Yes, yes, of course," he says, as if suddenly embarrassed.

He talks with a London accent. Definitely not a Geordie. For a second, I wonder if he might be Boydy's dad or something. But why would he be here?

"Bye, erm . . . I didn't catch your name."

OK, now this *is* getting a bit creepy. Dog chat doesn't normally extend to personal introductions.

"Ethel," I say, and I don't mean it to sound so cold, but that is how it comes out.

"Right," he says, his tone flatter now. "Right. Bye then, Ethel. And Lady."

"Bye."

I watch him go out onto the steps, and the old-tobacco smell lingers in the lobby after him. Lady and I go into the warm, carpety reception area and straight on towards Great-Gran's room. As we turn the corner, I look back. He's still there on the steps, lighting a cigarette, and he immediately turns his head, embarrassed at being caught looking.

"Eeh, petal—ye're soakin'!" says one of the staff when I walk in dripping rain.

Lady gives herself a good shake, and instead of being annoyed the woman just laughs. She knows me, but not by name.

"Y'come to see yer gran, petal?"

"My great-gran, yes."

"Well, she's just had her hot milk. She's sitting up now."

"How is she?"

The nurse pauses, clearly weighing up how much to tell me. Eventually she settles on: "Up an' down, pet. Up an' down. Not so good today. But she'll be pleased to see you. You're the second visitor she's had today!"

I don't know anyone else who visits Great-Gran, but I suppose I don't know everything about her.

Lady and I pad down the corridor, past old Stanley's room. He's there, as always, facing away from the window, and he lifts his hand weakly in a greeting—more to Lady than to me, I think, but I don't mind. This time I stop.

"Hello, Stanley," I say.

I would call him Mr. Whatever if I knew his last name, but I don't. He doesn't hear me.

Then a nurse pushes past impatiently, ignoring me completely.

"ALL RIGHT, STANLEY, LOVE! I'VE GOT THEM SUPPOSITORIES FOR YOU!"

I move away. I don't want to know more about Stanley and his constipation remedies.

Great-Gran is sitting almost exactly as I last saw her, but she's not responsive today. She doesn't seem to be expecting me, even though I phoned Priory View to tell them I was coming.

Her chair is facing the big window, and her hands are underneath the tartan blanket.

"Hello, Great-Gran!" I say, and Lady goes up to her, nudging her arm to be petted.

There is no response. Instead Great-Gran stares out, moving her jaw a little. I think she has a sweetie in there, probably a Mint Imperial. She likes those.

"How have you been? You look well. I like your cardigan. Is that new?"

I pause after each question, and if there's no reply, I sort of pretend there has been one. I've got all this from Gram—that's what she does.

So I start to tell Great-Gran about school. And that leads to telling her about Aramynta Fell and her "posse" and how tiresome they are. I try to make it funny, but it's hard when there's no reaction.

Telling Great-Gran about Aramynta leads on to Boydy,

and before I know it, I'm telling Great-Gran all about being invisible.

I know I shouldn't, but even if she tells anyone, who on earth would believe her? It would be dismissed as the rambling of a very old lady. This makes me feel guilty when I realize it: it feels like I'm taking advantage of Great-Gran's silence. She just sits there, gazing at the rain splattering on the window, sucking her sweet, which has lasted a good ten minutes already. Perhaps—without really knowing it—I meant to tell her all along.

Lady has settled at Great-Gran's feet and stretched herself out for a good nap.

We pause. Or rather, *I* pause. It's pretty exhausting maintaining a one-way conversation. What has she heard? What has she understood?

Then she says something.

"Invisible."

That's it. That's all she says. It's enough, though, for me to know that I have not been completely wasting my breath for the last ten minutes.

I prattle on.

"I hear you had another visitor today, Great-Gran? Who was that? Was it an old friend from Culvercot? I expect it's nice to get visitors, yeah?"

Oh dear, I am getting desperate now. It's OK, though,

because when I next look over, Great-Gran's head has drooped and she is asleep, upright in her chair. I get up to go and, seeing me, Lady scrambles to her feet as well.

Just then one of the nurses comes in.

"Hokay, Lizzie. You wantin' to come to lounge? *East-Enders* is on. We get you in wheelchair an' I take you along." She has a foreign accent. I don't know where it's from, but she talks a bit like Nadiya in Year Seven, who's from Lithuania.

"She's asleep," I say to the nurse.

"Asleep? I no think so—not Lizzie. YOU'RE NOT ASLEEP, ARE YOU, LIZZIE?"

Great-Gran's eyes flicker open, and seem surprised to see me.

"See? She just restin' her eyes, innit?"

"Excuse me," I say as politely as I can to the bustling nurse. "Who was my great-gran's visitor today?"

The nurse doesn't look at me. "She has a visitor, eh? Lucky you, Lizzie: that's two in one day!" Then she says to me, "Sorry, love, I just start my shift. Look in the visitor book, though. Everyone sign in."

I know I didn't sign in. The home seems pretty relaxed about it.

"Hey, Lizzie. How are you no boilin' under this blanket, hey? Come—I'll take it off you."

The nurse lifts off the tartan blanket. Great-Gran's hands have been under it the whole time, clutching a piece of stiff paper.

It's a photograph. An old one, with a shiny surface.

I know instantly who the man is—it's my dad, all beard and grungy hair—and he's holding a little child who could be me, but might not be (it's a bit blurry). And there's a woman behind him, and she's grinning and has a hand on my foot, as if she's wanting to be in the picture, wanting to show that she's part of this.

Except it's not my mum. This woman has dark, upswept glasses, an enormous auburn hairdo, and a heavily made-up mouth. She's vaguely familiar in a rock star/celebrity sort of way but I have no idea of her name.

Why would someone who is not my mum be in a picture like that? It could be some sister of my dad's, I suppose. Come to think of it, it could be anyone.

Anyone at all.

But it isn't, is it?

Great-Gran wanted me to see this photo, and that's why she told me to come.

CHAPTER THIRTY

Great-Gran shakily turns the photo over and over in her hands, and turns her head towards me slowly.

"Is this me, Great-Gran?" I ask, and I take it from her gently. "Who's the woman?"

Great-Gran is not looking at me. Her mouth begins to move, and she licks her lips. I recognize this: she's building up the energy to say something.

"Who are you?" she says. Her eyes have demisted and they're looking straight at me.

Surely Great-Gran knows who I am? My insides give a tiny lurch as I realize that perhaps she's finally losing her mind. Not recognizing her own great-granddaughter?

Gently, I say, "It's me, Great-Gran. Ethel. Your great-granddaughter." I add, a little louder, "*Ethel.*"

Her eyes narrow and her lips come together in what could be an expression of impatience.

"Who are you, hinny?"

I take the picture from her and look closer. It's definitely me; it's definitely Dad. I point to the woman with all the hair.

"Who's this?" I ask.

But Great-Gran's eyes have misted over, as if she's pulled a net curtain across her gaze, and she turns again to the window.

I hold the picture up close to get a better look. That's when I smell it.

Old tobacco. Sniffing the picture, I confirm to myself that there is a very faint but definite smell of cigarettes on it.

So I'm peering at the picture and sniffing it, which probably looks strange, and I become aware that the nurse from before is looking over my shoulder. She has been listening to our conversation, and I didn't realize she was there.

"You know who that looks like?" the nurse says as she plumps up a cushion and wedges it behind Great-Gran. "Aw, you so young. She die years ago. Probably before you are born, even. Is like Felina! Looks the spit. She did that song, *'Light the light . . . dad a dee dee . . .'*"

The nurse sings a line from the same song that Boydy sang that day. I've also heard of the name Felina, I think; obviously a stage name.

I nod to the nurse. "Oh, yeah. I've heard that."

I feel sure the picture is a present for me, so I put it in my pocket.

Then the nurse says something else. She just chatters on, making conversation.

"Destroy by show business, that's what they say."

"Who? Felina?"

"Yes. Drugs, alcohol . . . the whole lot. Ruin her. Kill her eventually, yes? Let it be a lesson, petal." She's wagging a finger at me, but she isn't being mean.

"I know she like the songs," she continues. She turns to Great-Gran and speaks a little louder. "You like Felina's songs, don't you, Lizzie? You quite the fan girl, aren't you?"

Great-Gran just blinks out of the window. I think she smiles a little.

"I am in here the other day and one of the songs come on the radio. Hey, I could tell she is listenin'. Her fingers start movin' with the music, I swear to God."

CHAPTER THIRTY-ONE

On the way home, I use up some of my phone's data allowance to listen to "Light the Light" by Felina. It's a slowish song, with lots of fuzzy guitar, a saxophone (I think), and deep drumbeats. And Felina's voice is throaty but beautiful.

"You always said that I never should,
And I always said that I would and I could.
You were never there
But I didn't want to care, so . . .
Light the light! Let me see you tonight.
Light the light! Let me put it right. . . ."

I'm not much good at analyzing song lyrics. So many of them seem to be pretty meaningless. But I think this is clearly an angry poem about a woman and a man she wasn't getting on with. It makes me sad, but I still listen to it three times.

I'm back shortly before Gram is dropped off by the Reverend Henry Robinson.

I don't tell her that I have been to see Great-Gran, and I don't show her the photo. I know it's significant, but I can't work out why, and it's pretty clear that it's some sort of a secret.

Why would Great-Gran ask me who I am?

CHAPTER THIRTY-TWO

I'm guarding a secret. Gram and Great-Gran are too. It's an isolating feeling. I wonder: If everything was out in the open, would I do what I do next?

That night before bed, in readiness for tomorrow, I drink two cups of Dr. Chang His Skin So Clear. I nearly throw it all back up, but don't.

Tomorrow I will be invisible again. Tomorrow I will make amends for being so mean to Elliot Boyd.

But it's more than that, isn't it? You know it, and I know it.

Making amends for being mean is nice and everything—and, yes, we should all try not to hurt other people's feelings in the first place—but it's hardly a good enough reason for such a risky venture.

So why am I doing it?

It is the last thing I think of before I fall into a fitful, sweaty sleep: *Who am I?*

Who am I?

I'm going to turn myself invisible again, and I'm going to find out.

CHAPTER THIRTY-THREE

And now, another confession.

I am a thief.

Not a bad one. It's just that the stuff from China on the Internet, Dr. Chang His Skin So Clear, I bought using Gram's credit card.

It's wrong, I know, and if Gram ever found out, she'd be so upset with me.

I don't think she will find out, though. Not for a while, at any rate. I know for a fact that she's truly hopeless at checking her bank statements: they pile up, unopened, in a drawer in the kitchen for weeks and weeks, and then she'll have a whole evening when she opens them all and puts them in a folder, which, once or twice a year, she hands over to Mr. Chatterjee, who does her accounts.

If I wanted to, I could probably use Gram's card to order all sorts of things, but I don't. In fact, this is the only time I have ever done it, and that was only because Gram refused my request to order it for me on the grounds that it was "stuff and nonsense" and "quite possibly dangerous."

So I am a thief.

I am now about to become a forger as well.

I have to forge a sick note from Gram to my school—I mean, if I'm invisible, they're going to think I'm absent, aren't they? This, as it turns out, is even easier, since the school accepts emails for absences.

Next morning, I'm up at six and downstairs on the computer before Gram gets up. I have opened up Gram's email account.

TO: admin@whitleybayacademy.ac.uk
FROM: beatriceleatherhead12@btInternet.co.uk
RE: Ethel Leatherhead, Class 8A

Please excuse Ethel from school today. She is unwell with a stomach complaint. I expect she will be back tomorrow.

Thank you.
B. Leatherhead (Mrs.)

I click SEND and then go into the "Sent" folder and delete the email.

Now the waiting starts. I need to wait for the school administrator to reply with an acknowledgment, then delete it immediately. That way it won't show up on Gram's phone if she checks her email at work.

The computer pings with an incoming email, but not the one I'm waiting for, so I turn the volume down.

Mrs. Moncur, the administrator, is usually at school by about seven-forty-five: I used to see her arrive when I'd go for early choir practice (until Gram stopped me because she thought I wasn't getting enough sleep).

Gram comes down at about seven-thirty.

I'm nervous but trying to act normally, while keeping an eye on the computer.

"Have you taken the paper in?" asks Gram when she comes into the kitchen for breakfast.

We have the newspaper delivered in the morning, and Gram reads it while eating a slice of whole-grain toast and half a grapefruit. Meanwhile, I munch my cereal.

"No," I reply.

The paperboy is totally unreliable, missing about one day a week. And when that happens, Gram goes to the computer to check the headlines online.

Time to think, quick. The router is on the other side of the kitchen from the computer, by the fridge, and as Gram pulls out the stool to sit down, I casually take my glass to get some juice and flick the router's switch to OFF.

It's only going to be a temporary solution. I mean, Gram's not a computer expert, but she can turn a router on and off.

I hear her tutting.

"Honestly. Ethel, can you have a look at this? I can't open the Internet."

"Have you run a diagnostics check?" I ask, leaning over her and clicking with the mouse. "It was acting up yesterday."

A diagnostics check takes a couple of minutes, but it'll come back with a message saying, *You are not connected to the Internet. Please check your router.*

While the check is running, Gram leaves the kitchen.

I'm going to have to act quickly.

I open up Word, select a boring font, and rapidly type the following:

YOUR INTERNET SERVICE PROVIDER IS TEMPORARILY DISABLED. ERROR NO. 809. PLEASE TRY AGAIN LATER.

I do a quick screen grab and import it into the "Photos" file.

Oh my, I forgot how long the photos take to load. . . .

Once it's there, I open it and hit EDIT, cropping the image so that it's just a rectangle of text, which I move to the desktop.

I can hear Gram coming back downstairs.

I position the notice bang in the middle of the screen and take another screen grab, which I open and enlarge to full screen just as Gram comes back into the kitchen.

I adjust my facial expression from one of TOTAL PANIC to mild irritation and I tut.

"Some problem with the server," I say. "Look."

She comes over and reads the error notice. It actually looks *nothing* like a real error notice, but if you're not suspicious, then it looks OK.

Thankfully Gram's not suspicious. She waggles the mouse a bit, tuts herself, then goes to put the kettle on again.

Result! At that moment, an "incoming message" alert appears at the top right of the screen.

Thank you for informing us of your child's absence. I hope she recovers soon.

Yours sincerely,

Mrs. D. Moncur (Administrator)

I hit DELETE quietly while Gram's back is turned.

Phew. All that for a day or two off school.

CHAPTER THIRTY-FOUR

Now that Gram has left for work (I "suddenly remembered" a geography assignment that I hadn't finished, so she left without me), I have chugged another two cups of what I now think of as Dr. Chang's Fantastically Foul His Skin So Clear.

I am getting better at keeping it down. I am not feeling sick so much, although my stomach is churning with nerves and is distended with gas, just like the last time.

I figure I will wait for the gas to start to make its escape, as it were, before I get in the tanning bed. I want everything to be the same as before.

I don't have to wait long. An hour or so after Gram leaves, I start on the burping.

I'm trying to back-time from the start of our school's Whitley's Got Talent show, which is at one-thirty, straight after lunch. Last time, my invisibility lasted about five hours, so really I don't want to get off the tanning bed till about ten-thirty or later. This means that so far, my timing is fine.

My heart is beating fast, my stomach is twisting, my

brain is racing, and as for my burps—you just don't want to know. This is not a normal smell. Even if you've been eating curried eggs or something, you could not produce a smell like this. It hangs in the air of the garage like a toxic fog.

Getting in the tanning bed this time is different from the last—mainly because I know what is going to happen, so I'm nervous, and also I won't fall asleep. Instead I just lie there with my eyes shut.

I've put the radio on this time and a caller to the radio station is saying: ". . . so I'd like you to play 'Light the Light' by Felina for me please, Jamie."

That's strange. I mean, I know it's just a coincidence, but still . . .

"Great choice! Great choice! One of my personal favorites. Why that one, Chrissie?"

"It's for my mum," says the caller. "It reminds me of her. She passed away when—"

But Jamie Farrow cuts her off, presumably because nine thirty in the morning is no time to be getting maudlin on Radio North.

"For your mum! That's lovely, Chrissie, what a nice thought, and I'm sure she appreciates it wherever she is. So, for Chrissie in Blaydon, and her lovely mum, here she is: the late, great Felina with 'Light the Light.'"

The song is already familiar to me: the slow *boom boom*

boom of the bass drum to start, then a deep, rusty guitar chord followed by Felina's throaty vocals, and for some reason—no doubt the combination of the fear I'm feeling and everything else that's happening—I find myself getting emotional. A lump forms in my throat, which I swallow back down, and I have to turn the radio off.

I lie in silence and let the time drift by, and I close my eyes because it's not good to stare at the UV tubes inside a tanning bed.

I know I don't fall asleep, but it's like waking up. I know it's happening, because the UV light starts coming through my eyelids, slowly at first.

I open my eyes to take a look at what's happening.

Holding my hand in front of my face, I can see through it: it's like it's made of a translucent plastic, getting clearer by the second. It's hard to see precisely, because my eyes are a little bit dazzled by the strong light, but it is definitely, *definitely* working.

I know the process is finished when I close my eyes tight and I am still looking at the mauvey light of the tanning bed tubes.

To be on the safe side—although I'm not sure if "safe" is the right word here—I lie there for an extra few minutes before lifting the lid and climbing off.

I go over to the mirror and marvel once again that I am totally, utterly, amazingly invisible.

And now I'm going in to school.

CHAPTER THIRTY-FIVE

I'm standing on the front step, and I discover that I just can't do it.

I can't confidently stride forward and out into Eastbourne Drive and turn right up towards school like I normally would.

I'm almost certain it's because I am naked.

Not that anyone can see me, of course. But I can feel the breeze on my bare stomach and it's just not right.

I try to imagine that I am wearing a swimsuit, which helps.

I get out the door and a few yards up the road before turning back when I see old Paddy Flynn shuffling down to the seafront on his walker. I know in my heart that he can't see me. It's all going on in my invisible head.

And while I stall on the doorstep, I run through the plan again:

1. Go onstage, invisible.
2. Take the guitar from Boydy, who will be murdering some song or other.

3. Make it look like he's levitating the guitar.
4. Boydy gets loads of applause and people say he's awesome, so . . .
5. He forgives me for calling him fat, which I didn't *really*, but I did more or less.

I couldn't tell you why it bothers me so much, what I did to him. I mean, it wasn't that long ago that I didn't even want to be friends. But it does. Maybe it's because if I *don't* try to make it up to him, then I'm just as bad as Aramynta and the others.

More than anything, it's the look on Boydy's face that day at lunch. The look of someone who has just discovered that everything is not as he thought it was. I can relate to that.

Whatever the reason, it seems like I'm doing this.

First, though, I have to get out of my front door, and perhaps the answer is clothes.

But I'm not doing the clown mask again, that's for sure.

CHAPTER THIRTY-SIX

Well, half an hour later I've made it to the school gate and it was a piece of cake, really.

Jeans, socks, sneakers, an old zip-up rain jacket that no one at school will recognize (see? I'm thinking ahead), a pair of Gram's white gloves, sunglasses, and . . .

A stocking over my head! Just like a bank robber (from back when people robbed banks). I've taken a pair of Gram's tights (clean ones), cut one leg off, and pulled the leg over my face. The color is sort of flesh-ish, so if I zip up the rain jacket over my mouth, and pull the hood's cord tight, there's only my (invisible) nose and the sunglasses showing.

I do look a *bit* odd, I'll admit. It's a muggy June day and most people are going around without jackets, but still, if I keep my head down, you don't really notice. That's what I tell myself, anyway.

And now I'm standing outside the school gate and it's locked. A year ago, this wouldn't have been a problem, but ever since some girl in Year Ten's uncle turned up to try and take her away, the school has had this massive security overhaul, which means thumbprint sensors and cameras on the gates.

My invisible thumbprint *might* still open the gate, but I'd be seen on the security camera, and I don't look like a regular student, not in this getup.

But—once again, if you'll excuse my boasting—I'm ahead of the game. I pull a plastic bag from my jacket pocket. There's a large rhododendron bush about ten yards along the high mesh fence, so big that there's a space inside it for about two people, which is used by the older kids who want to smoke. The ground is littered with cigarette ends, but I don't mind. It's time to go naked, and I have other things to worry about.

I quickly take off my clothes and cram them into the plastic bag, and shove the whole lot a bit further under the bush.

Then I emerge.

Naked and invisible.

The walk here has actually made me bolder, I think. I'm not feeling as nervous as I was before.

I head back towards the gate just before a van with *TYNE CATERING* written on the side pulls up. A moment later, there's a metallic *clank* and the gate opens. It's a simple matter to stroll in behind the van, and there I am: on the school grounds.

There's nobody about outside. Everyone is in class.

There's a longish drive that leads up to the main entrance and goes around the back, basically encircling the school, which is a two-story building with countless extensions and annexes, all built at different times and each with a plaque announcing which local councilor performed the opening ceremony.

The most recent addition was the Performing Arts Block, which is over to the right, and that's where I go now. This is where Whitley's Got Talent will be starting in about an hour.

The air is warm and sticky, and the sky is a glowering purply-gray. But so long as it doesn't start raining, I'll be fine.

Because if it starts raining, the raindrops will hit my invisible skin and make me visible.

CHAPTER THIRTY-SEVEN

Drip.

Drip.

Drip.

CHAPTER THIRTY-EIGHT

I haven't told you this before, because it hasn't really rained yet. But I kind of knew that it would eventually and I would tell you when it came up.

Well, it has come up, and so here goes.

Getting rained on—like, *really* rained on—is just about the worst feeling I can have. I mean, since forever, not just since being invisible.

One of the reasons I haven't mentioned it is so that you won't think I'm crazy, even though I am. Just a bit, anyway.

It's not as though being rained on gives me panic attacks or anything. It's not that.

It's that rain—heavy rain, not just a shower—makes me think of my mum. And it makes me sad. And I don't want to be sad when I think of my mum. So that makes me scared. Does that make *any* sort of sense?

I'm scared of the rain making me feel sad when I think of my mum.

I think it's because one of the very few memories I have of my mum is in the rain, and it's not a good memory.

It's the before-the-funeral memory I told you about. It's probably my very earliest memory of all. I must have been about . . . two and a half? Maybe even less. I'm walking, I know that, on a pavement somewhere. And Mum is walking too, gripping me by the wrist.

It's raining, like, *really* raining. There is lightning flashing around us, and people are shouting, and Mum is soaking wet and shouting back at them, swearing, telling them to go away, only ruder. She is holding my wrist so hard that it's hurting and that's making me cry, and Mum is crying too.

I think there must have been traffic too, when I was there on the street with Mum, because the smell of rain and traffic fumes can sometimes bring back this memory, especially if it's nighttime, and . . .

Well, that's about it, really. I was upset, Mum was upset, and people were not being nice, and my wrist hurt. That's all I can remember, and even then it's sketchy.

I was only little.

So when it starts raining, it immediately makes me feel sad.

But now it also starts making me visible.

I look down and there are droplets of water hanging in the air where my arms are, on my hands, making a sort of shimmery ghost-me.

CHAPTER THIRTY-NINE

As the rain descends, so does the air temperature. The weather goes from warm and sticky to cold and wet, and I'm huddled against the wall of the Performing Arts Block, where there's an overhanging roof, using my hands to brush off the rain as much as I can, and I'm feeling cold, shivery, scared, and angry.

Cold and shivery is obvious. The scaredness is the rain/Mum thing, which has made my breathing shallow and fast and made my heart beat rapidly in my chest.

The anger? That's just me. I'm furious with myself for having taken such a stupid risk. What the *hell* was going through my head when I thought that this would be a good idea?

I bet you thought *That's a crazy idea* when you read it, didn't you?

Well, congratulations. You were right.

I look down all around where I am standing and I think I have removed most of the rain from my skin. Except for . . .

Oh. My. God. My head!

My hair is soaking. I can feel it, but not see it. Carefully, I edge along the wall towards a window. It's one of the windows into the performance studio, and there's a dark blind pulled down behind it: it makes an almost-perfect mirror. And sure enough, when I stand in front of it, there's a silvery, watery fuzz of my hair—faint, but nonetheless visible.

It looks . . . weird. I peer closer, and my breath on the glass forms a cloudy patch.

The only thing for me to do is to get my hair dry, and I'll have to do that in the girls' bathroom, where there's a hand dryer.

I need to act quick, I know that, but I can't resist drawing my initials in the steam.

E.L.

And then I freeze. From behind me I hear a voice.

"Did you see that?"

I daren't turn, but I recognize the voice.

I can see their reflections—they're standing about three yards away. It's Aramynta Fell and Katie Pelling of the posse.

"See what?" Katie says.

They have both stopped and are staring right at me. Right *through* me, I should say.

"That." Aramynta points. "Them letters just . . . wrote themselves."

The steam patch is, thankfully, disappearing, and along with it the letters.

"What are you talking about?" Katie says. "What letters?"

"It was there, it . . . they . . . And what's *that*?" She is pointing right at my head now.

Right at me.

But Katie has lost interest. Barely glancing back, she's walking off around the corner.

"It's a wall, Aramynta. They hold roofs up, you know? Come on, we're going to be late."

Aramynta's having none of it, and I'm terrified because she's coming towards me. Slowly, hesitantly, with her hand out. And I know she's going to touch my head.

"COME ON!" shouts Katie.

I could run. But then she'd follow—she's got that determined, curious look on her face. Besides, my running route is blocked by Katie Pelling.

Or I could do something else. Something that'll stop Aramynta touching my head. I have no idea where this comes from, but I have only a second to act because her hand is just a few inches from my head.

Sticking my tongue out, I utter the loudest, strangest throaty gargle I can.

It's like: *Klaaaaaaghhhhghghghgh!*

And then, for good measure, I lick her hand.

It all happens at once, the gargle and the licking.

It's a combination of the two things, I think, that so utterly freaks her out.

It takes a second for it to sink in and then Aramynta Fell does something that makes me feel almost sorry for her. She lets out a little, terrified scream and she just sinks to her knees.

She is truly speechless with shock. I'm not sure it could be fright because *she's* not even sure that there is anything there to be frightened of. She starts panting and sobbing and staring at her hand while standing up and backing away.

"Mynt! What the heck has got into you?" says Katie, approaching her with concern.

Aramynta has not taken her eyes off my hair since it happened, but now she does. I take my chance to dash around the corner towards the door, but I stop to hear what she says.

"It . . . it . . . I mean . . . licked . . . eeugh . . . It did. Agh!"

Katie is suddenly all concerned. "Hey, babe. It's OK. Come on. What's wrong? Aw, look at you, you're in a puddle. . . ."

I can hear them go back the way they came, and I lean against the wall, breathing deeply and trying hard not to laugh.

Only, I'm not at all sure that what has happened is funny.

Satisfying, definitely.

But funny?

This invisibility business is more complicated than I thought.

CHAPTER FORTY

I have found myself the perfect spot in the wings of the small stage at the end of the school theater.

There's a stack of chairs, and a fake fireplace that was used in last year's lower-school production of *Oliver!* If I squeeze between them, I'm out of the way, and would probably be invisible even if I wasn't actually, you know, *invisible.*

If I lean out a bit I can see audience members filing in, noisy and excited. I'm nervous just from being almost onstage, and although I know—like, *really* know—that no one can see me, it's still a very peculiar feeling.

The way Whitley's Got Talent works is this:

Twenty acts, two from each class in the lower school, are each given a three-minute slot. With introductions and changeovers and the prizes at the end, the show lasts two hours.

They don't do judges' comments or anything like that—not this year, anyway. The first year of the show, before I was at the school, they tried that, but the judges—who were other kids—were trying to be too funny and cruel. Two acts left the stage in tears. Last year they switched to teachers being the judges, but the teachers were too kind and said that all the acts were excellent, even the ones that weren't, and the audience started booing the judges.

So this year it's a committee of three students and three teachers, voting in secret and not making comments.

Mr. Parker is in charge of introducing the acts. Today he has a bow tie on, and he skips up the steps to a cheer and applause, and at least one wolf whistle, which he acknowledges with a mock curtsy that gets a laugh.

(Honestly, Mr. Parker should just do the whole show. He'd win easily.)

"Thank you, thank you. A little bit of decorum, please, as we ready ourselves for a veritable *cornucopia* of entertainment! Indeed, we have comedians, crrrrooners, contortionists, and terpsichorean tunesmiths—kindly desist with the giggling, Mr. Knight, and look it up if you're finding that my choice of vocabulary obfuscates my lucidity!"

Half the time, I can only guess at his meaning, but I love listening to him.

He goes on like this for a bit longer, then gets to the first act.

"Please put your hands together rrrrapidly and rrrrepeatedly for Class 7A's mistress of melody—Miss Delancey Nkolo!"

Delancey is in the year below me, and she's good.

The lights go down and then up again as she comes onstage, and everybody cheers. Two boys from Year Eight are doing the lighting, and Delancey sings a Beyoncé song, complete with all the vocal swoops and trills and everything.

She finishes to a huge round of applause, and I'm thinking, *Poor Boydy.*

After two more acts—Finbar Tuley playing a really tricky piano piece, and two girls from Miss Hibbert's class doing weird, sort-of-yoga moves to music—it's Boydy's turn.

Mr. Parker introduces him.

"Ladies and gentlemen, you've heard of Eric Clapton, you've heard of Jimi Hendrix—well, those of you with any taste in music have. . . . Settle down, settle down. Now it's time to hear of Boyd, Class 8E's axeman of excellence, a guitarist of gargantuan greatness. Give it up for . . . Elliot Boyd!"

Wow. That's some introduction. As Boydy makes his way to the stage, I can tell he's nervous—and who wouldn't be after a buildup like that?

He starts to tune his guitar. *Ding-ding-ding. Ding-ding-ding . . . dong.*

Oh no.

(Tip to guitar performers: tune your instrument before you go on.)

Boydy does a few tryout chords, and then more tuning. Someone gives a sarcastic cheer.

Come on, Boydy, get on with it, I'm thinking.

A murmuring is starting in the audience.

He's losing them, and I know I have to act now. Coming out from behind the fireplace, I take a deep breath and prepare to do the scariest thing I have ever done in my life.

CHAPTER FORTY-ONE

Have you ever had a dream where you are naked in public?

It's not exactly unusual. Apparently, being naked in public is the most common bad dream people have. It sits ahead of falling, flying, being chased, and being unprepared for an exam.

In my recurring bad dream, I'm at school, although not this school—my primary school. I'm in the playground and, looking down, I realize to my horror that I am completely naked. Not a stitch on, and the funny thing is that nobody seems to have noticed. If I carry on walking, and dodging into doorways, people just ignore me. I don't have far to go until I get to the coatroom, where there will be some clothes that I can put on. But even though I am walking in the right direction, the coatroom gets no closer, while I am becoming more and more certain that people will notice that I have nothing on. The embarrassment builds into a real fear that everyone will turn and look, and I eventually wake up. I know the dream so well that sometimes I tell myself, in my dream, *Oh, Ethel, it's just that silly dream again. Why don't you wake up?* And I do.

I agree: other people's dreams are usually very boring. I wouldn't normally tell anyone about a dream, because I find myself getting bored stiff when other people tell me theirs. But this one is important because when I emerge from the wings onto the school stage, that is *exactly* how I feel.

I am naked as the day I was born, with one major difference: nobody can see me.

A strange feeling? You bet.

I am onstage, in front of the whole school, with no clothes on.

For a moment or two, I just stand there, rigid with fear.

I'm expecting at any minute to hear someone shout:

"Look! There's Ethel Leatherhead with no clothes on!"

But they don't.

Instead Boydy continues to stumble his way through a guitar piece, and it's awful. People are starting to giggle.

I come up behind Boydy and lean in close.

"It's me, Ethel."

He gasps and jerks his head round, causing himself to miss another note.

People in the audience are openly laughing now, and I

hear the first "boo," even though mocking the performers is strictly not allowed.

Then Boydy just stops altogether.

I reach forward and gently take the guitar from him.

"Let go. It'll be fine. You'll see." I'm whispering so that the microphone doesn't pick it up.

With his left hand, he releases his grip on the guitar's neck, and I slowly lift the instrument a bit higher.

The audience falls silent, and then I hear a small gasp, which builds.

Into his ear I say, "Now pretend you're making it fly."

I'll give him this: he's good. He gets it straightaway, and moves his hands in mysterious gestures as I make the guitar sway from side to side and pick up the tune where Boydy left off.

I can't actually do much playing while I'm moving the guitar around—I'm not that good. But I do manage to pull off some near-accurate chords and stuff, in between more elaborate twists and turns of the instrument, and the audience is loving it!

Boydy fixes a grin on his face and turns his head a little towards me, saying through his grin, "Ethel, are you, erm . . . are you naked?"

"*Shhh.* Yes. I am, obviously. Don't even think about it."

He keeps his fixed smile. "I wasn't. Honest. Until now."

"Shut up."

"Got it."

A ripple of applause starts, and then a cheer as I lift the guitar higher. I'm laughing inside as I imagine what the audience is seeing: it must look truly magical!

Boydy is grinning like mad, and waving his arms around as if he's conducting the guitar's movements as we go from one side of the stage to the other, and I'm feeling so confident that I tell him, "Follow me!"

There's an aisle up the center of the seating, and it leads to the rear doors of the theater. With Boydy following and waving his arms, and me strumming the guitar as best I can, I go down the steps at the front of the stage and up the aisle.

I know: it's a massive risk. But I've led a pretty risk-free life so far, and I have a bit of catching up to do.

I think it's the thrill that gives me the confidence. The thrill of doing something so outrageous yet being completely unseen.

At any time, someone could reach out and touch me, but they're all so awestruck that no one does. They just watch, openmouthed, as Boydy—grinning like a madman—conducts his floating guitar up the center aisle, through the audience, surfing a wave of amazement.

People are shaking their heads in astonishment, their mouths agape, eyes shining, just loving it, and loving *him*, and I just want this to go on forever.

Someone please tell me: Why is it that when I'm enjoying myself the most, there's a little voice in the back of my head telling me that it's all going to go wrong? It means I can never lose myself "in the moment," however much that's supposed to be a good thing to do.

Instead I always come back to what Gram would say at such a time:

"Pride, Ethel, comes before a fall."

It's not meant literally, obviously, but I should have seen it coming.

Or should I? I don't know—how could anyone?

I suppose it's just Jesmond and Jarrow Knight; wherever they are, you have to be on your guard, and I *do* spot them, halfway to the back, sitting at the edge of the aisle.

With water bottles. How innocent is that?

Not water pistols, or Super Soakers, or anything like that. Just water bottles, with those sports tops that have the little hole in them.

I see Jesmond out of the corner of my eye, but I'm too late.

He already has the water bottle raised, a stupid grin all

over his stupid face. He hands something to his sister—his phone, I think. Then he squeezes the bottle, a jet of water firing directly towards Boydy. It's just a thin spout of water, but it gets me right in the face and on my hair.

Beside him, Jarrow is holding the phone, filming.

CHAPTER FORTY-TWO

I don't think anyone notices at first.

Jesmond fires again, and again the water hits me. He could hardly miss—I am only about a yard away.

This all happens in a matter of seconds. I know, though, that I have been made slightly visible.

I throw the guitar, shouting "CATCH, BOYDY!" regardless of what will happen when people hear a voice from nowhere. The hubbub in the hall will be enough, I hope, that no one will be able to tell where my voice is coming from.

Except, at the exact moment I shout, the people nearest notice a strange watery shape appear, where the pistol's jet has hit me, and a silence falls over that part of the hall.

Aramynta Fell, who is in the next row up, just goes: "Oh my God. It's there again!"

Boydy catches the guitar by its neck, but by now I'm running up the aisle.

A few people are getting up out of their seats to follow or

simply craning their necks to get a better view of this weird thing. They probably think it's part of Boydy's act, another illusion.

Behind me I hear Mr. Parker shout, "SIT DOWN, EVERY-BODY, SIT DOWN! LET THE PERFORMERS PERFORM—SHOW THEM A MODICUM OF RESPECT!"

But he's never had a lot of natural authority, and the hall is now in a sort of pack frenzy, with people spilling into the aisle to see what it is that's causing the commotion.

The lighting guys brought up some of the lights in the auditorium as soon as Boydy started his move off the stage, but it's still not exactly bright.

Meanwhile, Jesmond Knight is firing his water pistol like it's a proper gun battle, and someone on the other side of the aisle, who has been hit in the crossfire, is returning fire from their own water bottle. Enough of it is hitting me to keep me at least partly visible to the mob advancing up the aisle.

I can hear people saying "What is it?" and "Look—there's a hand!" but mostly "Oh, God!" and a few other, much more extreme expressions. Mainly, though, no one is quite sure what they are seeing, and there's quite a few people saying things like "Awesome!" and "Whoa!"

Riley Colman, who won last year's physics prize, says loudly, as if he knows everything, "Oh, for heaven's sake—it's a trick of the light!" (He's right, of course: my invisibility is definitely "a trick of the light.")

I'm ahead of the crowd by a good few yards. If I can get outside and run, people won't be able to see me, I'm pretty certain.

There are double safety doors leading out of the auditorium, with one of those metal bars that you push to open.

I do open it, and I stop dead.

It's pouring outside—like, monsoon style. One step into the rain and I'll be totally visible, a rainy ghost figure.

I turn around, and there are about a dozen people right behind me.

I'm not even sure what they can see. A few drops of water on my face and hair? What does that look like?

Behind the small crowd I can see Boydy, fear contorting his face. At that moment he does something completely brilliant. He screams.

"*Aaaagh!* It's got me! It's the ghost of Jimi Hendrix and he's punishing me!"

Brilliant! Instantly the crowd turns around to see Boydy waving his arms, pretending to be attacked, and they all laugh.

I take my chance to edge along the back wall of the theater. I'm wiping water from my face and anywhere else I can, and I think I'm doing OK.

But then Jesmond turns back from Boydy and points at the ground.

"Footprints!"

I have left a trail of wet footprints, and they lead straight to me. Without waiting, I sprint to the main door of the theater and burst through it into the school corridor.

CHAPTER FORTY-THREE

Checking behind me, I see I am no longer leaving wet footprints, and the people in the crowd, led by Jarrow Knight, don't know which way I have gone. They stop in the doorway, and I can hear Mr. Parker and some other teachers trying to restore order.

Cautiously, I open the door of the girls' bathroom.

A couple of minutes later, I'm dry, thanks to the hand dryer, and I have checked everything in the big bathroom mirror.

I truly am invisible again, every last inch of me. I'm working out my options when the bathroom door bursts open and smashes me in the face, *hard.*

I let out a howl of pain and collapse on the floor, holding my face, as three girls rush in. I crouch down, holding my nose, and I can't see who's saying what. The hardest thing is making sure I don't moan in agony.

"Oh, sorry, I didn't . . ." "Hey! Did you hear that?" "What

was that? Did you hit something? I heard someone. . . ."

"Jarrow, did you just scream?"

"This is too freaky for me," says Jarrow.

I can feel the blood start to well up in my nose, and then it just bursts out. I remove my hands in time and jerk my head forward so that it doesn't drip on my skin. Instead it forms a long crimson splatter, becoming visible as it hits the floor—a growing red pool seeping over the white-tiled floor. Even to me it looks very creepy, and I both know what it is *and* am distracted by the agony in my face.

The one that's called Gemma notices it first.

"Oh, God. Jarrow, look. Blood!"

"Eeugh! Where's it coming from?"

I can't even look up, because to look up would involve lifting my face and that would mean blood dripping down it, so I'm stuck in this weird crouch. The pooling blood forms a little river through the spaces between the tiles and trickles towards the girls' feet.

"There's more of it, Gemma."

"Oh, God. That's gross. It looks like someone's . . ."

"Eeugh! I'm going to get Mrs. McDonald."

Two of them immediately leave the bathroom.

I can tell by her shoes that Jarrow is left behind. Her foot moves, tentatively kicking in my direction. She wants to see . . . what? I don't know. But she's getting too curious.

It worked with Aramynta Fell, so it might just work again.

I open my mouth and let out the throaty gargle. With the blood gathering in my nose, it's a more bubbly sound, and a fine spray of red with a few bigger globs lands on Jarrow's shoes.

That does it. She screams and runs out, stepping in the pool of my blood as she goes and leaving a red footprint on the tiles.

I can hear the sound system from the theater playing some thumping house music, and a microphone crackling, and Mr. Parker going, "Order! Come on, let's have a little order."

I'm just crouching and staying still, silently groaning as my nose throbs with pain and tears of agony sting my eyes.

That's when the tingling starts in my skin, and the early headache.

It's wearing off.

I'm going to be naked. In the middle of school.

Only, this time, I'll be totally, 100 percent visible.

CHAPTER FORTY-FOUR

I don't really have any choice, do I?

I have not exactly picked the best time to wander through the school naked, though, because as I open the door from the girls' bathroom, the bell goes and about half a dozen classes start emptying their students into the main corridor, along with the audience from Whitley's Got Talent.

There are two ways I can go: back through the Performing Arts Block, or follow along the main corridor to the big, glass-walled lobby, which is already filling up with students.

I consider waiting in one of the toilet stalls until the break is over, but the tingling on my skin is intensifying, and—based on the last time—I figure I have five minutes tops to make it back to the rhododendron bush to retrieve my clothes.

I check myself one last time in the mirror and remove a crust of blood from my nose.

All clear, I say to myself, and then—despite my nerves—

I smile. Because that's what I am: like a glass of water, I'm all clear.

I'm out the bathroom door just before four sixth-form girls barge in, and I narrowly avoid a second collision.

From now on it's a race against people and my soon-to-expire invisibility.

Dodging and weaving through the mass of bodies, I make my way down the corridor. I bump into people; I knock their bags. Some turn round and say, "Hey! Watch it!" But there's enough of a crowd for no one to be quite sure who bumped them.

In the lobby, the rain is hammering on the glass roof and I'm immediately gripped by my old fear, but now it's bordering on panic.

Stop it, Ethel. Not now, not now, I tell myself.

I dodge behind a large potted fern, where I'm kind of out of the way, and I take deep breaths, digging my nails into my palms until it hurts, and that distracts me from my fear.

I need someone to open a door so that I can squeeze through. Trouble is, no one is going outside. Why would they? It's bucketing down.

My head is throbbing, and my skin feels like a million ants are crawling beneath the surface. And . . .

Oh no.

No, no, no.

If I peer really closely at my hand, I can see the faintest beginnings of a shape.

A minute? Less? Until I'm actually living the world's most common recurring nightmare, and I'm naked in public.

I swallow. I take a deep breath and then . . .

I. Just. Run.

I'm at the side door in a second and I push it open. It seems like a hundred pairs of eyes turn to the noise of the door slamming back on itself as the rain gusts in.

Someone says, "What's that? Look!"

I'm out and running through the rain.

I can see the raindrops hitting my arms and legs and forming a brief, translucent outline that shifts and changes as I move.

In twenty yards I can turn a corner past the Science Block and be out of sight of the people in the lobby. Before I turn, I look back: faces are pressed against the glass walls, and some people have come through the door that I left open and are trying to get a better look at this ghostly shape moving through the rain.

And now I'm round the corner and heading to the main gate. It's shut.

The only thing I can do is open it with my thumbprint

and deal with any consequences—whatever they could be—later.

I can just see my transparent thumb as I press on the sensor pad. The gate swings open and I'm through, ducking under the rhododendron leaves to safety.

I'm done in, and I just collapse, flat on my back among the dead leaves and cigarette ends. I can hardly breathe, my brain feels like it's going to explode, and I screw my eyes shut before I roll over and throw up.

Then I sit up and look down.

I look down at me. I'm here; I'm back. There's my thigh. Here's my hand. I close my eyes and everything goes black, just as it should.

I'm visible.

I retrieve my plastic bag from where I left it, get dressed, and wait under the dripping rhododendron until the rain stops.

CHAPTER FORTY-FIVE

I'm back home before Gram gets in, and change into my school uniform as if I've had a normal day.

Normal day? Ha!

There's a text from Boydy.

That was AWESOME! Can u come round tonite? I'm cooking.

Seems like I'm forgiven, then. Plus, I'm super-curious to see what sort of house Boydy lives in.

Tea with Gram that afternoon is a strained affair, mainly because I'm dying to tell her what happened today but—obviously—I can't.

"Are you all right, Ethel?" she asks more than once.

"Yes, thanks, Gram. I'm just tired."

That, at least, is the truth. I'm exhausted. Otherwise, though, I feel fine. I keep checking myself over every time

I pass a mirror to make sure everything's in place. It seems incredible, but I really do seem to be able to do this invisibility thing without any ill effects, apart from being sick afterwards.

Best of all, my skin has improved even more. I have a slight rash of spots on my chin, but other than that, the acne has more or less gone. I grin at myself in the mirror. Gram catches me as she passes.

"Vanity, Ethel, dear. Too long in front of a mirror can be bad for you."

"Have you seen, Gram? My skin?"

"I told you it would clear up in time, darling."

She's off out this evening: another meeting, another committee, apparently. At least, that's what she says. I'm beginning to wonder.

Would you put on makeup for a committee meeting? Well, of course, no you wouldn't if you're a kid. But an adult? Especially if you're like Gram and don't often wear it?

And the thing is, she doesn't do it in her room. She says goodbye, that she'll see me later, and gets in her car, where, from my window, I see her adjust her rearview mirror and apply blusher, lipstick, and mascara. Then she drives off.

Months ago, when I first got my smartphone for

Christmas, Gram insisted on installing a tracker app—"Just for safety, Ethel, darling."

I'm pretty certain that she doesn't know that FindU works both ways.

Tonight will be the first time I use it. I'm going to find out where Gram is going.

CHAPTER FORTY-SIX

I'm not sure what I was expecting. I suppose the "Smelliot" thing still had me wondering if he lived in a horrible house, but . . .

Boydy's house is totally normal. Much smaller than I expected, what with his dad being a lawyer, but normal. With a very distinctive smell of scented candles.

"Sorry about the smell," he says, completely unselfconsciously. "Mum's got a client in."

He says that his mum is a reflexologist and Reiki therapist, neither of which I have a clue about, except that they clearly involve scented candles and whale song set to music—which you can hear everywhere in the house.

Boydy's dad isn't around much. I've never seen him, or heard him mentioned. I ask Boydy where he is and he answers quickly.

"He's away. He works away a lot. Will you pass me that knife, Eff?"

Boydy cooking is pretty impressive to watch, and I sit at his kitchen counter while he chops and fries. Because his mum is a vegan, Boydy's learned to cook stuff for himself; otherwise, he reckons, he would "starve."

She draws the line at having meat in the house but doesn't mind fish, so that's what we're having. Personally, I don't see the difference between meat and fish. I mean, if you don't want to kill something, fair enough, but what about the poor fish, gasping for life in the hold of a fishing trawler? I don't say this, obviously.

Anyway, Boydy's chopping up veggies for a prawn stir-fry and his hands are swift and deft, just like Jamie Oliver on telly.

"You should have seen it!" he gushes when we get to talking about that afternoon's Whitley's Got Talent, which takes about two seconds.

"I did. I was there!"

In case you were wondering, Boydy didn't win. I know: It seems crazy. The best illusion ever and *he didn't win.*

"I think it's because I told them it wasn't me playing the guitar."

"You *what?*"

I'm dreading what he's going to say: Has he spilled our secret?

"Everyone was raving. People were talking about ghosts.

Mr. Parker was in a right old state—it was nearly a riot. Honestly, Eff, I thought I was going to be burned at the stake."

I thought back to the bunch of people who were advancing on me, and the chaos in the hall. It certainly wasn't an orderly performance, if that was what they had wanted.

"Mr. Parker took me to one side and said, 'Mr. Boyd. While I appreciate the *theatricality* of your *rr*recital and the preparation that went into its *execution* . . .' "

I start to laugh because it's a brilliant impression.

Encouraged, Boydy goes on: " 'The invisible fishing line that you undoubtedly utilized to effect the levitation of the guitar was indeed *wily*, but as said instrument was out of your hands, I can only assume that the music was generated with more than a degree of *artifice*. Am I right?' "

"He reckoned you faked the music?"

"Right. But what could I say? 'No, Mr. Parker. It was Ethel Leatherhead, except she was invisible'? I said I had a recording on my phone and it was stuck with Blu-Tack inside the hole of the guitar."

"And he *believed* you?"

"Occam's razor, Effel. Occam's razor."

I give him a blank look.

He's buoyed with confidence now, and he dumps the veggies and prawns in the wok.

"Occam's razor. It's philosophy, innit? 'Once you eliminate the impossible, whatever remains—however improbable—must be the truth.' "

"What's that got to do with a razor?"

"Dunno," he says, expertly shaking and tossing the stuff in the pan without a spoon. "And he didn't say it, anyway. It was Spock in *Star Trek VI: The Undiscovered Country*, quoting Sherlock Holmes."

"So who's this Occam?"

"Doesn't matter. The point is, so far as Mr. Parker's concerned, the only way it *could* have happened is with some sort of ultrafine thread and a recorded track inside the guitar. And thus, as I was supposed to be a musical act, I was disqualified from winning."

"That totally sucks."

I feel angry that Boydy was denied his rightful prize, but he doesn't seem to care.

He shrugs. "Big deal. It was worth every second to see the look on Jesmond Knight's face when he fired that water at me and it hit you instead. It was like I had an invisible force field around me! Now, I hope you're hungry."

I've got to hand it to Boydy. His stir-fry smells delicious, and I am super-hungry.

Between mouthfuls, I ask him, "So what about the other stuff? You said the school was in a frenzy."

It turns out that there are three versions of the ghost story, all witnessed by different people, but none of the versions is quite consistent enough to make a solid, believable story.

The people who saw me get soaked in the hall are all arguing about what they saw, and Riley Colman the physics geek has convinced half of them that it was another part of Boydy's grand illusion—which Boydy isn't exactly denying.

The girls in the bathroom who saw me spraying blood are not what are known as "reliable witnesses." When someone tells you that a pool of blood just *appeared* on the floor, people won't believe you—as Katie Pelling discovered. Someone had a nosebleed. So what?

Aramynta Fell seems to have said nothing about my encounter with her outside the Performing Arts Block.

Which leaves me running through the rain from the lobby, which was seen by, I don't know, dozens of people?

Boydy swallows a big mouthful and waves his fork dismissively.

"Yeah, yeah, yeah—but what did they actually see? I mean, really? A shape? A squall of rain created by a gust of wind? One story I heard is that it's the ghost of some kid who drowned in Culvercot Bay, like, thirty years ago."

"Really? That happened?"

"Appaz. According to Dalton MacFadyen, whose dad

was at the school then. The point, my friend, is that nobody knows. Not for sure. And that means any of it could be true—or none of it. And my prediction is that, given a little time, it'll all die down and go away, and your secret will be safe."

Next to him on the table, Boydy's phone pings, and he looks at it, scrolling through a message quickly.

His face falls.

"Ah. Or *not* so safe."

Hi. We r on to u and ur little unseen assistant. V clever. No wonder u r desperate to keep it secret. Thing is, we think this video shud b seen by every1. Youll b famous! 4 now it stays on my fone. If u want it 2 stay there 4ever meet us tonite 8:00 at the bandstand. J & J

Boydy and I look at each other. Jarrow and Jesmond. Who else?

Then we look at the clock on the wall.

It's seven-forty-five.

CHAPTER FORTY-SEVEN

Even though it's June, and the rain has stopped, there's a bleakness about Whitley Bay's seafront that makes it seem like it's permanently February. Perhaps it's the boarded-up hotels, which look like they were once grand but now remind me of the old people in Great-Gran's home: crumbling and unloved.

Perhaps it's just my mood.

Why is it, I ask myself furiously, *that these twins seem to make everything worse?*

The rain has given way to a clear, cool evening, and the seagulls have fallen silent. A weak sun is starting to set behind us, giving a pinkish tinge to the lighthouse.

We head down to the Links. Bang in the middle is an old, flaky bandstand.

Jesmond and Jarrow are already there, watching us as we approach.

"So . . . what do we say?" I ask Boydy, who has developed this strangely calm manner that I am finding unnerving.

"Relax, Eff. We deny everything. They can't have any proof at all."

"They've got a video—that's what their message said."

"Yeah, well, even if they do, it's not going to show much, is it?"

"Hmm . . ." My mind goes back to Jarrow filming on her phone. I can't share in Boydy's confidence. "So what are we going to do?"

"We just bluff it out and tell 'em to go to hell."

"We could have done that by text. Why are we meeting them?"

"Well. We want to see exactly what it is that they've got, don't we? Just in case. Assess the evidence before coming to a verdict an' all that."

We are a few yards from the bandstand now.

"OK, just let me do the talking," Boydy says.

"No. I'll talk if I want to."

"Fair enough, Effow."

We step up into the bandstand, where the twins are waiting. Honestly, if I wasn't so tense I'd have to laugh. They're both standing there, feet apart, arms folded, like they're posing as a pair of sinister blond Bond villains.

They nod at us curtly.

"Evening, Jarrow. All right, Jesmond?" says Boydy.

"A'reet, Boyd, Ethel," says Jesmond. (The boy twin. Don't worry, I used to confuse them all the time. And incidentally, "Boyd"? That's just a blatant attempt at intimidation. No one calls him by his last name—at least, not without a *y* added, and that's only me, I think.)

I straighten my back and refuse to be intimidated.

Jarrow says, "It's nice to see you, Ethel. That is, to see *all of you.*"

I don't reply. It seems like a good strategy: say as little as possible so as not to give anything away.

Encircling the bandstand are slatted wooden benches covered with graffiti and with a snowdrift of litter gathered underneath.

We sit down, and Jarrow continues.

"Y'see, it all makes sense now. Well, sorta. That day we found your dog for you. We thought there was summin' up wi' yer hand, didn't we, Jez?"

Jesmond nods.

Jarrow blinks hard behind her glasses. "Like, we couldn't see it when we shoulda been able to."

I look down at both of my hands and turn them over, as if to say, *What's wrong with my hands?*

Jarrow ignores this. "And then today at the School for Show-Offs. That thing wi' the guitar. Fishin' line? Are you kiddin'? Ah know a bit about fishin', and there's not a line in the world that's thin enough *and* strong enough to do that."

I glance over to Boydy, and our eyes meet. He's chewing his bottom lip.

"Anyway," she continues, "we heard yuz. Well, you, at least. 'CATCH, BOYDY!' Definitely your voice, and all caught on camera!"

It's like they've rehearsed it. At the mention of the camera, Jesmond pulls out a phone. In a moment he's brought up a video clip, and I lean in to watch with a mounting feeling of sickness.

It starts when Boydy begins his walk down into the audience, the guitar floating in front of him. The footage is wobbly, but it's still a terrific illusion. I was worried that somehow the camera had "seen" me in a way that the human eye cannot—that it would see and record light in a slightly different way, and that somehow I would be visible—but no.

I am as invisible on the video as I was in real life.

There's the noise of the audience, and then the chaos starts. People pushing their seats back with a squeak; Mr. Parker telling everyone to sit down. Then the image tilts wildly as Jesmond hands the phone to Jarrow, before fixing on Boydy coming ever closer.

And the water.

For a brief second after it hits me, the water creates the outline of half my face before running off and dispersing. You can't really tell what it is. I start to allow myself to hope that I have been worrying for nothing.

And then my voice: "Catch, Boydy!" I must have said it very close to the camera's microphone because it's very clear. Unfortunately, it's also unmistakably me, but so what?

Then the scene changes. It's a few seconds of video, shot from the school lobby during the downpour. You can hear someone saying "There! Did you get it?" and there's the slightest blur of *something* moving away and around the corner, but you can't tell what it is.

I'm working on a little half smile, bordering on a sneer. I'm going to turn to the twins and say, "Is that it? Is that the best you can do? That proves nothing other than you two being a couple of crazies with fantasies of invisible people. Got any leprechaun films as well? Ha! Losers!" Or something to that effect, anyway.

But my sneer is frozen, half formed.

Because the video is now repeating, in slow motion. At the point the water hits the side of my face, it slows again, to a frame-by-frame rate. That's when it's clear. Unmistakable, in fact. My face, or half of it, at least, outlined in water.

Just for a few frames. You'd miss it otherwise, but slowed down, there's no question.

The slo-mo and enlarged version of the video shot in the rain reveals even more.

There I am. Almost completely transparent, but outlined by the torrential rain, running away from the school's lobby. It's definitely a person. A half-invisible, naked person.

Definitely me, in fact.

That's where the film ends. Jesmond replaces his phone in his pocket.

"It's you, isn't it?" he says, and *he's* the one smirking now.

Boydy and I exchange glances, but neither of us says anything.

"It's pointless denying it. You can tell it's you. It's obvious from the way you run. Besides, it was your thumbprint that was used to open the school gate."

Boydy goes on the offensive. "Rubbish! You don't know anything. How the hell can you know it was her thumbprint?"

Jarrow chips in now. "Easy, if you've got a little bit of leverage over Stuart in Security. A little bit of persuasive power, if you know what I mean."

Old Stuart Hibbert is the night security guard. He's a nice guy who doubles as a crossing guard at the busy back entrance.

"Old Stuart? What on earth has he done?"

"Not for us to say, is it, Jez?" says Jarrow. "But let's just say fifty quid goes a long way when you're a security guard on minimum wage."

"You *bribed* him?"

I can hardly believe what I'm hearing. Basically, the Knight twins have paid the school's night watchman to hand over security information.

All four of us are so silent that the only sounds are the competing swishes of the traffic on the road and the sea on the sand.

Jesmond Knight speaks first. "So I'll admit this much: we've got no idea what's *really* going on. But it seems to me that *you*"—and he jabs his finger at me—"have got some weird invisibility thing. Is it a magic spell? Is it some sort of suit you put on? Is it some military thing? Haven't a clue. But I'll bet it's top-secret, and I'll bet you want to keep it that way. Otherwise we'd have heard about it."

I'm glaring at him while he says this. He is, of course, more or less spot on, and I'm terrified.

"So here's the deal," says Jarrow. She takes a long pause while she removes her glasses and polishes them with a hankie, making us wait. Finally, she says, "It's on Jez's phone right now. That's where it'll stay so long as you play nicely. Or should I say, *pay* nicely."

"Pay?" says Boydy.

"Oh aye. We reckon a thousand quid should do it, don't we, Jez? It's manageable, if you do it in installments."

I feel sick. Not just upset, but really sick, like I want to throw up.

A thousand pounds. Where would I get that?

"You're mad," I say eventually. "There's no way we could get anything like that amount. No way at all."

I'm furious, but I'm also very scared, not to mention utterly stunned. This is proper blackmail. Not behind-the-bike-shed-stealing-your-sweets stuff, but the sort of thing real criminals do.

"It's not a negotiation. You realize that, don't you, Little Miss Invisible? It's not like we're going to haggle."

"I can't do it."

He shrugs. "This is the sort of thing that goes viral instantly. A couple of calls to the *Evening Chronicle*, you know? 'Local Girl's Invisible Secret.' All over YouTube, easily. There'll be reporters camped outside your house. You'll be Invisigirl from *The Incredibles*, only in real life, you know? And it'll stay with you all your life, Ethel. Stuff like this never goes away."

"Get stuffed."

The words come out, but—maddeningly—they wobble in my throat. Somehow the Knight twins have zoned in on my one big fear. They've worked out that I'd truly hate to be famous like that, and they're going to exploit it.

"Have it your way." Jesmond takes out his phone and mutters to himself as he prods the screen. "OK . . . upload . . . preparing to upload . . ."

"Stop!"

He stops, finger hovering over his phone, his face a picture of innocence. "Yeah? What?"

"Give us time. Time to think."

The twins look at each other, and they both nod. Jesmond puts the phone away.

"OK. Three days. See yuz. Well, not you, obviously," he says, pointing at me. "Not if you're invisible, anyway."

Without looking back, they saunter off, laughing at Jesmond's joke, leaving me and Boydy in shocked silence.

CHAPTER FORTY-EIGHT

Back home, I'm in my pj's, playing through the events of the evening while I wait in the living room for Gram to get back.

Ten minutes ago, according to FindU, she was in Tynemouth, though it's a bit late to be visiting Great-Gran. Visiting ends at nine, and it's already nine thirty. Perhaps they allowed her to stay a bit later.

Boydy and I hadn't really said much on the way back to his house. The only thing *to* say was "Oh my God, what are we going to *do*?" And as both of us knew that the other didn't have an answer, it seemed pointless to say anything.

Boydy's mum was up when we got back, and Boydy introduced us. She's OK, his mum, just a bit dippy. She's got dark rings under her eyes and an exhausted look about her. She gave me this soppy, lips-together smile with her head on one side, and said, "You have a lovely aura."

"Um, thanks." I had no idea what she meant, but I think she was being nice.

As an aside to Boydy, she added, "Lovely manners. See, Elliot—you could do a lot worse."

I had no idea what that meant either, but Boydy rolled his eyes at me in solidarity.

The last thing his mum said was "I'll leave you two . . . alone." And I swear that she left out some words, as if what she wanted to say was "I'll leave you two lovebirds alone," but she didn't dare.

The very idea that Boydy and I might be a couple is just so completely ludicrous that I almost laughed.

Anyway, with his mum out of the way, Boydy and I sat opposite each other, with a mug of tea each, and decided on a plan of action.

Apparently, I'm going to break into the Knights' house and steal Jesmond's phone.

It took a while to get there, as you've probably guessed. I wasn't thrilled, as you can also guess. But neither of us could think of another way to ensure that the twins don't show everyone that video.

In fact, I'm a bit surprised that it isn't all around the school already, uploaded onto YouTube, and being viewed in Tokyo or somewhere. But then, I'm not factoring in the Knight twins' willingness to wait and see what they can extract from the situation. Exactly how long they *will* wait is anyone's guess.

"It's perfect," said Boydy, when we came up with our plan, smacking his lips after gulping his tea. "You make yourself invisible, get into their house, and get their phones. Piece of cake."

"Oh yeah. Piece of cake. If you're not the one doing it, that is."

He looked hurt. "I'll help."

"How?"

"Dunno, exactly. I'll be your wingman."

"My *what*?"

"It's an expression my dad uses. I think it means 'helper.' "

I simply could not think of a single way that Boydy could help me stage an elaborate burglary with the victims still in the house, but I didn't say so. Instead I drew his attention to another problem that I had spotted.

"That clip they showed us—it was edited."

It definitely had been: the slow motion, the enlarging, the stitching together of the separate clips.

"So?"

"So how do you do that?"

"I dunno. You use an editing program, iMovie or whatever. You upload the clip to your comp— Ah."

"Ah indeed. That film is *not* just on Jesmond Knight's phone, is it? It's on his laptop, or the family's computer, or *somewhere* else too. And for all we know it's backed up on the cloud."

Boydy sucked his teeth. "You're gonna have to wipe their computers. Wipe them clean completely. Erase all the data."

"How do I do that, Bill Gates? What if they've got backups?"

We talked this through for another half hour. Some people never back up their computers: Gram, for example. She wouldn't know how. Some people do it every now and then. That's what Boydy does: he has a plug-in hard drive that every few months he uses to back up the music and movies and homework that he has on his laptop. Some people set their computers to do it automatically, for example with Apple's Time Machine.

And some people have everything backed up automatically to the cloud.

"We just have to hope it's not the cloud option," said Boydy.

"We? *We?* I like that!" I don't know why I was so indignant.

"I'm trying to help, Eff," said Boydy, and he sounded sad. "But face it, knowing what you know of the Knight twins, do you reckon they're the sort to rig up their computers to auto backup?"

I thought for a moment, and agreed with him. It wasn't impossible, but it also wasn't very likely.

Terrifyingly, it made the burglary a viable option.

Even more terrifyingly, it made it our only option.

CHAPTER FORTY-NINE

And as if that's not enough to be dealing with, when Gram gets back I can tell she's been crying.

All her mascara has gone and her eyes are red, which makes me think that she smudged her makeup with tears, then wiped it all off.

Other than her red eyes, though, she's pretty good at hiding it.

"You OK, Gram? You look . . . upset."

She turns away. "Upset? No, no, no. I'm fine, darling. Just a little tired, that's all."

I try to trick her. "How was Great-Gran?"

She's cleverer than that.

"Your great-gran? Well, she was fine when I last saw her, on the weekend. What do you mean?"

"Nothing. I thought you said you were going to see her, that's all. My mistake."

Gram's busy with the kettle, so I can't see her facial expressions from where I'm sitting.

"No. I've been to a church bazaar meeting. It rather went on. Half the time seemed to be taken up with talking about Queenie Abercrombie's dog."

"OK, my bad."

"Don't say that, darling. It's rather common."

"Sorry, my mistake. Where was the meeting?" It *might* have been in Tynemouth, which is where the FindU app had said she was.

"Goodness, aren't you curious tonight! It was at the church hall. Why do you ask?"

Not Tynemouth, then. Gram is lying.

"No reason. Good night, Gram."

I go up to bed but I can't get to sleep; I'm just lying there wide awake. You would be too if you had as much on your mind as I have. I hear a rummaging coming from Gram's room.

It's not her normal going-to-bed noises. This is different. Each of the noises I have heard before, but not combined in this order.

First of all, she checks in my room to make sure my light is off and that I'm asleep. I'm not. I'm just lying in the dark, but that seems to satisfy her.

Next there's a creak and a little clanging noise. That's the small stepladder that's kept in the built-in cupboard on the landing along with the vacuum cleaner and the Christmas decorations.

She walks quietly back to her room, the floorboards creaking.

Then I hear the key turn in her bedroom door. Why on earth is she locking the door? The only conceivable reason is in case I get up and go in during the night.

That is not at all likely, but whatever she is doing must be so top-secret that she cannot take even the slightest risk, and therefore she locks the door.

Well, *that's* got my attention. I'm up in an instant and pressing my ear to my bedroom door.

She'd only get the stepladder out in order to retrieve something from one of the high cupboards. Sure enough, I hear the click of the catch as one of the cupboards opens, and . . .

That's it, basically.

There's a bit more rustling and some footsteps around the room, and then she takes the stepladder back to the landing.

After that it falls silent, and eventually I go back to bed and fall asleep.

According to the clock on my phone, I wake an hour later.

I have a fierce thirst and I go to the bathroom to get a drink. A thin light is coming from under Gram's bedroom door, but as I pass by on the landing, it switches off.

I mean, really: *What's* going on?

CHAPTER FIFTY

Until recently, Gram has never really struck me as one for secrets.

On the other hand, she does think that everyone should be discreet, and that you shouldn't "make an exhibition of yourself."

Making an exhibition of yourself is, in Gram's world, one of the worst things a person can do. It goes with "showing off," "demanding attention," and "being a drama queen."

Growing up with Gram meant I was encouraged never to draw attention to myself. Even stuff that all kids do—cartwheels, silly dances, jumping off a stool—came with a warning.

In fairness, I did fall once, and it really upset Gram. I must have been about six, and the council had put up a new jungle gym.

To a tiny six-year-old, this jungle gym was *huge*. There was even a sign saying it was for kids over eight, but everyone ignored the sign, even Gram.

While I played, she would sit on the bench, reading a book, and Lady would lie underneath. On the day it happened there were a couple of other kids there that I knew, and we dared each other to climb to the top, where there was a little platform.

I was halfway up when the other kids' mums called them, and by the time I reached the top, the kids had climbed down again. They were walking to where their mums were, almost at the exit, and so I shouted.

"Amy! AMY! Ollie! Look at me! Gram! LOOK AT ME!"

I was waving and shouting, and I could see other people in the park turn to look, but still Amy and Ollie hadn't seen me, and Gram was looking around because she had heard my voice but hadn't thought to look up.

"UP HERE!" I yelled. "LOOK AT ME! I DID IT!"

That's when I fell. My foot slipped and I toppled over. I banged my head on a metal bar, and then some rope netting, so I didn't hit the ground with full force, but the fall was still hard enough to knock me out for a few seconds. Underneath the jungle gym was that soft, spongy surface, and I sprained my wrist, but I guess it could have been worse.

When I came round, there must have been a dozen people crouching, standing, kneeling all around me. Gram was cradling my head and going, "Not again. Please, God, not again," which—at the time—seemed a bit odd.

I lay there a little longer—far longer than I wanted to, in fact, but the park attendant had to do all these tests that he had probably learned about in his park-qualification course. Things like checking: Was I breathing properly? Did I have blurred vision?

All I wanted to do was get up and go home and cry about my hurt wrist.

Eventually, the crowd thinned out, and it was just me, Lady, Gram, and the attendant. There was no blood, and Gram wanted to get home to put ice on my wrist.

On the way home, I asked Gram, "What did you mean back then? When you said 'not again'?"

She seemed a little taken aback, now that I think about it, but it was a while ago.

She just said, "Nothing, darling. I didn't mean anything by it. I just don't want you to get hurt, all right?"

Even then it struck me as unusual. So unusual, I suppose, that I have remembered it quite clearly.

That, and also what she said after that:

"People only look in case you fall."

CHAPTER FIFTY-ONE

Next morning, Gram is as nice as pie, all smiley and morning-brisk. As if nothing at all is going on.

I almost convince myself that I'm imagining all the odd stuff over the last few days and weeks, and the rummaging sounds coming from her room the night before.

I'm still off school "sick," you'll remember, but I'm downstairs in my school uniform as usual.

Gram leaves before me, and I'm left to lock the house and take Lady to the dog-sitter. (It occurs to me that I could save the ten pounds that we pay the dog-sitter and keep it, and I'm on the verge of doing just that when my conscience speaks up and reminds me that I'm already involved in a web of deception. I don't really need to add to it. Besides, I'd just get found out.)

So I drop Lady off at the normal time, but instead of carrying on to school, I double back and I'm home again, before school has even started, standing in the middle of Gram's bedroom and staring at the high cupboards.

Gram's room is by far the neatest and tidiest in the house, probably because I never go in there. Everything is put away: there are no blouses slung over the back of a chair, no stray socks, or books on the floor. The top of her dressing table is home to a silver-backed hairbrush and a carved box with a lid, full of loose change. Everything is blue or gray. The carpet is gray, the bedcover is blue stripes, the cushions are blue and white, the curtains are gray and white and blue. It smells nice, like Gram's perfume and deodorant.

There are built-in wardrobes along one wall, with a row of cupboards along the top going up as high as the ceiling.

I grab the little stepladder from the cupboard on the landing. There are only three steps on it. Even on the top step, I have to strain to see into the first cupboard I open. It contains pretty much what I expect to find: blankets, a spare duvet, and a long puffer jacket that Gram bought, wore once, and then saw someone on TV wearing one similar and never wore again.

The second cupboard is empty. The third has more sheets and a cardboard box containing my old picture books from when I was little. I spend a happy half hour looking through them and remembering how Gram used to read them to me. (Gram said she was going to give them to the church book sale, but that was ages ago, so I suppose she has just forgotten.)

The last cupboard is just cupboard junk. There's an old sewing machine that never gets used, a bag of old clothes, and a pretty brass vase thing with carving on it and a lid.

That's it.

Can Gram really have been taking down the box of old picture books to look at? I hardly think so.

Frustrated, I'm up on the stepladder again, putting the book box back, and it's not an easy task when you're as small as I am. As I lift it, it tips back and a few books slither out and land on the floor, so I have to come down the steps and put the box down to retrieve them.

One has skidded across the carpet and under Gram's bed, and I'm on my knees to get it.

That's when I see it.

A metal box. I know it is what I have been looking for. Don't ask me *how* I know. I don't even know myself. But I just know.

Gram must have taken it down from one of the cupboards and put it under the bed—why, I don't know. Maybe so she can access it more easily?

I reach under and pull it out. It's quite big: the top is about the size of a tea tray, and it's about six inches deep.

And it's locked. Of course it is. It had to be.

There's a padlock with a combination lock securing the

lid to the box with a little latch, and my heart sinks. If it was a key lock, I could at least look for the key, but it's not.

Can I guess the code? It's four digits.

I try some obvious ones: the year of my birth, the year of Gram's birth, then each year either side in case I got it wrong. The last four digits of her mobile number. The first four digits of her mobile number, then mine.

Then 1066 because of the Battle of Hastings, and 1815 because of the Battle of Waterloo, and 1776 because we've just done the American War of Independence at school.

It's hopeless. I'm never going to just guess.

But . . .

I *could* try every number from 0000 to 9999.

Every single one.

How long will that take? I do a quick check on my phone's calculator. Assuming two seconds to input each new number (might be quicker?), and rounding 9,999 up to 10,000, that's 20,000 seconds. Divide that by 60 to find out how many minutes . . . that's 333 (point 3 recurring, actually) and divide *that* by 60 to get the hours and I'm looking at . . .

Five and a half hours.

On Tuesdays, Gram's back by lunchtime.

I'll just have to hope she hasn't chosen a high combination number.

I get to work immediately.

0000

0001

0002

0003

0004

After each turn of the dial, I give a little tug to see if it has worked. I can't be slapdash—I don't want to get to 9999 and realize that I have missed one, or failed to test the lock on each number.

So here I am, sitting on Gram's bedroom floor, with my back against her bed and the box in my lap, turning the combination dials and tugging, again. And again. And again . . .

An hour goes past.

2334 *tug*

2335 *tug*

2336 *tug*

I get up and stretch and go to the loo and then make a cup of tea.

Another hour.

3220 *tug*

3221 *tug*

My shoulders are aching and my fingers are hurting from the sharp edges of the number cogs.

Another hour.

I'm looking at the clock nervously as it ticks towards midday. I'm thinking, *So long as Gram doesn't come home early, I'll be OK.*

No sooner do I think that than I hear her car outside.

CHAPTER FIFTY-TWO

Oh God oh God oh God.

I'm on my feet in an instant and running downstairs to lock the front door, because if the door is *not* locked when Gram comes in, then either:

a) I'll be in trouble for not locking it when I left for school, or

b) Gram may think I'm already back, for some reason, and come looking for me.

I can see her coming up the path through the bubble glass of the front door. She has Lady with her, which means she has finished for the day and will be home for the rest of the afternoon.

I turn the key quickly, extract it, and dash upstairs again, where I kick the box—still locked shut—back under her bed and close the high cupboard door, and I've just managed to put the stepladder away when she comes through the front door and *immediately starts up the stairs.*

She's taken her coat off, but that's it. She's in a proper hurry.

I have no choice but to dive under Gram's bed.

OK, yes, I *do* have a choice. It would involve hiding in my own room, but I can't get there without being seen, with Gram already on the stairs. Or it would involve jumping into a cupboard.

Which, now that I think about it, would have been a better idea, because what if Gram is coming up to get the box? It's clearly something that's on her mind at the moment, and if she looks under the bed she'll—

Shhh.

She's coming in. Lady has followed her, and Lady is sniffing the carpet. I can see their legs—Gram's and Lady's—and Lady seems agitated, probably because she can smell that I'm in the room.

"What's the matter with you, Lady? You're very sniffy today," says Gram.

There's a creak, and above me the bed sags as Gram sits on it. She kicks her sensible shoes off and then goes over to one of the wardrobes. Next she sits down again and puts on a pair of sneakers.

Gram laughs. "You know, don't you, Lady? You know this means a walk! Well, you're going to have to be very good today, because we're meeting someone else and I want you to let me know if you like him."

Then she gets up, because the doorbell has rung, and she's going downstairs.

I can hear all of this, but very muffled, from my position under the bed, and my mind is already reeling.

Gram: "Hello. Do come in. I'll just get my gloves from the kitchen."

Man's voice: "Hello, Bea. This must be Lady. Hello, Lady—nice to see you again. You wanna tickle?"

I gasp, because I have heard this voice before. I can't place it, but I have definitely heard it before.

I squeeze out from under the bed. I need to see who it is, but I'll have to look out of Gram's bedroom window. I can't risk looking down the stairs.

I hear Gram say, "Come on, then."

The front door closes.

Together, Gram and Lady walk down the front path, followed by the man, whose face I cannot see but who has short sandy hair.

Yes. It's him.

The guy I met in the doorway of Priory View.

What the heck is he doing here? With Gram?

CHAPTER FIFTY-THREE

An hour. That's how long Gram normally walks Lady for. Down the street, across the Links, down onto the beach, along to the lighthouse, and back. You can do it in less. A lot less. But with ball chucking, letting her play with other dogs, and so on, it's about an hour, usually.

But who knows? Gram might go with this bloke down to the bandstand and turn around. Or might continue on to Seaton Sluice and be gone all afternoon.

I'm telling myself this to distract from the pain in my fingers.

5004 *tug*

5005 *tug*

5006 *tug*

Then there's the man himself.

I'll come straight to the point. And I know it seems like a strange conclusion and it's not even a conclusion, but . . .

Is Gram *dating* him?

The thought makes me shudder. For a start, he's *years*

younger than she is. I do *not* like to think of Gram as some elderly lady with a young boyfriend. To be honest, I wouldn't be keen even if he was the same age as her. It just wouldn't be right.

And he's a smoker. Gram would never date a smoker.

(I once asked her if smoking was common. She thought for a while and then said, "When it was very common, it wasn't actually 'common.' Now that it's less common, it's actually much more 'common.'" She smiled at her own joke, and so did I. I understood what she meant.)

Thing is: Gram is Gram. Straitlaced, strict, very proper. And, importantly, *single.*

6445 *tug*

6446 *tug*

6447 *tug*

I'm trying to piece together all the instances of Strange Things That Don't Add Up. The thing with Great-Gran; the lie about being at the bazaar meeting at the church hall when she wasn't, and coming home looking as though she had been crying; the date with a younger man; and this *flippin' box that JUST WILL NOT OPEN.*

7112 *tug*

7113 *tug . . .*

Pop!

It opens. On the seven-thousand-one-hundred-and-thirteenth try.

My throat is dry. My hands are even shaking a little bit as I pull the padlock out of the latch, and open up the lid.

If you'd asked me before what I expected to see, I would not in a million years have said "A photograph of the pop star Felina." Yet that's what it is, staring right at me.

A color picture of a dead pop star, in all her cat makeup, hands held up like a cat's claws, but with a sneaky glint in her eyes and a cheeky smile.

Felina.

CHAPTER FIFTY-FOUR

As well as the photo in my hand, there are loads of others, some of them cut from magazines. There is a copy of *Soul* magazine, with a picture of Felina on the front, and a load more photos and text inside; a copy of the *Sun* newspaper from ten years ago, with a black-edged picture of her on the front and the headline "RIP Felina."

There's a copy of the *Whitley Guardian* as well, folded over on a page headed Obituaries, which is where anyone famous who has died gets their life story printed.

I read the whole thing.

FELINA

Smoky-voiced pop singer whose catchy hits could not hide her inner torment.

Another name has been added to the sad list of victims of the wild rock-and-roll lifestyle: pop and soul singer Felina, who has been found dead at the age of twenty-four. The cause of her death is not yet clear.

She was one of the most successful artists of her generation. Her distinctive voice—and equally distinctive appearance—created an appeal across generations, making her the top-selling pop artist of recent years. But Felina suffered from serious drug and alcohol addiction that plagued her life.

Her second album, *The Cat's Whiskers*, occupied the number-one slot for four weeks, and propelled her to a level of fame that—some would say—became her downfall.

She was born Miranda Enid Mackay to a middle-class family in south London. Her salesman father, Gordon, and her mother, Belinda, later divorced.

By the age of seven Felina was attending drama classes locally, but it soon became clear that music was her first love. Rebellious instincts surfaced in her early teens: at fourteen, by her own admission, she was smoking cigarettes and had acquired her first tattoo: a cat on her upper arm. "My parents couldn't control me, and that was that," she said later.

Her singing teacher passed an MP3 file of her singing to a record company. Aged just seventeen, she signed a deal with Slick Records, but her rebelliousness had already caused a rift with her parents, and she moved out of the family home, beginning a relationship with fellow musician Ricky Malcolm.

Her first song, "Say You Can," was released just after her nineteenth birthday. As "Felina," she burst onto the scene, and her "cat" makeup and costuming was immediately both mocked and admired.

It certainly got her noticed. Headline appearances followed, plus a string of hits, including the song that will now be forever associated with her, "Light the Light." That song began a US breakthrough that was to be cut short by her death.

The hits continued, although it was becoming clear that the showbiz lifestyle was taking its toll. A string of canceled concert appearances led to rumors—strongly denied at the time—that she had drug and alcohol problems.

Paparazzi were soon following her around the streets of London. She seldom appeared in public without her trademark "cat" makeup, usually accompanied by extravagant sunglasses.

Felina won a Brit Awards nomination for Best Female Artist, and was nominated in the same year for a Mercury Music Prize and the Ivor Novello Award for Songwriting.

A child with Ricky Malcolm soon followed, a girl they named Tiger Pussycat.

Motherhood did not seem to come naturally to Felina, and she attracted hostile comments when she embarked on a world tour, leaving six-month-old Tiger Pussycat to be looked after by her grandmother.

After an apparently drunk Felina was photographed on the street at night with her young daughter, record sales plummeted.

At the time, her mother laid the blame squarely at Ricky Malcolm's feet, blaming him for "leading my daughter astray" and "infecting her with the virus of instant fame."

At the time of her death, Felina and Ricky Malcolm had separated. He was on tour in New Zealand and returned to the UK yesterday.

Felina's body was discovered in her home by police on Saturday morning. The official cause of death has not been established, although a drug overdose is strongly suspected. In a view that many will share, however, her mother has said in a statement that the talented Felina had been "killed by celebrity."

Miranda Enid Mackay, "Felina," is survived by her parents and her daughter.

It has taken me ages to read this, and I'm staring at the page wondering why it is making me so deeply sad.

It's more than the story of a singer's life ruined by celebrity excess. There is something about that story that touches me in a place I can't identify.

I replace the newspaper in the tin and start looking at other items. There are reports of Felina winning awards, stories of Felina coming out of a nightclub with Ricky Malcolm, with his long hair and all-over tattoos, and in all of them she's in her cat getup.

I've got to hand it to her: she did very well at concealing who she really was—or anyway, what she really looked like. It was a façade, a disguise. Always wearing—at the very least—the dark, feline glasses, and lashings of crimson lipstick.

I want to know more. I keep rummaging in the metal box, there on Gram's bedroom floor. More photos, more clippings.

I'm checking the clock on my phone. Gram's been gone an hour, and I don't want to risk being caught, so I'm putting everything back the way I found it when one last article catches my eye.

It's taken from the *Daily Mail* and the headline is:

"Felina—The Unseen Pictures of Pop's Tragic Princess."

I open the folded paper, and in that second my whole life changes.

Felina—Miranda Mackay—is my mum.

CHAPTER FIFTY-FIVE

So.

Felina is my mum, my real name is Tiger Pussycat (for goodness' sake), and Gram has been keeping this secret all my life.

It's the picture in the article: it's Felina without makeup, in the days before stardom, and it's the same one as we have downstairs on the mantelpiece. I don't even need to go downstairs to check.

It just is.

She's pretty, probably about sixteen, with an optimistic smile and a cheeky look. I can easily see the resemblance. It's there in the pale, bright, gray-blue eyes, the same shape as mine. Her hair too: strawberry blond—or, as Gram likes to call it, "spun gold."

There are even some spots on her chin that her concealer has not quite succeeded in concealing.

I pick up the photo of Felina in full makeup and sunglasses, hair dyed deep auburn, and hold the two pictures side by side. It's obvious, once you know. It's in the shape of the face, the slightly pointed chin.

But if you *didn't* know? No way could you tell.

I read the accompanying article as quickly as I can, but there's nothing new in it that I haven't read before. It's just that picture, and the caption: *In happier times: a teenage Felina.*

I turn the page, and my stomach lurches.

There's a headline:

Did This Picture Cause Felina's Downfall?

And there she is: snapped by the paparazzi, and looking startled. Her hair is wet and hanging in strands. It's nighttime, and the roads are wet from rain. Her left hand is holding a cigarette, and her right hand is gripping the wrist of an unhappy-looking child of about three.

The caption to the photo reads: *Felina last night with her daughter, Tiger Pussycat.*

That's what Great-Gran was saying: Tiger Pussycat.

My name.

Me.

CHAPTER FIFTY-SIX

I look at the pictures in the articles of the man with the long hair and unkempt beard—Ricky Malcolm, my father.

I don't even need to get my own photo from my room, where it has been on my shelf since forever, because I can see it in my mind.

In it, I'm a baby. Mum is holding me in her arms and looking down at me, a half smile on her contented face. Obviously she's not in her Felina outfit for a baby picture. Sitting on her left is a bearded man in a turtleneck, his long hair held back in a ponytail, and he's looking at Mum. His right arm is around her shoulders, and he's smiling too, but his shoulders are turned away.

It's as if he can't wait to get out of the picture. I've always thought that, actually, although I have never, until now, put it into words.

There is no doubt it is the same man, though. The same man who features in the newspaper articles in Gram's tin. In those, he is usually snapped leering aggressively at the camera, angry at being photographed by the paparazzi, or holding up a hand to block the camera's lens.

There is only one photo of him doing his job—as a musician. He's onstage, head down, playing the bass guitar, wearing a denim shirt open to the waist, and he looks exactly like what he is.

My dad. The rock star.

Well, not so much the star, actually. The caption below reads: *Ricky Malcolm: reclusive failed rocker.*

I read the accompanying article cut from *Heat* magazine. It's very short, and dated five years after my mum's death.

Where Are They Now?

Ricky Malcolm, husband of tragic star Felina, has not been seen in public since the inquest into his wife's death five years ago.

Cleared by the court of any involvement or blame in the death of Felina, New Zealand–born Malcolm is believed to have returned to his homeland, where sources say he has cleaned up his life and lives as a recluse near the remote community of Waipapa on the country's sparsely populated South Island.

I scrabble urgently through the rest of the clippings in the box, searching for more articles.

There are none—this is the most recent.

But there is a card at the bottom. One of those greeting cards that people use for thank-you notes—except Gram, of course, who has a special box of expensive writing paper with matching envelopes.

On the card is a picture of a stormy gray sea, and right in the middle is a tiny lighthouse being bashed by the waves. The words on the front read: *You are my calm in the storm.* Inside, in big, loopy handwriting, is a message.

Thank you, Mum, for everything. I have made mistakes that were not your fault. If it all goes wrong please take Boo far away from ALL of this. M xoxox

Carefully, I replace all the clippings in the box, fasten the latch with the combination padlock, and put everything back exactly where I found it.

I'm in my room when I hear the front door open and Gram come back in with Lady.

And now I have to work out what to do with this information.

I do not know which new fact has stunned me the most.

Is it that my mother was a famous singer who died in tragic circumstances?

Or is it that my dad was a bass guitarist who is probably now living in New Zealand?

There's another that I'll add: That my grandmother has been lying to me all my life? And possibly my great-grandmother too, for that matter?

What would *you* do?

Whatever it is, it shouldn't be what I do. Really.

CHAPTER FIFTY-SEVEN

I'm lying on my bed. I can hear Gram puttering around downstairs. There's the *chink* of teacups, and I remember I'm supposed to be making supper tonight.

Do I tell Gram what I know?

That would involve admitting to snooping around her room, but on the scale of "crimes of deception committed in my house," a spot of bedroom snooping comes in way down the list compared with "lying to my granddaughter for her WHOLE LIFE."

What difference will it make?

Why has she lied?

Can I ever trust her again?

Will she be angry? Upset? Hurt? Sorry? Defiant?

What about me?

Will anything change?

What about Great-Gran?

All these questions are swirling inside my brain. The tuna-and-pasta bake that was supposed to be for supper seems pretty insignificant. No wonder I forgot it. Perhaps I can just stay up here all evening?

"Ethel!" comes the call from downstairs. "Will you come down, please?"

I decide to postpone the big confrontation until I have had a little more time to work out what it all means. Until then, Gram and I will be living in a state of complete dishonesty with each other.

She is lying to me about what *she* knows, and I am lying to her by not telling her that *I* know what she knows.

I'm not supposed to know about my mum. Nor about my dad. Nor about Gram's young boyfriend.

Gram can't know—yet—about my snooping, nor about the invisible stuff.

It makes for a tense evening at the kitchen table.

"Sorry, Gram. I fell asleep."

She doesn't seem to mind at all. Her mood is light, even—dare I say it?—playful.

"Never mind, dear. We'll just have sandwiches. How does that sound?"

I busy myself making tuna sandwiches, replying as believably as I can to Gram's questions about school today.

"You're back late," I say, hoping that her response might reveal something about the man she met earlier.

She doesn't look at me when she says airily, "Oh, you know—these meetings can go on forever! Honestly! *Tsk!*"

She actually does that—says "*tsk.*" I probably wouldn't have noticed before, but now? I'm looking out for every little bit of evidence that will reveal my gram to be a serial liar.

When we're done, she gets up from the table and starts clearing the plates.

"We'll just clear these away now, shall we? Thank you for making the sandwiches. Goodness, look at the time—it's almost time for *Robson Green's Country Walks*, eh? I'll just pop this in the fridge. . . ."

She's giving a running commentary on what she's doing in order to avoid more questions.

Now I get it. She's nervous. She is acting carefree because she's hiding something. I know then that I will not be able to raise the issue of my mum and dad with Gram. Not now, at least.

I feel almost sorry for her. Yes, I am angry and confused, but I can see that there is confusion and conflict inside her too.

It's going to have to wait.

Besides, I have just received a text from Boydy. Which changes EVERYTHING.

Call me call me call me. Big prob re twins.

CHAPTER FIFTY-EIGHT

I'm in my room, phone on speaker, fingers tap-dancing on my laptop keyboard as I speak to Boydy.

"I can't find it."

"Just take my word for it."

"I want to see for myself. Are you absolutely sure?"

"Sure as sure."

And there it is on the school website, but it's not what I feared when I nervously put the call in to Boydy. I thought he was going to say that the video was already posted online, especially when he said, "Have you seen the school website?"

Whitley Bay Academy Trip to
High Borrans Activity Center
14–19 June

The following students have paid and submitted their consent forms to Mr. Natrass . . .

After that is a list of about twenty names—including Jesmond and Jarrow Knight.

"They're going to be away for six days from Thursday," says Boydy.

"And . . . ?"

That's all I can think of saying for the moment.

Boydy breaks the silence.

"That means it's *got* to be tomorrow, Eff."

"If they're away, it'll make breaking in easier."

"They'll have their phones with them when they're gone. And on a school trip, can you *imagine* the temptation to show everyone?"

"But if we agree to pay them . . . ?"

"Have you got the money, Effow?"

"Well, no. Obviously not."

"So there's your answer. There's no way you can pay them, and they know that. Unless we get ahold of it, that little video is going viral—if it hasn't already."

I think about Jarrow and Jesmond on the school trip. Boastful, cocky. On the bus, in the dorm, with everyone still talking about the "ghost" in the school.

I swallow hard.

Boydy's right, of course. It would be shown round, there's no doubt, and then what? I have no idea how much newspapers or websites pay for stuff like that, but it's definitely the sort of thing you see on dailymail.com or *BuzzFeed*, under a headline like *Haunted School: Is This a Ghost Caught on Camera?*

My heart is fluttering. I'd thought we had days to plan it, to work out the best way to achieve this. Basically, to summon up the courage to do it.

As Boydy and I talk, and try to work out reasons why we shouldn't go through with the plan, my phone pings with a text from Jarrow Knight.

First payment: 24 hours from now.

I read it out to Boydy and we both know what that means. It's tomorrow—it's got to be—and I feel sick with nerves. I look at the clock. It's just nine.

"Can you get to the back lane behind my road in five minutes?" I say. "We have to check tonight if we're going to do this tomorrow."

"If I pedal hard enough."

"Get pedaling, Boydy—this is crucial."

CHAPTER FIFTY-NINE

Five minutes later, Boydy, Lady, and I are heading towards the back of the house, and Boydy is looking at me intensely.

"You OK, Eff? You look a bit, I dunno, pale?"

I haven't said anything to him about what I've learned. I mean, what would I say? "I just found out my mum was really famous. Can you guess who it is? And by the way, my name's not Ethel. It's Tiger Pussycat." It's not the kind of thing you just come out with, is it? Besides, I need to focus on stopping the Knight twins from making *me* famous, and in the worst way I can think of.

Gram is watching her favorite TV show, and it's on the BBC, so there are no ad breaks. She won't be moving. I tell Gram that I'm taking Lady out for her nightly wee and she nods absently at me.

There's a back lane that runs behind Eastbourne Gardens, then turns left, and a hundred yards further along it's the back of the Knights' backyard. There's a high wall with a door in it.

"I can't get over that," I say, craning my neck to look up. "Besides—look!"

All along the top of the wall are lumps of broken glass set into concrete—jagged edges and shards sticking out at all angles—an oddly vicious-looking form of homemade barbed wire.

I try the handle of the door. As I expect, it's locked. I try it again, then leap back in fear. On the other side, there is a *thump* as a dog—a massive dog, I'd guess—hurls itself at the door and snarls.

Lady yelps and jumps back, jerking my arm with her leash.

Boydy sucks his teeth and says, "Hmm. That'll be Maggie, their, erm . . . tosa cross." He says the last bit quietly.

"Their *what*?"

"Just their, erm . . . tosa cross."

I just look at him, eyebrows raised, waiting.

"It's a dog. A tosa crossed with something else."

"You mean, the Japanese fighting dog? The Knights own a dog that's a banned breed in Britain because it's so vicious and you didn't think to tell me? How do you know it's a tosa?"

"I'm sorry, Eff, I just didn't want to worry you. I heard Jesmond boasting about it. Apparently the dog's got a heart of gold and their dad rescued it from a shelter. And it's crossed with something else, so it's not actually illegal. Probably not as dangerous."

He says it as if that makes it safe. We can still hear Maggie snarling, and Lady's pulling on her leash.

We follow the wall around till it joins onto a fence belonging to another house's yard. That might be one way in: get into the adjoining yard, and then gain access to the Knights' yard. Like it makes a difference with a snarling devil-dog, albeit one with a heart of gold.

The back lane ends and we're on the street that's parallel to mine. We follow the road around to the right onto the coast road, where the front of the Knights' house overlooks the Links. The house is big but ratty, with peeling paint and a rusting car in the driveway.

The sun has just about gone down, but it's still twilight for another hour. The sky's a deep royal blue and the streetlights are coming on, so Boydy and I cross the road and sit together in the darkened bus stop, hoping to be able to observe the house unobtrusively.

Above us, an airplane follows the line of the coast before banking left, high above the lighthouse, and I watch it, mesmerized by its silence and grace.

Beside me, there's a loud crunch as Boydy bites into an apple.

"Not long now, eh?" he says.

I follow his gaze to the lighthouse, but I don't say anything.

"Had you forgotten?"

"No, no," I lie. I *had* forgotten. "Day after tomorrow? Light the Light?"

Boydy grins. "S'gonna be awesome! You'll be there?"

I have been so caught up in my own stuff, but I nod. "Wouldn't miss it for anything."

Boydy turns his attention to the Knights' house. "It's the back or the front, basically," he says after a while.

Over the next ten minutes, we devise a plan for tomorrow night. Whether it's going to work or not remains to be seen.

One big question is: Can this all be done in the time after school? The invisibility lasts about five hours, or it did last time. It takes about two hours to activate.

So assuming I'm back from school at about four-thirty, start the process at five, invisible by seven . . .

We could be OK.

Only, Gram gets in at about six, right in the middle of the turning-invisible process.

It's unlikely she'll go into the garage. Not impossible, but unlikely. So I need to be in there, in the tanning bed, by five, and hope that she doesn't come in. Once the process is complete, I can go out the back way, hopefully avoiding Gram. And Lady, who might just go crazy but I'll have to hope not.

I'll give Boydy my phone during the Operation. That way, if Gram texts or calls, Boydy can text back as me to say I'm on my way, or have been held up.

I'm going through this in my head, wondering what will go wrong, counting on my fingers the potential traps I can fall into, worrying about that enormous Japanese tosa that might—or might not—be OK with invisible people, and wondering how—how on *earth*—I'm going to achieve the near impossible.

And that is: gain access to the Knights' computer(s).

It's a gamble. It's all a huge gamble, with the odds stacked against me, and it's my only choice.

Here is the plan (such as it is). Boydy writes it down and texts it to me so we both have it:

19:50—Ethel leaves home by back door
20:00—rendezvous with E. Boyd in back lane. E. invis. Go to Knights' house
20:15—B. knocks on door and begins plan. E. slips through open door
20:15 onwards (part 1)—E. locates J & J's computer(s).

Mac or Windows? Is there a shared family computer?
Execute Operation Wipe, as discussed
20:15 onwards (part 2)—locate J & J's mobile phones.
These will be password-protected. Steal them or destroy them.

To which, of course, has to be added:

- Don't get caught.
- Don't get mauled to death by some weird ninja–wolf hybrid.

It is ridiculous. Monstrously, impossibly stupid.

But it's going to have to work.

CHAPTER SIXTY

Boydy and I walk back up the lane in near silence. Before he gets on his bike, Boydy hands me a folded sheet of paper.

"It's the translation of the Chinese tea box. Danny Han's dad did it for me."

Danny Han lives above the Sunrise Chop Suey House. Boydy is one of their better customers.

We stand under the yellow streetlight in the back lane while I read it. Where Mr. Han did not know the correct word he put in question marks:

DR. CHANG HIS SKIN SO CLEAR
Very old remedy/medicine for many skin and scalp problems including:
acne, boils, psoriasis, vitiligo, mange, (???), and (?rash?).
Using historic and traditional plants and minerals,
Dr. Chang from Heng Shan Nan has created a mystical (?magical? ?unknown?) blend of (???) that will bring clean and (?smooth?) skin to those who use it.
This is how you use: one to two qian (5 g?) in water one time in day.

Carefully: do not eat more.
Contains: powder of mushroom, (???),
lime stones, (???), salt of lake, horn of rhinoceros, plus
secret mixture.

And that's it. Terrific.

Not only is there no indication of an address, the "secret mixture" could be anything. Plus, of course, I had—without knowing it—been taking rhino horn, which is just about the worst thing you can do if you have any respect at all for endangered wildlife (which I like to think I do. I once did a sponsored walk in aid of elephants of somewhere or other).

Worse are all the question marks.

"Mr. Han explained those," says Boydy, and he sounds quite proud. "Thing is, unless you know the symbol, you can't necessarily tell what it is. In English, even if you don't know what a word means, you can still look at it and know how it sounds. Doesn't work the same in Chinese."

"Where's this Heng Shan Nan, anyway?" I say.

It's just about the only clue to anything at all. We look it up on my phone.

Heng Shan Nan, or Nan-Heng-shan, or any of the other combinations, is a mountain in southern China, the southernmost of the Five Great Mountains of China. At the foot of the mountain is the largest temple in southern China: the Grand Temple of Mount Heng.

"So Dr. Chang lives by a mountain. Big deal. I'll bet he doesn't even exist. You haven't told anyone, have you? This has to be secret."

He gives me a hurt look. "You gotta trust me, Eff. I ain't told no one. Honest."

I do believe him. I'm just on edge, I guess. After all, tomorrow I have to drink more of this stuff with rhino horn in it.

Then I have to break into a house belonging to psychotic twins, with a Japanese fighting dog inside.

"So," says Boydy. "See you tomorrow night. Or I *won't* see you, actually."

"Ha-ha," I say.

But I'm not feeling very funny.

CHAPTER SIXTY-ONE

I'm in my room, later that night, staring at the packet of Dr. Chang His Skin So Clear, and my heart sinks.

The gray powder is almost gone. In my head I do a rough calculation, which involves guessing how much I have swallowed of this stuff in the past to make me invisible. I haven't really been scientific about it: I just guzzled as much of the vile brew as I could without it making me sick.

Four, five full mugs? More? I don't really know.

What I *do* know is that there's enough of the powder left for one more go, and no more.

There's another thing that's bothering me too.

This stuff—this herbal concoction, tea, gloop, whatever. It's pretty special. It deserves to be investigated, surely? I mean, investigated properly, by a proper scientist, from a university or the government or something like that.

But here's the thing: Why would anyone believe me?

Who would I go to? A twelve-year-old girl cannot just

wander up to a random professor and say, "Excuse me, Professor. This powder, when made into a tea and consumed in quantities that make me burp—sorry, *eructate*—powerfully and pungently, and combined with a long session on a sketchy tanning bed, makes me invisible."

It's not going to happen, is it?

Who else would I go to?

I run through the possibilities in my head (for the umpteenth time, by the way—this has been on my mind for a while):

- The police. Yeah, right. I walk into a police station and give the same spiel as above? I'd be lucky not to be arrested for wasting police time.
- My doctor. Dr. Kemp at the Monkseaton Surgery is a nice man, but why would he believe me? Why would anyone believe me without proof?
- Mr. Parker, our teacher. It sounds like a classic teacher windup, doesn't it? I can hear him now: *Very amusing, Ethel. Very* droll. *If only you put as much effort into learning physics as you do into the creation of such whimsical* folderol, *you might make quite a successful student. Until then . . .*, etc.
- Our local parliament representative. He'd have contact

with government scientists, but I'm too young to vote, so he wouldn't take me seriously and he'd probably be scared of being mocked if he did.

- Finally—and I suppose most obviously—it's Gram. Force her to watch while I do the whole invisibility thing. She'd certainly have to believe me then. Trouble with that is, I wouldn't then be able to rescue the evidence from the Knight twins—that requires secrecy. It'd be like: "OK, Gram, you can see I'm invisible now. Just wait around while I go out to do this really important thing. Back soon! Honest!"

It all comes down to proof. People are going to demand that I show them.

"Extraordinary claims require extraordinary proof," said some guy, sometime.

So this is what I'm going to do. It sounds crazy, but bear with me.

I'm going to use the rest of the powder to become invisible one last time, for the break-in at the Knights'. All but one teaspoon, which I shall keep for analysis by the experts. That's about all I can spare anyway. (Later, perhaps someone can track down Dr. Chang, if he's even real.)

I shall then film myself turning invisible.

I know. It sounds crazy, seeing as one of the reasons I'm becoming invisible once again is to destroy the video of my invisibility.

But this will be under my control. It will not appear on Facebook or YouTube, or Vimeo or Instagram, or any other thing like them that might come along in the future.

It won't be all *Tragic Star Felina's Daughter Turns Invisible.*

Once something's on the Internet, you've lost control of it: it's not yours anymore. And I wouldn't be me anymore. I'd be the Invisible Girl, which would make me anything but invisible.

And this is mine. My invisibility, under my control. It will be private, secret. I will find an investigator, a scientist, a researcher—someone I trust completely. I will *own* it.

It will be on my terms alone.

Part Three

CHAPTER SIXTY-TWO

I have hardly slept *at all.*

(I don't think you would, either, if you had to do what I have to do this evening.)

I was kept awake by another rainstorm. It's turning into one of those English summers that you get in the old comedy films that Gram likes: that is, the unfunny ones where people go on holiday to resorts like Whitley Bay used to be, and it rains just as they're setting up their deck chairs.

Anyway, all night I was torn between thinking *Please stop, rain, please stop* and *Rain as hard as you can so there's none left tomorrow.*

Rain, as I discovered at school, is not a good companion to invisibility.

As for explaining why I'll be out all evening, this has taken a bit of thought. In the end, I settle on a text to Gram, which I send to her during morning break.

Boydy's having a gathering tonight for his birthday. Movies and pizza. His mum will drive me home. Back by 11. Don't wait up. E xxx

Normally—that is, with Gram behaving normally—a text like that would produce an avalanche of further questions, probably starting with "What on earth is a gathering, Ethel? Is it like a party?" But lately I've begun to trust that Gram will react anything *but* normally. It's kind of like "expecting the unexpected."

She texts back:

Will there be others there?

Easy.

Yes, there will be about seven of us.

Plausible? I think so. So does Gram.

All right. Have fun. x

I've been staring out the window during the physics lesson, gazing at the flat gray sky and trying, by force of will, to ensure it stays dry. Soon I'm practically falling asleep, even though the subject is one very close to my heart: the nature of light.

"I hope you all understand this," says Mr. Parker. "There'll be a test at the end of term, you *lucky duckies*."

Groans all round.

Light is energy, I've got that.

It's a type of radiation—the type we can see, because our eyes have evolved to be able to see it.

Then Jesmond Knight puts his hand up. He's in the same class as me, but his sister isn't.

"Mr. Parker," he begins, and then he turns his head to look straight at me. "Do you think it's possible for a person to be invisible?"

"I'm over here, Mr. Knight, thank you. Do you mean like Harry Potter's cloak of invisibility? Or the one that occurs in the legend of King Arthur? Or the 'cloaking device' in *Star Trek*? A splendid question, and the answer is—get ready to have your gobs smacked and your flabs gasted—yes! In theory, at least. You see, researchers have been working—"

Jesmond interrupts him—always a dangerous move with Mr. Parker, but he gets away with it. "Sorry, sir. I didn't mean that. I meant the whole person." Again, he turns and looks at me, a sly smile on his face—one that doesn't reach his eyes.

"Ah! An invisible person? Well, that would require both

biological and *technological* breakthroughs that have so far proved elusive to even the finest minds in science. So the answer to your question, Mr. Knight, is—for the time being, at any rate—a disappointing and resounding no. Continue with this inquisitiveness, however, and you may yet be the scientist who makes the discovery that—"

"So, sir, if someone had the ability to become invisible—"

"That is a BIG if, Mr. Knight."

"I know, sir, but *if* they did, they'd be, like, famous an' that?"

"I very much expect that indeed such a person would be, like, famous an' that. It would be a worldwide sensation, without a shadow of a doubt. And talking of shadows, who can tell me the difference between the *umbra* and the *penumbra* of a shadow? Yes, Miss Wheeler?"

And he's off again on the nature of light, leaving Jesmond smirking at me in the most creepy way. It makes me feel sick.

People are still talking about the strange events of Monday:

- Rafi McFaul tells me I missed the freakiest thing, like, *evah*, even though she didn't see any of it, while those who do claim to have seen something—mostly people in the lobby who were looking out at me running through the rain—are exaggerating their accounts alarmingly.

- Sam Donald says he saw the “ghost” (for this is what I am becoming) turn and laugh, pointing at someone in the crowd.
- Anoushka Tavares insists it was not the figure of a human, but something larger, like a big ape.

I have to hand it to the Knight twins: they are showing incredible willpower not to just play everyone their video. But they’ve only given me and Boydy till the end of tonight to make the first payment of money we don’t have, and once they go on that school trip there’s no *way* they’re not going to end up getting out the video when everyone’s around the campfire or whatever.

It all makes it even more essential that I act tonight.

CHAPTER SIXTY-THREE

After school, the evening is warm and hazy, with a salty breeze coming off the sea. Normally I'd love an evening like this. I'd walk Lady on the beach, have a "summer salad" for supper with Gram, do my homework, watch a bit of TV, go to bed when it's still a bit light.

There's a lot to be said for "normal." Normal is nice, normal is reliable, and unsurprising, and comforting. Now I am wondering if anything can ever be normal again.

I am treating this whole thing like I'm a commando on a raid or something, and it is very far from normal.

First of all, I shower. I don't want any tiny bits of dust or dirt clinging to me to give away my presence. I check my nose for snot, my ears for wax, my hair for dandruff, my nails for dirt trapped beneath them. You may think it's gross, but tough: I'm not taking any risks.

Which is a stupid thing to say. What I mean is, I'm not taking any risks *apart from* entering someone's house invisibly and wiping their computers. That's risk enough for me.

I brought some Dr. Chang His Skin So Clear to school in my water bottle and I drank it at lunchtime. It hadn't improved. It was still foul.

By the last period, I could feel the familiar gut-rumbling and I knew what was coming. The lesson was English, and Mrs. West had allocated parts for us to read from *Othello*, which is Shakespeare. Tyrone Bower always gets to do *Othello* because he throws himself into it and doesn't care about sounding like a complete clown, e-nun-ci-at-ing his Shakes-pee-ahh like he's appearing at the Theatre Royal.

And I did something that—only a week ago—I would not have dreamed of doing.

Bored with Tyrone and his overacting, I had skimmed ahead in the text, and seen something coming up that I thought, well . . .

Here's what happened. I would normally never burp in class. Who would? And what made me suddenly decide that now would be a good time?

I held on and held on, while Tyrone shouted his lines. He was even doing arm actions *at his desk*. I really couldn't hold on any longer—it was giving me stomach cramps. If I say so myself, when it finally came, it could not have been timed better.

Othello, if you didn't know, is the name of an army general, and he's crazily in love with a woman named Desdemona. Take it away, Tyrone:

Othello: If after every tempest come such calms,
May the winds blow till they have wakened death!
Me: *Buuuuurp!*

You know when you drink a cold Coke on a hot day, and guzzle it too quickly? It was like one of those burps, but doubled. It was loud, and perfectly timed. But that was nothing—*nothing*—compared with the smell, which was worse than ever.

People laughed at first, because of the line about "may the winds blow" and its perfectly timed follow-up.

But then the odor began to spread.

Have you ever seen on the news when police fire tear gas at protesters? It was like that in Mrs. West's English literature class. People were actually getting up from their desks and moving away, coughing.

And best of all, I didn't get the blame. Everyone thought

it was Andreas Hansen, who was sitting next to me, mainly because he turned and pointed at me, and no one—and I mean *no one*—would ever imagine that I, quiet little Ethel Leatherhead, would do such a thing. I helped it by coughing a bit and looking accusingly at Andreas.

At least I know that the drink is working.

CHAPTER SIXTY-FOUR

Boydy has come round, and we have gone over for a third time the process for wiping content from both Windows and Mac computers:

Open up this drive, locate this file, locate this backup file, and so on and on. . . .

Check for video-editing software: Windows Movie Maker, iMovie.

Check for video files: mpgs, jpgs, avi files.

Check if they've been backed up when transferred to the editing programs.

And all the while hoping—*hoping*—that at each stage, the computer doesn't ask for passwords for the different functions.

"You'll probably be all right," says Boydy, but I don't like the "probably." "I looked it up last night. Hardly anyone sets their personal computers to have passwords for different commands. It's too much hassle. One password to get in, and then the computer stays open, and most people don't even bother to shut their computers down properly: they just let them go to sleep on their own."

It's a bit reassuring.

Downstairs in the garage, the tanning bed is in position, and we have rigged up my laptop with a webcam recording directly onto a plug-in hard drive. I want the whole thing in HD.

Two more scoops of the drink mixture mean that the packet is pretty much empty, apart from the little bit I have left for analysis once I have all the evidence I need on film.

"Look after this for me, will you?" I say to Boydy, and I hand him the near-empty packet. I'm not completely sure why: I think I want to show him that I trust him, and that I appreciate his involvement.

I certainly wouldn't be able to do this alone.

He takes it, folds it, and shoves it in his blazer pocket. He's still in his school uniform. He keeps hitching his trousers up with his hands, and it's then that I notice.

"Have you, erm . . . Have you lost weight, Boydy?" I say, before draining the last of Mr. Chang's vomitous creation and swallowing hard.

I have never seen anyone blush so fast and so hard. Poor Boydy doesn't just go pink—he goes *fuchsia* (which, in case you didn't know, is a type of bright, deep pink).

"Ca-can you tell?"

"Either that or you're going for an eighties 'baggy look.' They don't fit anymore, I can tell you that much."

"Just eating a bit healthier, you know?"

I smile at him, and he blushes even more, for some reason.

"Right," I say. "Time for me to get undressed and onto that tanning bed. I don't need you for this bit."

"Eh? What? Yeah, of course, Eff. All in the name of science, eh? Ha-ha."

He's gone weird. I give him a quizzical look.

"Whatever. See you at our rendezvous spot in two hours. Oh, hang on—hold on to your hat."

I let rip with another huge burp.

"Nice one, Eff. Very, erm . . . Yeah. Bye."

He leaves, with his hand over his nose, and I don't blame him.

Even Lady whimpers and retires to her basket.

CHAPTER SIXTY-FIVE

It's eight o'clock. The evening shadows are long, and the threat of rain has receded. The sky has cleared to a pale mauve with long streaks of gray cloud. The sea is gray-brown and still, like freshly laid concrete.

Boydy and I are standing outside the front door of the Knights' house. He's holding a clipboard and a pen.

"You there?" he says.

"I'm here, behind you."

"Where?" He reaches out his hand at chest level. "Oops, sorry, Effow."

"It's OK. Just, you know, a bit higher next time, eh?"

"Got it. You ready?"

"I'm ready."

Boydy rings the doorbell, and for a brief moment I wonder if the sound of the bell will be drowned out by the banging of my heart.

From inside the house comes a loud barking, which gets

nearer and nearer; then two paws thump against the door and the barking continues. Instinctively I shrink back, but then I move closer when I hear a deep, posh-sounding voice coming towards the door.

"Maggie! Maggie! Be quiet, will you, darling? Get out of the way. Jesmond! Come and get the dog, please!" It's a man's voice—I'm guessing it's Tommy Knight, their dad. I remember the time at the school bazaar when he bought the soaps and was softer-spoken than I expected: like a lion that purrs like a cat.

There are sounds of a struggle and then the same voice, but tinny, crackles out of a brass panel that has a little screen with a camera behind it.

"Hello. Who's that?"

Boydy grins at the brass panel.

"Hello! I'm from Light the Light, the campaign to reinstate a light in St. Mary's Lighthouse, and I was wondering if you could spare a minute to—"

"Yes! Hold on."

There's an electronic beeping, and then the door opens just a crack while a balding white-blond man eases himself into the space, blocking it off from the growling dog. The man gives a shy smile and jerks his head towards the dog.

"Sorry, old son. She's a bit excitable. Now tell me about

your campaign: I'm all ears. I love it when youngsters take the initiative."

Youngsters?

So Boydy does tell him all about the campaign, and Tommy Knight listens intently, and chuckles, and says it all sounds "splendid," and all the time I'm looking at him and his swept-back hair and his expensive-looking teeth, and I forget myself. I forget that I'm invisible and start to say, "Are you Jesmond and Jarrow's dad?" because it seems so unlikely.

I get as far as "Are," then I remember, and I stop.

Tommy Knight, who has stopped talking, glances in my direction and Boydy fakes a coughing fit to cover the strange noise.

"Anyway, I'm happy to sign!" he says.

He takes Boydy's clipboard, signs his name with the ballpoint pen and hands it back.

"Jolly good luck to you. I wish I could get my two off their phones to do something like this!" Tommy Knight is grinning and good-natured.

He's about to close the door, so Boydy pipes up:

"We—that is, I—ah . . . I'm a friend of Jesmond's. I wonder if he'd like to sign as well?"

"Good idea! Look, I'm going to take the dog into the back

room. Jesmond will be down. Jesmond! Friend of yours at the door!"

Tommy Knight retreats down the hallway, pulling Maggie by the collar and shooting a friendly "Cheerio!" over his shoulder.

Footsteps thump down the stairs and Jesmond is standing in the doorway.

Any warmth that Tommy Knight had given to our encounter is immediately dispersed by the chill in Jesmond's eyes.

"Boyd? What do you want?"

"All right, Jez?" Boydy lowers his voice. "It's about, you know . . . the payments."

Jez glances back to check his dad's not there.

Boydy keeps up the friendly approach.

"I told your dad it was about the lighthouse campaign, but really it's about how me and Ethel get the money to you."

Jesmond looks over Boydy's shoulder, and left and right.

"Where is she, then?"

"She's back home. She sent me as negotiator. Come on, man."

Boydy's pleading works, but only up to a point. Jesmond opens the door fully but stands, arms folded, blocking the way. Boydy hands him the clipboard and peels back the top sheet with the Light the Light petition on it. Beneath is a sheet of printed paper.

Jez looks at it and reads aloud: "'We the undersigned formally declare that on receipt of the agreed sum of one thousand pounds, we will surrender all physical and digital copies of the video clips featuring Ms. Ethel Leatherhead . . .'"

I have to hand it to Boydy. He can do this legal-sounding stuff really well. Jesmond's voice is flat as he reads. I don't think he understands a word, and I'm not surprised.

"'. . . and in addition will relinquish all claims, moral and legal, with respect to said intellectual property in perpetuity henceforth from this day forward, signed . . .'"

He stops and looks at Boydy closely.

"That it? That's yer legal document, is it? I'm not signin' *that*. It's just a bit o' paper."

"Well . . . we've had some problems at the printer's. Still waitin' for the proper version."

"Well, come back when you've got summin' worth signin'. Y'know what, you can save yourself a trip and not bother comin' back at all, Boyd, because I'm not signin' anyth—*OOOOF!* What the HELL?"

Seeing our only chance slipping away as Jesmond backs off and starts closing the door, I do the only thing I can think of. With all my strength, I barge at Boydy right in his back.

He, in turn, stumbles forward into Jesmond Knight, and the two fall through the doorway, ending up in a mess on the floor. I take the chance and hop over them into the hallway.

"Are you completely mad, Boyd? What are you doin'? Gerroff me."

"Sorry, Jez, sorry . . . I just, erm . . . tripped up, like."

"Tripped up? On what? Get out, you fat idiot!" Jesmond hustles him out the door and slams it shut, then stands looking at the wood, shaking his head.

I'm in. I'm actually in the Knights' house, and invisible, standing on the dark tiles of the hallway and staring at Jesmond, trying to anticipate where he will move next so I can get out of his way.

The Knights' house is pretty big, and the hallway is wide. The stairway runs up the right side of the hall, and there's a full coatrack right behind me.

Jesmond turns away from the door. Unless he reaches for a coat, I'm safe. He walks past me towards an internal door a little along the hall. When he opens it, there's a blur of tan fur as Maggie, the huge Japanese tosa, bundles out and runs right at me.

"Oi! Maggie! Calm down. What's the matter with you?"

The dog has stopped about half a yard away from me and is sniffing the air, turning her huge head from side to side, then dropping it to the ground, inching a little closer and snarling.

I can do nothing but stay absolutely still. I look down and, horrified, I can see that my bare feet have left faint, sweaty footprints on the tiles.

"What is the matter with you, Maggie? Come here. *Come!*"

The dog doesn't budge, but continues sniffing and snarling.

Jesmond's voice gets harsher. "Maggie! Come here *now!*"

No reaction. Jesmond strides forward to grab Maggie's collar. Honestly, he's close enough to hear me breathing, so I hold my breath as he wrestles the massive hound away from the coats and me. As the dog reluctantly succumbs, Jesmond gives her a vicious kick in the backside.

"Stupid dog. Get in there!"

I hear his dad's voice from inside the room, gently chiding: "Jesmond, old son. Be nice."

The door slams behind them both and I am alone in the hallway. Now I just have to wait for Boydy to enact the next part of the plan.

Sure enough, exactly five minutes later, I hear the ringtone of a mobile phone. Jesmond's is first. Boydy has both of the twins' numbers from a class list that went round last year, and I hear Jesmond, through the shut door, answer and say a brusque "Hullo."

Boydy has concealed the caller number, and as soon as the call is answered, he hangs up.

That's all. The only purpose of the call is to make Jesmond's phone ring so that I can locate it, and it's worked. He has it on him. Not ideal, but it's kind of what we expected.

Jarrow's phone is next. I hear it ring upstairs, a jaunty preset tone like a sea chantey. It rings and rings and rings and then stops. Excellent!

That puts me in a good mood. It means that at least one of my tasks has become a little easier. I relax a bit, and even sit down on the third stair to calm my breathing. I try closing my eyes, forgetting that my eyelids are transparent. So I just breathe through my nose a bit, and although I can still see when I close my eyes, the *feeling* of them being closed is oddly calming.

I get my bearings. The Knights' house is *not* how I expected it, and that is both comforting and disturbing at the same time.

I was expecting it to be messy and dirty, because that's how it looks from the outside—but it's not.

Apart from the dark red tiles on the floor, everything in the hallway is brilliant white: the walls, the skirting board, the radiator, the ceiling. The stair posts are white; the stair carpet is creamy white. At the end of the hallway there's a mirror, and in front of the mirror is a big bunch of white lilies in a white vase.

Arranged in a line on the wall are photographic portraits of the entire Knight clan: the ones where you go to a studio and everyone has to wear blue jeans and a white shirt. Second along are Jesmond and Jarrow, looking on point, like teen models.

Everything smells of lilies and floor polish and disinfectant. It's like the sort of place you see in *a magazine*—where film stars live.

Attached to the wall of the hallway is a glass-fronted cabinet, with a light inside it and a brass plaque saying, *An A to Z of Man's Best Friend.* Arranged on four glass shelves are loads of tiny china dogs, each a different breed, with little brass labels in front of them: AFFENPINSCHER, BORDER COLLIE, CHIHUAHUA. There's even something called a xolo, as well as a Yorkie and a zuchon. It's the sort of thing that people collect, and I think of Tommy Knight's doggy soaps and know these must be his.

Further along the hallway are doors leading to other rooms—I'm guessing the kitchen, living room, and so on. That's where the noise of the TV is coming from, and where Jesmond went.

I'll come back down and check it out later. Right now I want to go and find Jarrow's phone.

The plan says that if the phone doesn't pick up, it's safe to call it again two minutes later to help me find it. If I have *already* found it, I'll turn off the volume so that it doesn't ring again.

See? This plan is *slick*.

CHAPTER SIXTY-SIX

Upstairs, exactly two minutes later, the phone goes again, the sea chantey louder now and easily identifiable as coming from the doorway right ahead of me. I don't dare open the door yet: it might make the ringtone sound loud enough for Jarrow to hear it downstairs and come looking for the phone.

I'm feeling a calmness that is unusual as I wait for it to ring out, then open the door. The room's light is on, but the smartphone's screen is still glowing from the phone's having rung. It's right ahead of me on the desk, and I stride forward and almost scream when a huge swivel chair spins round and Jarrow, in an oversize onesie with a zebra pattern on it, leaps to her feet. She takes off her headphones in the same action as reaching for the phone and turning it on with her passcode.

She looks quizzically at the screen for a few seconds and sees that it shows "number withheld" (at least, it should, if Boydy's done it right), puts the phone down, picks up her laptop, gets back in her swivel chair, and spins around again, so her back is towards me.

This is a *huge* opportunity. The smartphone is unlocked, and will stay that way until it locks itself, usually after about half a minute of not being touched.

All I need to do is cross the room to the desk and touch the screen to stop the smartphone from locking itself; then I can access all Jarrow's phone data.

Four steps, I reckon. Five, maybe.

I'm going too slowly. At three steps, there's a creaky floorboard and I don't know for certain if Jarrow's headphones are back on: the back of the chair is too high. And now I can't wait any longer: the screen goes half-dark, preparing to shut down. I take one big step, the floorboard creaks, and the minute I touch the screen to reactivate it, the chair swivels round again.

"Jez?" she says.

She must have heard something. I stand stiller than I have ever stood in my life, holding my breath until she swivels back—but only halfway.

She can't see me, obviously. But she will see the screen on her phone changing if I do anything. She's not looking at it, but it will attract her attention.

All I can do is stand there. I'm about a yard away from

her, and my finger is hovering over the phone, preventing it from shutting down by touching it now and then, and I'm watching Jarrow *very* carefully in case she makes a sudden move in my direction.

Any calmness I had begun to feel has melted away, and I'm so tense I swear you could twang me like a guitar string.

This goes on for *nine whole minutes.* I know because there's a clock on the front of Jarrow's phone showing the advancing time. Eventually, just as a cramp that started in my left foot is spreading up my leg, Jarrow sighs. She snaps shut her laptop, removes her headphones, and stands up. She's about to reach out for her phone, so I take my hand away, but then she changes her mind and leaves it on the desk.

The minute she is out the door, I've flipped open her laptop, and if I weren't so nervous, I'd probably do a little jig of joy because it springs to life again, meaning I won't need a password to access her stuff.

Result. Yay. Brilliant. Etc.

Now get on with it, Ethel.

I've got her phone in my hands, and I'm scrolling through and trying to find where she might have the video of me.

It's not a model I'm familiar with. I've got Gram's old iPhone and I can find my way round one of them easily. This one's an Android phone, and not even a well-known Android phone. Most of the app icons are the same, though, and I quickly work out where the video clips are.

And there it is! The one taken in the school theater has been sent to her on a clip-sharing app, and it's easiest to delete the entire app and its contents. The whole video, including the security footage and the close-ups, is in a "Videos" app, and that gets sent straight to the bin.

There's a "deleted" file in "Settings." Empty that . . . *click.*

I search her emails for video attachments. Nothing.

Now for her laptop. That's an Apple Mac, so it's iMovies. Nothing there: the film wasn't made on this, then.

Emails: There it is! Sent two days ago. *Click,* gone.

And iTunes: There it is again, saved from the email. *Click,* gone.

OK, OK, where else could it be?

Could there be a copy in a video player? I don't know, but I open up QuickTime just in case. Nothing there. Good.

Next I search the whole laptop with the search tool. Nothing. Even better.

Finally, empty "Trash."

I can hear footsteps on the stairs, and Jarrow saying, "Night, Jez! Night, Daddy!" Her voice sounds different from normal: softer, and much less Geordie.

(*Daddy?* Jarrow Knight does *not* strike me as the kind

of girl to call her father "Daddy." In Jarrow's normal accent, "Dad" would be right, maybe even "Da," but "Daddy"?)

Oh, Jarrow, I think. *Why do you choose* tonight *to have an early night?*

How do you empty "Trash"? I'm pressing buttons frantically, and the progress bar is telling me there's *loads* of trash to delete, and it's taking forever, and I tell you this: I have *no idea at all* how Jarrow Knight did not see her laptop mysteriously closing itself as she came back into the room, or for that matter hear an anxious panting.

But I've done it.

Well . . . one part of it, anyway.

I've got Jesmond's to do next. Then I still need to check the family computer, if there is one. And deal with a huge, badly trained dog.

Oh, whoopee.

CHAPTER SIXTY-SEVEN

I'm back downstairs now, in the white hallway, and the only open door leads through to a huge kitchen, decorated in the same no-color color scheme—pale grays and sand. It's a sort of L-shaped room, and there are double doors leading to the sitting room. The lights are off, apart from one above the cooker, which casts a yellowish glow over the whole room.

There, in the corner of the room, is a large computer screen resting on a countertop with papers and stuff littered around it: the family's computer.

I'm tiptoeing across the floor when I hear the dog growl and, in a second, she has burst through the double doors and is bounding straight for me, a string of drool flopping from her jaws.

"Maggie! Maggie! Oh, for heaven's sake, that dog!" It's Tommy Knight's voice but it doesn't sound angry. Impatient and amused, I'd call it.

I'm paralyzed with fear when Maggie just skitters to a halt on the white kitchen tiles, sniffing and snarling by my feet, angry and puzzled.

"What is wrong with you, eh?"

I get a better look at Tommy Knight now that he's not shielded by his front door. He's tall and slightly stooped, wearing jeans high on his waist like an old man, although he's just normal dad age. His checked shirt is tucked in and his eyes are crinkled as if he's half-smiling at a private joke. I thought the Knight twins' dad would be twice as scary as they are, but he isn't. In fact, only his white-blond hair gives any indication that they are related at all.

He is heading straight towards me and I edge backward. Maggie follows, snuffling at the ground. I really think she'd attack if she could see me, but she keeps looking up and around, completely baffled at the absence of anything to accompany what she can clearly smell.

"Come on, you—out!" murmurs Tommy Knight, walking past me and opening the glass door to the backyard, but the dog just stays put, making threatening noises in her throat.

"Come on. Stop that, you big silly!"

Tommy takes the dog by the collar and coaxes her away, shoving her gently out the door and slamming it shut. The dog whines at the glass barrier, and Tommy turns away, shaking his head in wry amusement.

In my fear, a little more internal gas has escaped via a silent burp.

Tommy sniffs, then looks at Maggie through the glass pane. "You filthy beast," he mutters, smiling. Then he says, louder, "Jesmond! What have you been feeding Maggie?"

He pulls out the chair in front of the computer and sits, wiggling the mouse to bring the screen to life. It's an ancient computer: like, a truly prehistoric old Mac. I figure: *This is Tommy's computer, and only Tommy's.* There's no way at all that Jesmond or Jarrow would do any video editing on it, and I can safely leave it alone.

He opens up an email program and starts scrolling through, opening emails, writing stuff, and it looks like he's settling in.

Carefully, I edge away. I'm sensitive to every tiny noise I make, from my breathing to the slight sound my feet make on the tiles when I lift them up, but he doesn't notice.

From the TV room, I hear a mobile phone's ringtone.

I stick my head around the door. Jesmond's laptop is next to him.

Then something happens that turns all my terror on its head.

"Oh, hi, Mum. . . . No, she's gone to bed. . . . Just, y'know, hangin' out. . . . When are you back? . . . Midnight? I'll be in bed. . . . Yeah. . . . Love you too. Night."

Hearing that conversation suddenly changes Jesmond Knight from a fearsome brute into . . . well, a normal thirteen-year-old. "Love you too"? To his mum? I smile. I become less scared.

More than that, though, it's his voice—the same as his sister's earlier. Gone is the earthy, broad Geordie accent in favor of something much gentler. Not posh, exactly, but well on its way.

Along with Jarrow calling her father "Daddy," I'm beginning to think that I'm not the only one here who's invisible: there are parts of the Knight twins that are unseen as well.

I'm still stuck, though. For a whole hour, as it turns out, I'm trapped in the kitchen, while Tommy Knight fiddles on his computer and Jesmond lies on the sofa in the living room, playing some game on his phone, then flicking the channels on the TV.

Eventually, Jesmond hauls himself upright on the sofa, opens the cover of his laptop, and quickly types in the password. I can sort of see over his shoulder, but his fingers move too fast for me to get any idea of what he's typing.

I'm looking so intensely, though, that I miss his father

coming back towards me. For a tall guy, he moves very quietly. I just manage to squeeze aside as he comes through the double doors and his arm brushes mine.

Tommy Knight stops. With his other hand he touches his arm where it touched mine, and he looks around, frowning, but then carries on into the living room, where he lowers himself into a black leather armchair.

"Did you see that thing about the missing dogs, Jesmond?" says Tommy. "It's all over the *Whitley Guardian*'s website."

It's the way he says it, though, that makes me really pay attention. He's looking carefully at Jesmond, as if trying to measure his son's reaction. This is not an off-the-cuff conversation-maker.

Now, you have probably already made the same connection I have, but I haven't mentioned it yet because it was just a hunch and I wasn't sure how relevant it was. My hunch is this: that the Knight twins are *somehow* connected with the missing-cats-and-dogs thing. It was the encounter on the beach that day, when I was invisible and they had Lady. The other events of that day have kind of overshadowed everything, but it's been there in the back of my mind, nibbling away like a rat chewing through an electric cable: you know, nibble, nibble, nothing, then . . . *pow!*

Jesmond either is a very good actor or genuinely has

nothing to do with it all. His attitude is completely relaxed. He barely looks up from his laptop.

"Hmm? Dogs and cats? Haven't seen it, Dad." Then he changes the subject: clever. "Can you run us to school tomorrow, pleeease? We've got luggage for the school trip."

But Tommy is not distracted.

"You know, Jesmond—if I do find out you're mixed up in this, I'll . . ."

Here Jesmond does look up. What threat will his dad make?

". . . I'll be very disappointed."

Jesmond doesn't reply. Instead he gets to his feet and closes the cover of his laptop. But there's no chance I can pull off the same trick as I did upstairs with his sister—not with his dad sitting there.

"I'm off, Dad. Night," says Jesmond, and Tommy Knight's brow wrinkles in puzzlement.

Jesmond goes through the other door, the one that leads to the hallway. He's got his phone in his hand.

How am I going to do this? Without a proper shutdown, most laptops will turn themselves off after a few minutes. I haven't got long to act.

I walk quickly to the back door and open it just the tiniest bit, as quietly as I can. There's a security chain at the top, which I engage so that the door won't open more than a few inches. Then I start to taunt Maggie.

"Hey, Maggie," I whisper. "You are one horrible, ugly hound—do you know that?"

That's all it takes. Maggie starts growling, barking, and whining, poking her huge muzzle through the gap between the door and the frame, trying to locate the source of the sound.

In a second, Tommy Knight is shuffling back through the kitchen, and I pass him as I head to the living room.

"Maggie! Do be quiet, love. How did you get that door open? You want to come in, do you?"

No, please! No!

"Sorry, love. You stay out there a bit longer. And *shhh!*"

Phew.

It buys me enough time to open up Jesmond's laptop. Trouble is, the DVD drive starts up too, and the whole thing is glowing and whirring when Tommy comes back in.

Now, I can't say for certain that Tommy Knight is spooked, but he just stops dead in the doorway, staring at the laptop. The screen is only half-opened, at a forty-five-degree angle to the keyboard, giving out a glow to the room.

He stands there for maybe ten seconds—which is a long time if you count it out—then he looks back into the kitchen towards the back door, then he touches his arm again where it brushed mine, and the frown on his face gets so intense, his eyebrows practically fuse together into one.

Then he sighs, goes back to his chair, and flicks through the channels until he finds something he likes: an animal documentary.

Now I'm in trouble. I can't see the angled screen unless I get on the floor.

This I do, very cautiously. There is no way I can do all the searching that I did on Jarrow's laptop. Not at that angle, and with all those keystrokes, each of which will make a noise.

It's the "wipe" option. Wipe everything off the laptop, restore it to factory settings. With Tommy Knight about two yards away.

He can't actually see the screen from where he is sitting, which is a good thing, but hitting the keys silently is practically impossible. If you don't believe me, try it sometime.

You're probably not interested in how to wipe a computer. But the whole thing involves pressing certain keys, holding them down till the DOS appears (it's basically just a whole bunch of operating commands), and then pressing DELETE and ENTER till everything's gone.

Which would be fine, and (just about) doable—even lying on a white carpet peering at an angled screen and hitting the keys *very gently* with a man two yards away—except it requires the hard drive to be pretty active as it deletes stuff, and that makes a whirring noise that no amount of sound from the TV will cover, especially if the man is already spooked.

I have to press the command to delete, and I know this will set the hard drive off.

I just have to do it.

My finger hovers above it, and then I hit it. The drive whizzes to life with a loud *SHHHHHH,* and Tommy Knight spins round and leaps to his feet.

It's being so close to the carpet that does it, I think. But I really couldn't have picked a worse time to sneeze.

CHAPTER SIXTY-EIGHT

It's just a little one: not a huge comedy *WWWWACHOOO!* More of a cute panda-sneeze: *ichhha!*

It is definitely a sneeze, though.

Tommy Knight just stands there. I have no idea what else he's doing, because I'm in a crouched position behind the coffee table and I dare not look up.

I know, I know: it makes no sense, really. He can't see me, so why shouldn't I move my head from being curled up? I think it's just ingrained in us, an instinctive thing: if you feel threatened or unsafe, then you curl up, kind of defensively, and that is what I do.

At first, anyway.

After a few seconds, I realize the silliness of what I am doing, and I lift my head. My nose is tickling again.

Tommy Knight is still standing there, head cocked, very alert and suspicious.

Then it comes again, another sneeze, and I have held this one in so hard that it explodes, not so much as a sneeze sound but as a splutter, and a fine spray of spit lands on the laptop, becoming visible immediately.

Cautiously, Tommy Knight steps over and picks up the laptop and looks at it. It's still whirring while it deletes everything. Holding it in one hand, with the other he draws his fingers across the spray on the cover. He rubs his fingers together, sniffs them. Slowly replacing the laptop on the coffee table, he backs out of the double doors, through to the kitchen, where I hear him fiddling with the chain to let the dog in.

I take my chance and scuttle out to the hallway, closing the door behind me, just as Maggie barrels through the other doors, with Tommy behind her, saying, "What is it, Maggie? Go seek, girl. Go seek!"

I can hear the shower upstairs. Jesmond's in the bathroom, and his phone will be in his bedroom. Now's my chance and I run upstairs, not caring about my feet thumping on the thick stair carpet.

I open the bedroom door. It's the smell that hits me first. It's not exactly dirty. It is a combination of things. Cologne of some sort, for sure. Lynx? Something more expensive, probably. But there is something else going on there as well. Something more . . . earthy. Animal-y.

I quickly scan the room to see if Jesmond has left his phone on the bed or the desk.

He hasn't.

He has a big double bed jutting out from the wall, and I go round to the other side, and that's when I see the source of the animal smell.

An animal.

I don't see the dog at first, just the small carrier it's locked up in. Then it comes to the front of the carrier, and I see it. A little Yorkshire terrier.

With a missing leg.

Mrs. Abercrombie's Geoffrey. No doubt about it at all.

He gives a little whine. Can he smell me? It's a sad whimper, and the result is a whole new sensation for me: feeling sorry for the loathsome Geoffrey.

How can their dad not know? I guess smuggling a puppy carrier in and out of a house isn't so hard, and I don't suppose either of the twins' parents actually goes into their rooms much. The smell would be enough to put *me* off. Although, given the conversation in the living room, their dad clearly suspects *something.*

But enough about the dog. That's not why I'm here.

It's Jesmond's phone, his phone, his phone. Where is it?

His jeans are lying discarded on the bed and I start to go through the pockets. Nope, not there.

And then I hear from the landing the lock on the bathroom door click open, and before I can make it out the door, he's there, in the bedroom, towel around his waist, another one being used to dry his hair, while with the other hand he's holding his phone and talking. The strong Geordie accent has returned.

"As I predicted, my friend, as I predicted. All you've gorra do is go round there with it tomorrah, hand it over, collect the reward, an' you'll get y' ten quid finder's fee. First thing in the mornin'—it cannit stay here, cos we're on the school trip. How's that? . . . Aye. . . . Sweet as! . . . See ya, Mynt."

Mynt? *Aramynta Fell?* How's she caught up in this?

He throws the phone onto the bed.

I'm on the other side of the room being as still as I can and dreading what's coming next, and . . .

OHMIGOD! He's dropped the towel from around his waist and I'm staring at Jesmond Knight's white, naked bottom and this is just *so embarrassing.* I can't close my eyes, so I turn my head and . . .

OHMIGOD, that's even *worse*! I'm looking straight at a mirror and I get a full-frontal of Jesmond.

Inside my head I'm screaming, *Put some clothes on!*

He struts up and down the room, then he stops in front of the mirror and flexes his arm muscles. Then he goes into that sort of gorilla pose that bodybuilders do: curled arms pointing downwards, chest expanded, and the whole thing is just so appalling that I have to turn my head, while watching his movement from the corner of my eye so that I can dodge if he comes close.

I think I'm safe. I've found a little position near the curtains in the corner, which is out of the way, and it's a pretty big room. I just *do not* want to see any more of a naked Jesmond Knight, especially when—*aaaghh!*—he bends over to pull a pair of shorts from under his bed.

Somehow, through my disgust, I still manage to piece together what I will do next. It's a long shot but it's my only shot. I'm going to wait for Jesmond to fall asleep, then take his phone and leg it out the back door. Or the front door—I don't really care at this point. To be honest, I think I'd try leaping from the window if it meant I didn't have to see Jesmond Knight's buttocks anymore.

Then I hear Geoffrey whine in his pet carrier and I feel this rage boil up inside me. How *dare* they do that? Kidnapping pets for the reward money? *Seriously?*

Jesmond sniffs the air.

"Jeez, mutt," he says, peering down at the pet carrier. "You don't 'alf stink." Then his tone softens slightly. "Wanna come out?"

Oh no. Please, no. I tense as Jesmond opens the carrier

door, but when Geoffrey trots out on his three little legs, he ignores me, and snuffles around the bed instead.

Eventually—to my huge relief—Jesmond gets his pajama shorts on. I haven't noticed that I'm standing on the end of his pajama top, which is splayed out on the carpet. He stoops to grab it and, because I'm standing on a sleeve, he has to tug it out from under the weight of my foot, and that is odd. I suppose it looks a bit like the arm of his pajamas was stuck to the floor with chewing gum or something.

He has the same puzzled look on his face as his dad did a few minutes ago when he heard me sneeze.

I know that there is no reason for Jesmond to think I am in his room, invisible. But, unlike his dad, Jesmond at least knows that invisibility is possible.

He stands in the middle of his room, holding his pajama top, staring at the floor where it had appeared to stick to the carpet.

I follow his gaze down to the floor, and I see what he is staring at.

There, imprinted in the thick pile of the carpet, are two perfect footprints where I am standing.

CHAPTER SIXTY-NINE

It's probably only a few seconds, but it feels like about a year.

"Hello, Invisigirl," he says, a sneering half smile on his face.

Then he gently throws his pajama top at me. It hangs on my shoulder for a second before falling to the floor.

Jesmond swears under his breath, and what happens next is so fast that I can barely keep track.

He darts forwards, both hands outstretched, and I dash to one side and move over next to his bed.

"I know you're there," he whispers, and his eyes scan the carpet again for my footprints.

Meanwhile, Geoffrey has finished his snuffling and squats in the middle of the room, back arched in readiness for a poo.

Jesmond sees this and is distracted momentarily.

"No, no, no. Oh, you dirty little—"

The words freeze in his mouth as he draws back his foot

to aim a kick, and this is not just a little kick. It's going to be a big one—I can tell from the angle of his foot that he's putting a lot of force behind it.

And I just cannot stand by and let Geoffrey be harmed, so I shout, "Hey!" and push Jesmond with all my strength, and he topples over, cracking his head against his dressing table, sending his deodorants and hair gels scattering.

I've got only seconds to act. I reach down and grab his phone from the bed. Jesmond sees it rise spookily from the duvet and he is scrambling to his feet when Geoffrey—little, brave, yappy Geoffrey—gives a tiny, furious growl and launches himself at Jesmond's ankles.

It's all the distraction I need. I run to the bedroom door, yank it open, and I'm off down the stairs, followed about three seconds later by Jesmond, who is calling out for his sister and swearing at both me and Geoffrey, who launches himself again at his captor, sinking his teeth into Jesmond's lower leg, causing him to yowl with pain.

By the time I'm at the bottom of the stairs, Jarrow's bedroom door has opened, and she's calling out, "What the hell is going on? I'm tryin' to sleep!"

But she sees the commotion, and maybe notices the mysterious floating phone, and joins in the pursuit.

Front door or back door?

The front door is closer, but as I'm nearly there, I see the entry panel and the keypad that they use instead of flippin' *keys*, and I quickly turn around, dodging past Jesmond, who has reached the bottom of the stairs, pursued by a very angry three-legged Yorkshire terrier.

"Give it here," he snarls, grabbing for his phone, which he can see levitating along the hallway.

As I shimmy out of his way, the rug beneath my feet slips on the highly polished floor and I put my other hand out to steady myself. It connects with the glass-fronted cabinet of china dogs and the whole thing comes smashing down to the ground with a huge *crunch*, shards of glass and little dogs showering everywhere.

I'm barefoot, but I can't worry about it. I plow straight through, stabbing my heel on the broken neck of an Irish wolfhound and limping through the door of the kitchen.

By now, Maggie has joined in the chase but hasn't worked out who to attack yet. She decides to go for Geoffrey, who is having none of it. Courageous little lion-heart that he is, he emits such a volley of yapping that, for a couple of seconds, the big dog—which could probably devour Geoffrey without even chewing—backs off.

It's all the time I need, and I'm out the back door, legging it down the backyard, pursued first by a cursing Jesmond Knight, then by a snapping, snarling terrier (who is managing a few nips of Jesmond's ankles), then by a massive, slavering devil-dog. Behind them are Jarrow and, last of all, Tommy, who is shouting.

"WHAT is going on? Jarrow? Jesmond? Who smashed the cabinet? And where did that other dog come from?"

And there is Boydy.

Boydy? I've no idea what he is doing in the backyard, but he's already running with me. I press the ON button of the phone as I'm running and the start-up light lets him know where I am.

"Come on, there's a hole in the fence. Follow me!" he gasps, but his excess weight is holding him back.

I overtake him, heading for where I think he means.

"TO YOUR RIGHT!" he yells.

In the dark, I can see where he means. There's a gap between some bushes and a section of broken fencing, and without looking back I'm through it, but I have to stop because I can't just leave him.

"COME ON, BOYDY!" I yell through the gap.

He's nearly made it, and he dives to the ground just as Maggie makes a final, snarling leap.

Boydy howls as the dog's teeth penetrate his jeans and grip his backside. I can see Jesmond closing in, and he's about to grab Boydy's ankles when Geoffrey once again snaps, this time at Jesmond's outstretched hand, and he screams.

I have grabbed Boydy's hand through the gap, and I'm pulling as hard as I can while he kicks his legs at Maggie. For a second the only sounds are two snarling dogs and our panting; then Maggie releases her grip to prepare for another attack.

It's all Boydy needs. With a final, desperate kick, he's through the gap. I have picked up one of the missing fence posts and I'm poised, like a baseball player waiting for the ball to be pitched.

An instant later, Maggie's head comes through the gap, and I bring the fence post down on her head with all the force I can muster. She emits an unbearable howl, but still she keeps coming further through the hole in the fence, and I find myself saying, "I'm sorry, Maggie, I'm sorry" as I whack her again.

The huge head sinks to the ground and for a horrible, dread-filled moment I think I have killed her; but then, groggily, that huge head lifts up and she retreats, whimpering but alive.

Geoffrey's yapping continues but gets more distant, moving further from the fence and back to the house.

Boydy's lying beside me, but instead of moaning, he just says, "You got it?"

I nod.

He can't see me nodding. "Well, did you?"

"All done!"

I put the phone in his hand, and he grins, then moans in pain. On the other side of the fence . . . nothing. No shouts, no threats. In fact, there's no one there.

"They've gone out the front way. They'll be here any minute," I say.

CHAPTER SEVENTY

Boydy drags himself up, and we both clamber over the next-door yard's wall. My heel is sore where I stepped on the broken china dog, and I stoop to pull a piece out of the flesh. It's bleeding, but not badly.

Two minutes later, wheezing and moaning, we're through the door into my backyard, and a minute after that, we hear footsteps pounding up the back lane.

"She lives somewhere around here. One of these," I hear Jarrow say.

But they don't know which one. We hear them rattling all the back doors up the lane, but none of them opens—and certainly not mine.

No . . . mine is shut tight. Nothing to worry about there.

All I have to worry about is right behind me.

Gram. She's standing on the back step, with Lady.

"Elliot? Oh my goodness, what has happened to you?

And where is Ethel? I've been worried sick. I was about to call the police. Have you seen the time?"

For a second I think it's strange that she's asking where I am . . . and then I remember.

She can't see me.

CHAPTER SEVENTY-ONE

I've got to hand it to Boydy. Lying under pressure: it's quite a skill to be so good at it by the age of thirteen. Mind you, the story he comes up with is so utterly far-fetched that I just stand there, invisibly openmouthed at his fluent deception.

"Ah, you're up! Oh good—I didn't want to wake you. Ethel's fine, she's just, erm . . . a bit poorly and has gone to bed in our spare room."

I'm standing right next to him as he says this, of course, and my gaze darts from one to the other.

"You'd better come in," says Gram.

She's not buying this, I can tell. Not yet.

I follow Boydy through the back door into the kitchen, and stand in the corner, watching all of this. This time, Lady doesn't freak out, although I see her nose go up as she smells my presence. Instead she just slinks away to the front room.

In the light, the extent of Boydy's injuries is more apparent. The back of his jeans is torn and soaked with blood.

"Get those off," commands Gram. "We'll clean you up and you can tell me exactly what is going on."

So far, I have got to the age of nearly thirteen without once having to see a teenage boy's bare bottom. Now I get to see two in the space of one evening.

Oh, lucky me.

"How did this happen?" asks Gram quite kindly.

It does look bad. There are puncture marks on the top of his thigh, and there's a tear in the flesh of his large, pale buttock. Boydy leans over the kitchen table as Gram gets some witch hazel and cotton wool. He directs his comments over his shoulder.

"I was attacked by a dog in the back lane."

"Good heavens. We should call the police! An attack like this is very serious."

"Erm, no . . . don't do that!" He sounds desperate.

"Whyever not, Elliot?"

"I was, erm . . ."

Honestly, I can almost hear the cogs turning in his head as he thinks on his feet.

"I was . . . taking a shortcut through someone's backyard and it was a guard dog!" He ends up sounding very pleased with this fib, and continues, "You see, I was coming round to tell you about Effow, because—ooh, that stings!—because Mum told me to take responsibility."

Good. Clever. Invoke the command of a responsible adult.

"Responsibility for what, Elliot?"

"I think she—in fact, I know she—erm . . . drank some alcohol. Ooooow!"

Oh, thanks a lot, Boydy. Thanks a huge, great, gift-wrapped bundle.

"Alcohol? Oh, Elliot, oh no, no, no."

I now know that, of all the things you could say to Gram, this is probably the worst, given what she went through with my mum. The color has drained from her face, and she stands holding the bottle of witch hazel, shaking her head.

"I'm sorry, Mrs. Leatherhead. It was only one beer. She didn't even like it, and then she threw up and my mum put her to bed."

"Where did she get it? Did you give it to her?" Gram renews her nursing with extra vigor.

"I don't know, Mrs. Leatherhead. Ooooow! Honestly, it was just her. We only had Sprite and Fanta. I'm really sorry. I should have stopped her. Aaiiieee!"

Good, I'm thinking. *I'm glad it's hurting.* It's bad enough that he lied about me drinking alcohol. For a start, it's disgusting. (I've never had any, but I have smelled wine and I don't think I will ever drink it. Why would you drink fruit juice that's gone off, which is all it is as far as I can tell?) And for another thing, why choose *that*? He could have just said

I'd overindulged on the pizza. You know, one slice of pepperoni and mushroom too many and up it all came; then I got shipped off to bed.

Too much imagination, that's Boydy's problem.

Gram's got a bandage out now and is applying it to Boydy's bitten bum.

"Well, frankly, Elliot, I am surprised and disappointed. I thought you were more responsible than this. Although I appreciate your coming round to tell me in person. Right, you're all patched up. It's too late now, but I shall be calling your mother in the morning. And tell Ethel to come here before she goes to school."

Boydy—to my great relief—has pulled his trousers back up and is hobbling to the back door.

Gram has her back to us both as she puts the witch hazel away.

Boydy takes out Jesmond's mobile phone from his jeans pocket and holds it up to me. He points at it, then to himself, and then makes a wiping motion with his hand.

He's going to wipe Jesmond's phone. Good. You can do that without a passcode. In fact, that's pretty much all you can do without a passcode: restore it to a blank phone, erasing all saved data.

He then takes out my phone that I gave him before and puts it out of Gram's eye line, behind the toaster.

"Thank you, Mrs. Leatherhead. And, erm . . . sorry."

"Goodbye, Elliot. Pull the back door shut behind you."

And if I thought I had had enough heart-stopping tension and excitement for one day, what comes next makes this whole evening, in comparison, seem like a quiet evening watching *Robson Green's Country Walks.*

I'm still in the kitchen, remember, trying not to put weight on my sore heel.

I have decided. Now is the time to bring Gram on board with the invisible stuff.

I can prove it, because I'm invisible.

I'm just thinking about what words to use: "Hey, Gram, remember what I said about being invisible?" But I'm still kind of . . . what? Shy? No. Not shy, but . . .

Anyway, it doesn't matter because Gram starts talking to someone who—apparently—has been in the sitting room all along.

"It's OK. He's gone. You can come through."

CHAPTER SEVENTY-TWO

And he does. Gram's boyfriend, the guy from the Priory View doorway, comes into the kitchen and says, "What was all that about?"

"Ethel is staying at a friend's tonight. She's . . . she's not very well."

It's the first time I get a good look at him since I first saw him at Priory View.

"We'll have to do this another time, eh?" he says.

"Yes. Perhaps you could come round tomorrow?"

The boyfriend grins: it's a nice smile. "Sure thing. Gimme a call."

Last time I saw him, he was dressed smartly: jacket, pressed trousers. Now he's just in a T-shirt and jeans. To my surprise, I see that his arms are heavily tattooed, which makes me wonder. Body ink is *so* not Gram's thing. Surely she can't—

Then he turns. Meandering up his neck, from out of his

T-shirt up to his hairline, is another tattoo. A distinctive, unmistakable twist of green ivy that I have seen before, somewhere.

I gasp out loud, and both he and Gram look round, but each probably thinks it is the other.

As soon as I have the thought, it begins to make sense.

The accent. It's not a London accent at all. It's a New Zealand accent.

It is all I can do—and I mean that: it takes ALL of my effort—not to call out, "Dad?"

But I cannot forget that I am standing naked and invisible. It's not how I want my dad—for the first time in ten years—to see me. If you see what I mean.

I hear Gram at the door say, "Good night, Rick."

I'm still standing in the kitchen, and I haven't moved a muscle. I don't think I have actually breathed. My heart is racing at least as fast as my mind, and I am *definitely* not going to have the "invisible" conversation now.

Gram comes back in to turn off the light before going to bed. A blue glow comes off the digital clock on the cooker. It's 11:45.

I wait a few minutes for Gram to settle in her room; then I sneak upstairs and into bed as quietly as I can.

And a thought that has been nagging at the edge of my

mind becomes clearer: *Shouldn't I be starting to get the tingling feeling?* The itch, accompanied by a headache, that precedes the return of my visibility?

For the moment, I try to put it to the back of my mind. I'm exhausted. Mentally and physically drained. Besides, there's a whole new thing I've got to think about now.

My dad? Ricky Malcolm?

I go over it again and again. The change in appearance is no mystery. From a guy with snaggled teeth, a long mop of red hair, and a huge, dirty-looking beard to a clean, shaved man who could be a teacher or, well . . . anything but a rock rebel. The difference is astonishing, and I wouldn't believe it anyway, if it weren't for the tattoos.

In my room, I quietly open my laptop and search Google Images for Ricky Malcolm.

There he is: the hairy rocker.

I enlarge one picture in which, onstage, his hair is swept back, revealing the tattoo on his neck. It's definitely the same.

And now I look at his eyes: the same gray-green. In this picture, he's looking directly at the camera, and I enlarge it even more, till the pixels begin to show, and the eyes are life-size. I rotate the picture until the eyes are level and I just stare and stare.

That's the same look he gave me when we chatted about Lady at Priory View. He had peered intensely into my eyes, because he knew. He knew that his were the same as mine, and that I was his daughter.

Why hadn't he said something?

I'm lying there, and there's a part of me that knows beyond a doubt that I may not have another chance to show Gram that I am really invisible. Yes, I have the recording of me *becoming* invisible—it's right there on my laptop, the thing I filmed in the garage. But will that be proof? I've looked at it and, well . . . I'm not sure.

I'm about to close my laptop when it pings softly with an incoming email.

From thomasknight@ringmail.co.uk. *Tommy Knight* is emailing me?

Well, no. It's Jesmond and Jarrow, using their dad's account.

V clever, Invisigirl. We'll admit that. Is it you that's done our laptops as well? Thing is, Invisigirl, how do you know we don't have a copy of it all?

You have stolen my phone. I want it back, or it all goes on YouTube tomorrow.
Jesmond

It's past midnight, but I text Boydy nonetheless, attaching the email.

He doesn't reply. He must be asleep. On his front, presumably.

I'm on my own, and the mood I'm in is not one to start giving in to anyone.

So I email back.

Thanks for your dad's email address. That'll come in handy when I want to tell him about your dog-and-cat scam. Or perhaps I'll call round in person and tell him myself—after telling the police, obvs.

I don't believe you about the copy, BTW. But even if you have got one, I'd keep it to yourselves.

Ethel

I hit SEND. What do I have to lose? I have a feeling that this is the end of the whole affair.

I should know *much* better.

CHAPTER SEVENTY-THREE

Gram is still up. I can hear the cupboard door opening as she extracts the tin box of Mum's memorabilia.

That's when I know that I can't confront her. Not yet. It's like it's too much at once, to go into her room and say, "Hi, Gram. Look at me—I'm invisible. And by the way, we need to talk about the contents of that tin box and then you can explain to me why you have been lying to me all these years. Oh, and by the other way, that was my dad, wasn't it?"

I practice it—at least I get that far. But I just can't do it. Not yet.

I lie on my bed and await the itching and the headache.

They don't come.

Not by midnight.

Not by 2:00 a.m., when I am still awake and have heard Gram put everything away and go to bed.

By 4:00 a.m. I am still awake, and by the grayish dawn light coming through my curtains I look down to check if I have somehow become visible without the itching and headache. But no: I am still invisible. The birds are waking up outside.

It's OK, I tell myself. *It's just taking a bit longer to wear off.*

At some point, I fall into a light, restless sleep. I don't think I dream, or if I do, I don't remember any of it.

I hear Gram getting up, and I hardly dare to look down to see if I'm still invisible.

I am.

I am overcome with a fear that is somehow more than a fear. It's like knowing something, but without knowing how you know it.

This is what I'm afraid of: that the invisibility is now permanent. I have messed around too much with the cells that make up my body. They have lost their ability to . . . to what? Regenerate? Renew their light-reflecting capacity? How would I know?

Exactly. How would I know? What was I even *thinking*?

And why, at times of stress, do I keep on hearing Gram's voice in my head?

What's done is done, Ethel. A strong person doesn't moan and mope, but deals with the first problem at hand, and then the second, and then the third. Some people either attack everything head on, or they run away. That's not our way.

The first problem at hand? That'll be my invisibility.

Well, actually: there is a closer one. According to Boydy, I'm supposed to be coming home to change before school after disgracing myself at his birthday gathering.

Gram, who I can hear making tea downstairs, will be expecting me in about . . . ooh, now-ish.

CHAPTER SEVENTY-FOUR

I've sneaked downstairs—and, despite the fact that I am invisible, sneaking is much, much harder than you'd think. Lady is out in the backyard doing her morning wee. I have just sent Gram a text. I want to see her reaction.

> Hi Gram. I am so so sorry about last night. I know Boydy told you and it wasn't as bad as all that, but I am very ashamed. Too ashamed to talk to you at the moment. I have my uniform with me. See you later. Love E xx

I have left my phone at the top of the stairs. I pressed SEND and then hurried quietly downstairs, and I am there in the kitchen, standing in the doorway, when Gram's phone goes *ping* with the incoming message.

She is sitting at the kitchen table, dressed in her smart work clothes, and she picks up her phone in her usual way: as if someone's smeared something unmentionable on it.

She reads the message and purses her lips, but the rest of her face doesn't really do anything.

Then her fingers move over the screen and she puts the phone to her ear. She's calling me . . . *and I've left my phone on the stairs.*

As soon as I have the thought, I hear my ringtone loud and clear, and Gram is getting up. I dodge out of her way as she stomps up the stairs, where she glares at my phone ringing merrily.

Picking it up, she goes into my room, where she will see my slept-in bed.

Oh no, oh no. This is getting worse. Gram comes downstairs quickly (I'm already in the kitchen) and she picks up her phone again. Then she puts it down. My phone is in her other hand and she looks at it, then at hers, sheer bafflement clouding her face.

She goes back into the hallway.

"Ethel?" she calls up the stairs. "Ethel? Are you there?"

I'm on the point of just saying, "Gram! It's me! I'm here, and I'm invisible!" but her whole manner has been so brisk, no-nonsense, and I am so terrified that I might be permanently invisible that I just can't bring myself to do it.

Two minutes later, and Gram is out the door with both

my phone and hers in her pocket. Lady gets left at home on Wednesdays because Carol the dog-sitter goes to college. I think Lady is getting used to invisible me. She hasn't freaked out, at any rate.

I have to act quickly.

CHAPTER SEVENTY-FIVE

Unless I turn up at school, Mrs. Moncur the administrat
will be on to Gram in about an hour to find out where I a
Then things will really start going wrong.

Wronger.

I'm *not* doing the whole walking-through-the-st
naked-but-invisible thing again. I just can't face it. For a
it looks like rain, and for another, my feet are alread
from running around last night barefoot and stand
broken china dogs.

So it's back on with the disguise. Stocking ove
hood pulled up, sunglasses on, coat, trousers, shoes

Head down, I'm out of the house and running t
I can do it in eight minutes.

The main entrance is teeming with my classm
don't take any notice as I scuttle past on the other
road. Better try the back entrance. There, it's less

This time, I can't worry about the security

besides, a cloud of smoke emerging from above the rhododendron bush tells me that there are people inside what I have come to think of as my changing area, smoking cigarettes.

I wait for a lull in the trickle of students approaching the gate, and then I'm there. I press my invisible thumb on the entry pad. How does the machine read it? I have no idea, but it does, and the gate swings open. I don't go through, and no one takes any notice at all.

That's me registered as present, then. It's double physics first and there is a chance that Mr. Parker will notice my absence, but then there's also a chance that he won't.

Back home, I take off my disguise and put on some slippers and pajamas instead. It just feels less weird. Lady approaches me and actually wags her tail, which cheers me up.

I'm at the house phone, the one that uses the landline. I want to call Boydy, but Gram's got my phone and I don't remember his number. Meanwhile, I have another number I'm looking for.

The house phone keeps a memory of the last twenty calls made, but only the numbers come up on the little screen. I've just got to hope. One by one, I start to call them, preceding each call with 141 so that the caller is unidentified. Some people don't pick up those calls. I'll just have to risk it.

0191 878 4566. Voice mail. "This is the Reverend Henry Robinson. I'm sorry I am unable to take your call, but please leave a message after the tone."

0191 667 5544. "Hello, Diane speaking. . . ." I hang up.

0870 . . . no, that's not a personal number.

118 118 . . . no, that's directory inquiries.

I'm down to the fifteenth number, and I have still got nowhere. They all seem to be friends of Gram's, or voice mail, or company numbers. The sixteenth and seventeenth just ring and ring and ring with no response at all.

The eighteenth I recognize as the school lobby.

The nineteenth is my mobile, which Gram must have called.

And so this is the last one in the phone's memory.

A mobile number that I don't know. I had actually seen it on the displayed list and hadn't dared call it because I wanted to do it all methodically, and because I was nervous about what might happen if someone *did* pick it up.

07886 545 377. If I could see my fingers, I would watch them trembling as I pressed REDIAL.

It picks up straightaway.

"Hello. Richard Malcolm speaking."

My dad.

CHAPTER SEVENTY-SIX

Why call my dad?

Well, who would *you* call in an emergency? I know, I know: mums are great. In fact, most mums I know are brilliant at most emergencies. Tax Goodbody's mum actually gave birth to him on the backseat of a minicab from A–Z Taxis (hence his nickname), and Holly Masternak's mum used to be a paramedic. It's just that, having grown up with neither a mum *nor* a dad, I think I should be allowed to choose, and right now I want a dad.

(I don't mean to be insensitive here. It could be that you don't have a dad. I get that, and I'm sorry if that's the case. Don't forget: up until last night, I pretty much didn't have one either.)

I think about people I know who don't have a dad living at home. Hayley Broad, for example: her dad was a soldier killed in Afghanistan, and she hates her stepdad.

Without thinking too hard, I can come up with at least

six people I know whose dads are not around. I'm not including stepdads: stepdads (apart from Hayley Broad's) are just dads, so far as I can see. (As for Boydy's dad, well—there's something going on there, I'm sure, but I just don't know what.)

Any man can be a father. But I don't think every man can be a dad.

And I want to give my dad a chance. I don't even know yet what has gone on between him and my mum, him and my gran, even him and my great-gran—because she's had something to do with it all, and a hundred years old or not, she's got some questions to answer next time I'm around at Priory View. Come to think of it—that could be sooner than she expects.

I can only assume he wants to see me. Doesn't he? Why else would he turn up after ten years living as a recluse in a place that's about as far away from me as possible without going into space?

I want to give my dad a chance to help me in this—the hardest time I have ever faced in my life.

So *that's* why I call him.

CHAPTER SEVENTY-SEVEN

"Hello," I say, when he answers the phone. "This is Ethel. Ethel Leatherhead."

Long pause.

"Does your gran know you're calling me?"

"Um . . . no."

"So how did you get my number?"

This was not how I had imagined it, to the extent that I had imagined it at all. I had expected (hoped for, perhaps) more of an "Oh my God, my long-lost daughter, it's so good to hear your voice. My heart has ached every hour we have been apart. . . ."

I wasn't expecting a sort of interrogation.

"Your number? It was stored in the phone's memory."

"I see, and . . . Look, this is a bit awkward, you see. . . ."

"Are you my dad?"

I hear a sigh come down the phone. A long sigh that seems to contain ten years' worth of regret.

"Yes. And I'm sorry about—"

I cut him off. His apologies can come later.

"Where are you?"

"I'm in a hotel in Newcastle."

"How soon can you get here?"

"Look, erm . . . Ethel. I'm not sure your gran—"

"Dad. It's an emergency. I really need you. Now. I'll explain everything when you get here."

CHAPTER SEVENTY-EIGHT

When the doorbell rings half an hour later, my invisible heart is in my invisible mouth, because I know it's him on the other side of the door and I have no idea how he'll react when he sees me.

I can see him through the bubble glass. I'm back in my disguise: the hoodie, the sunglasses, the gloves. I'm going to tell him about the invisibility thing but I want to ease him into it gently.

No, in case you are wondering, I don't fling the door open and rush into his welcoming embrace. It is not like that at all.

The first thing he says is "Oh!"

That's it. Just "Oh!"

It could have been "Oh, good God—what are you dressed like that for?" but it isn't. Just "Oh!" (Although I think the rest of those words are sort of bundled up in that one syllable.)

He's standing there, and I hardly dare look at him, but I do, and the expression on his face is one of total bewilderment.

"Come in," I say after a second or two, and he steps into the hallway and follows me into the kitchen.

"Why the, erm . . . the, you know, unusual clothes?"

He's sitting at the kitchen table, and I make tea while I tell him the story, just like I have told you, starting with the acne, and the tanning bed, and Dr. Chang His Skin So Clear, and it turns out he's a really good listener.

He just sits there, holding his little teacup in his big hands, and nods, asking a few prompting questions, but not too many. He doesn't interrupt me when I pause, wondering what comes next, but sooner or later I just have to say it.

"And then I became invisible."

I watch his expression carefully. I realize that I'm using it as a sort of test to see if he's going to be the dad I want, and I know that's not really fair, but it's how I feel. And as Gram is forever telling me, "Feelings are always genuine, Ethel, but talking about them too much is rather common. It's how we deal with them that makes the difference."

He nods slowly and takes a big gulp of tea. Then he pulls a packet of gum from his pocket, pops a piece in his mouth, and chews thoughtfully.

"So . . . underneath all of that, you're . . . You are invisible, is that right?"

"Yes."

"And no one else knows this?"

"Boydy knows."

"OK. But not your gran?"

"No."

"Are you going to show me?"

And his tone is so gentle, so reassuring, that I nod. He could have mocked, he could have been sarcastic, and I'd have had to show him anyway, in a mood of angry defiance: "Yeah? You wanna see? You want me to prove it to you? Well, here you go."

But it is not like that—not at all. He's just sitting there, Ricky Malcolm, my dad, and he has his head slightly cocked to one side, and he's chewing his gum. Skeptical, perhaps, but definitely interested and, most of all, respectful.

I know now that *this* is why I haven't told Gram. I love my gran, for sure, but what I want—what I *need*—is a calm reaction, without judgment. . . .

Without blame.

I start with the gloves. He angles his head to look up my sleeves. Next comes the hood, lifted back to reveal a space where my head should be, then the sunglasses and the stocking leg.

That is enough. I don't exactly want to strip down.

He reaches out and touches my hand in wonderment, and I grip his hand back. Then his other hand touches my head and my face, tracing the shape of my nose and my ears, feeling my hair, and my cheeks, and all the while he is saying nothing at all.

I look at his handsome face and I don't think I have seen anyone look so completely stunned in my life. His gray-green eyes with the pale lashes keep darting around where my head should be, before settling on where he thinks my eyes are. He must be guessing, but it's right. I stare back, and I grip both of his hands across the table, hard, because I can feel myself wanting to cry and not wanting to at the same time.

His eyes are moist and I *really* don't want him to cry. I've got nothing against men crying: it's not that. I just don't want my dad to. Not now, anyway.

He gets up and comes around to my side of the table, and we don't let go of each other's hands. I stand up. The top of my head is about level with his chin. Then he throws his arms around me and strokes my hair.

"You poor girl," he says as I dissolve into a crying heap, sucking in gulping sobs and seeing his shirt darken with my tears.

He doesn't cry. He just stands there, solid and firm,

stroking my hair and breathing steadily. I can smell his minty breath.

"It's going to be OK. We'll get this sorted out, just wait and see."

Well done, Dad. You've passed.

CHAPTER SEVENTY-NINE

Getting it "sorted out," though, does not mean acting hastily. There are a few things that need to be dealt with.

Gram, mainly.

And then where do we go? Hospital? The police? It's the same problem I had when this all started, and have had all along.

Who do you turn to for help when you become invisible?

Yet before we do any of that, I want some answers from my dad.

We're up in Gram's room, and I've taken down the tin box, which Gram had put back up high in the cupboard, but Dad's eye has been caught by something else: another box right at the back, which Dad can see because he's taller than me.

Carefully, he lifts it down, and holds it gently. It's a flight case: one of those silvery boxes with rounded edges and black reinforced corners. It's not very big—a cube of about twelve inches on each side.

"This was your mum's," he says.

Sitting on the edge of Gram's bed, he opens it. Inside is just a load of makeup, with brushes and sponges, and tubes of color, and mascara, and blusher, and foundation.

"This is how she would transform herself: Miranda Mackay would become Felina, and the one would hide the other. I'd do it for her sometimes." Dad speaks quietly.

I reach forward and lift up a pot of foundation, the flesh-colored makeup that is the base layer. I touch it with my fingertip and then I look at Dad.

Have we had the same idea simultaneously? Or has he thought of it before me? I can't tell, but he's grinning at me.

"Come on, we'll do this together," he says.

Seconds later, I'm sitting on the stool in front of Gram's dressing table with the contents of the box spread out over the surface before me.

Foundation goes on first, with the aid of a little sponge pad. (It's a bit like applying face paint, but not as cold.) Bit by bit, streak by streak, my face becomes visible again.

It's not perfect, obviously. For a start, there's still a gaping space where my head and hair should be, but still . . . it's working.

We try lipstick, but that looks weird on me—it's like I'm

dressing up as an adult, so we go with a type of dark blusher, which is totally convincing.

Dad's good at this. He even mixes a slightly darker shade for my ears. There's a light brownish-red for my eyebrows and lashes.

The glitter wig is mad, but at least it covers up the space, and now all that's left are my eyes and mouth.

Both of these look disgusting and scary. My eyes are just these dark holes in my face. If I part the wig at the back of my head, you can see right through. As for my mouth, that's no better: I can't put makeup on my tongue and teeth. So the sunglasses will stay on, and my mouth will stay shut.

I stare at myself in the mirror, and it looks fabulous. I give a huge grin, which looks much less fabulous, like I've had all my teeth knocked out.

I even do my hands. There's a whitish polish I can put on my nails.

Dad's got this soppy half smile as he watches me turning my head to see the effect from other angles.

"You look just like your mum," he says, and I figure now is a good time to ask him the question I have been dying to ask.

Because, it's not like everything is suddenly OK, you realize?

I'm not like, "Oh, my dad's turned up out of the blue, so I'm now going to live happily ever after, and never question him, and trust him forever. Whoop-di-doo! The End."

No. I have some questions that—so far as I can see—only he can answer. Well, only he and Gram, and Great-Gran, but seeing as Dad is the only one within asking distance, it's going to be him.

I take a deep breath and ask:

"Why did you run away to New Zealand and leave me?"

CHAPTER EIGHTY

I was living with Gram when Mum died, though I don't really remember much, as I think I have said—I was only three.

"Your mum always wanted the best for you," says Dad. "She wasn't able to look after you properly—not with the touring and the recording, and, well, you know. . . ."

I don't know. Not really.

"So having me around was . . . what? Inconvenient?"

Dad looks hurt, and I know I have touched a nerve. "Try 'impossible.' The life we were living wasn't exactly suitable for a little girl."

"So why not change your life?"

Dad gives a small grunt of laughter. "That's what your gran said. She loved your mum's success, but she hated the world she was in—entertainment, show business, music. People who were jealous of everything; people who will cheat you. You've got to be strong to survive it. I think your gran blamed herself because your mum wasn't stronger."

"That's crazy."

"Maybe. But we're all a little bit crazy. If we weren't, how boring would life be?"

We're still in Gram's room, and as Dad speaks he keeps taking out clippings and pictures from the tin and turning them over in his hands. He comes to the one of me in the rain with Mum and just stares at it.

"They said she was a drunk. A drug addict," I say.

"No," says Dad. "Not your mum. Oh, everyone *said* that, and—well, she sailed pretty close to the wind. But after you were born? She cleaned herself up pretty good."

"So how did she die, then?"

"Heart attack. That's what the doctors said. I think, to be perfectly honest, she was pretty weak, physically. But do you know the expression 'mud sticks'?"

"Get a bad reputation and it stays with you?"

"That's it, spot on. And she wasn't helped by the one person who could have helped her." He has picked up the card with the message to Gram: the one with the lighthouse on it and the message saying *If it all goes wrong please take Boo far away from all of this.*

"Who was that?" I am *so* hoping he will not say Gram. I couldn't bear it if he blames Gram.

"Me. I was messed up. I was pathetic and lost and completely incapable of bringing up a little girl. I mean, I tried. I told the judge that I would provide for you and give up the music business, but I turned up in court drunk, and that was it. Your gran, God bless her, did *exactly* what she'd promised your mum she would do. She took you far away, gave you a new name, a new home, a new *history*."

This is all coming a bit fast, I have to say. I'm not sure I like it, but I need to keep listening. Dad's voice is soft and reassuring. It's what he's saying that is *not* soft and *not* reassuring.

"Gram chose my name?" I say.

He looks at me. "Come on, do I look like the sort of guy who'd call a kid 'Ethel'?" And then a shy half smile comes onto his mouth, and I get that he is testing me, and I grin.

"Not really." I look at his ordinary clothes and his neat hair. "But then you don't look like the sort of guy who'd call a kid 'Tiger Pussycat.' Not anymore, anyway."

He smiles, and it turns into an embarrassed half grin. "You got me," he says.

"So what am I meant to call myself now?"

"You can be any name you want. Me and your mum? We always called you 'Boo'—like on this card." He holds it up. "After the girl in *Monsters, Inc.* Your mum loved that film."

"Me too," I say. "As a name, though . . . it's all a bit, I dunno . . . showbiz. Isn't it?"

He laughs. "Yup. Lost in showbiz, we were! I prefer 'Ethel' now."

"Really?"

He looks at me closely, through my sunglasses. "Really, I do."

This is nice to hear, but I'm not letting him off the hook.

"And now? Why do you turn up now?"

There is the longest pause. So long that I wonder if Dad has heard my question.

"Dad?"

He turns to me and nods. "I heard you. I'm just not sure that my answer will be good enough."

"Try me."

"I was scared. Scared you'd hate me; scared you'd blame me. Once I got myself straightened out, it became clear to me how I had let you down. I figured you must be better off without me, and besides, your gram had done such a good job that you weren't exactly easy to find."

"So how *did* you find me?"

"You know what, Ethel. I think there's someone who can explain that better than me. But we're going to have to go out."

He stands up and takes another piece of chewing gum from the packet. That's when I notice: it's nicotine gum, used by people to help them stop smoking. I look at Dad's fingers: the yellow stains are much fainter, and he no longer smells of old cigarettes.

"You've stopped smoking," I say.

"Doing my best" is all he says, and he starts chewing again.

I stand up too. "So where are we going?"

"To see your great-gran," he says.

CHAPTER EIGHTY-ONE

Great-Gran turns her small white head towards us as we walk in. Her nodding seems to increase in intensity and her eyes are fixed on Dad, who is smiling broadly. We've brought Lady with us; she's totally relaxed with me now, and she immediately goes and flops down by Great-Gran's slippered feet.

"Dear old Mrs. Freeman! Twice in as many days, eh?" says Dad. "You're lookin' pretty good today. Well, certainly a lot better than you have a right to expect at your age."

I look across at Dad, horrified at his . . . his what? His cheek, I suppose. He carries on in the same manner: blunt, teasing, funny.

Even, dare I say it, a little bit *common.*

"I've brought Ethel with me—or, as she now knows her name to be, Tiger Pussycat. She knows everything, an' don't go havin' a heart attack on me, not with *your* ticker."

It's his New Zealand accent: he's sort of laying it on a bit thick—the no-nonsense, straight-up, tell-it-like-it-is bloke who can have a laugh with everyone. He's not even shouting at her—he's just speaking clearly—and Great-Gran seems to have no problem hearing him.

And you know what? She is *loving* it! I can see it in her eyes, and the smile that is dancing round her old, cracked lips, and the little color that has returned to her cheeks. I even think she is *blushing.*

I honestly don't think Great-Gran has been spoken to like this in years.

He's being friendly, funny, and respectful. He calls her Mrs. Freeman. He is talking to her *as if she is normal.*

Which she is, of course. Just very, very *old* and normal. Perhaps I had forgotten.

I've still got my shades on, and my hood over the glitter wig.

"Sorry about the sunglasses, Great-Gran," I say. "I've got a bit of an eye infection," I add, by way of explanation. She barely takes her eyes off Dad, though.

He has brought an iPad with him from the glove compartment of the rental car that we drove in to Priory View.

"I thought I'd show Ethel how I found you all," says Dad, switching on the tablet and typing rapidly.

A few seconds later, the front page of a newspaper comes up: *The Whitley Bay News Guardian.*

Scrolling down, Dad's fingers stop at a story and a picture.

One Hundred and Not Out

Century Celebration for Local Woman

Mrs. Elizabeth Freeman celebrated her 100th birthday last week at the Priory View Residential Care Home, where she has lived for the last nine years.

A stroke several years ago affected her speech, but care-home staff reported her to be in "excellent health and spirits" when the big day came.

Born during World War One—in the reign of George V and before the invention of television or commercial air travel—Mrs. Freeman has lived through the terms of *nineteen* prime ministers, the first being David Lloyd George.

She received a cake baked by the staff of Priory View, and a message of congratulations from H.M. the Queen.

She is pictured with her daughter, Mrs. Beatrice Leatherhead, and her great-granddaughter, Ethel Leatherhead.

"That's it?" I ask, incredulous. "That's all it took?"

"All it took? Her old house was turned into flats, and letters were returned to sender. I tried calling all the nursing homes once, but Priory View wasn't on my list because it's a 'senior community residence.' So for three years, I did a twice-weekly Google search for 'Elizabeth Freeman.' I had a feeling that she'd make it to a hundred, but I couldn't remember exactly when her birthday was. I also knew that when she did, it would be in the local news. So I just kept checking and checking. For that, or . . . well"—he lowers his voice—"for an obituary." He turns to Great-Gran and speaks louder. "But I was totally confident you'd make it, wasn't I, Mrs. Freeman?"

Great-Gran's nodding seems to intensify (though it's a bit hard to tell sometimes).

He goes on: "And that photograph? Well, your gran may have cut her hair and changed her glasses, but there's no mistaking her. As for you: a bloke can recognize his own daughter anywhere!"

"And you came back?"

He fixes me with his pale gray-green eyes.

"I was on the next flight, Boo. It was just a question of persuading your gran that I was a changed man, and that she wouldn't be betraying your mum's wishes by letting me meet you."

All this time, I'm looking at my great-gran, whose expression has changed. The shaking has stopped for a while, and her eyes are even wetter than normal. She is looking straight at me and her trembling left hand seems to be beckoning me.

But I don't move. I just don't know how to react. I mean, Dad's being nice and everything, but it's dawning on me that this old lady, pretty much locked in her own mind for nearly a decade, has been deceiving me all along. Amid all the happiness of rediscovering my dad and of having at least some of my millions of questions answered, there's a quiet anger building up inside me.

Then I hear Gram's voice behind me and that anger finds a focus.

"Oh, my darling Ethel. I was about to tell you, I really was . . . and my goodness, what *are* you wearing?"

CHAPTER EIGHTY-TWO

So that's who Dad was frantically texting before we drove here.

Gram continues, "Are you wearing *makeup*, Ethel?" Then she says to Dad, "Richard, how did this all come about?"

And even if now is not exactly the right time, and the circumstances not exactly perfect, I don't really have much choice.

I'm face to face with three adults. I'm twelve. Their combined age must be nearly two hundred, and I still feel that it's me who has more sense, me who is doing the right thing.

"How? How could you?" I say softly, and turn to include Great-Gran. "How could you both?"

Perhaps it's Dad's bloke-ish banter that gives me the confidence to speak to them as directly as I do.

Gram hasn't even sat down yet, and no one says anything, so I go on.

I practically whisper. "You knew. You and Great-Gran,

the two of you, conspired to keep the truth from me. All my life I have been living as . . . as *someone else*. And you knew?"

No one says anything, so I hiss, "How could you?"

My voice is losing its calm.

Dad has raised his hand in a *calm-down* motion. "Steady, Boo," he says. "She's an old lady."

That's when something releases inside me. It really feels like that, as well: like when a stretched elastic band pings off your finger. Everything that I have been concealing, all of the tension that I have been holding on to, all of the times that I have wanted to share my secret but never felt able to—it all seems to come loose with that one gentle gesture and the soft words of Dad.

"Don't 'steady' me!" I say, much louder. "And I *know* she's an old lady. Old enough to know better, that's what I say."

I look at Great-Gran, and speak directly to her. "One hundred years old and you haven't learned not to lie? Everyone thinks you're just a sweet little old lady, sitting there in your shawl, but you're no better than anyone else. Just because you can't talk? You think that's an excuse?"

Dad has stood up now. "Boo, that's enough." He's right, of course. It was mean. But I just keep going.

"Enough? I haven't even started. And don't call me Boo. It's Ethel. And I *like* my name! My name—the one that's on that stupid fake birth certificate!" I'm shouting now, and Great-Gran's expression is horrified, but there's more to come, I can feel it.

I turn my anger towards Gram.

"Have you seen this?" I say, pulling off my sunglasses to reveal the dark sockets of my eyes. "What about *this*?" I open my mouth wide and lean in to Gram. "This is *me*! What are you so horrified about? Is being invisible a bit too 'common' for you? Or is it just 'vulgar'? Well, I don't care—*this* is what is going on, and I'm sick of lying! I'm sick of hiding!"

I pull off the glitter wig and Gram's hands go straight to her mouth as she sobs a gasp of pure terror.

CHAPTER EIGHTY-THREE

I'm on a roll now, and I don't think I could stop even if I wanted to.

I stride over to the basin in Great-Gran's room, where, as always, there is a tub of Nivea skin cream. Removing the lid, I plunge my fingers in, then smear a glob over my face.

"Boo? Ethel? I really think we should talk this through." Dad's voice is not loud, but I can tell he's super-anxious. "Think about your gran, eh?"

I'm ignoring him. I want to reply along the lines of "Why should I think about her? She's turned me into someone I'm not," but I can't because I'm vigorously rubbing off all the carefully applied makeup, leaving pinkish-brown smears all over Great-Gran's hand towel.

And then it's done. Off come the hoodie, the jeans, the shoes, and I am standing in front of them all.

They stare, dumbstruck. For like five, ten seconds.

Just.

Completely.

Awed.

"This is me!" I say eventually. "Can you see? I'm nothing—nothing at all. And you know what? I think I prefer it this way. At least it's the truth."

I check in the mirror and remove the last traces of makeup while Dad is pacing and saying stuff like "Boo. Think about what you are doing."

Poor Great-Gran looks terrified. Gram has sat down on a low chair and is looking straight ahead and blinking hard.

I *am* thinking about what I am doing. I'm thinking that if this invisibility is permanent, I'm going to have to get used to it. And more lying won't help.

Lady has retreated to the far corner of the room, scared off by the raised voices.

"Come, Lady," I say, more gently, and even though she cannot see me, she's used to me now, and she comes to where I am. I like it that there is at least one person in the room (if you count Lady as a person, and I kind of do) who doesn't seem to care whether I am visible or invisible.

I'm halfway to the door when I see Gram stand up and take a shaky breath. What she says is almost too quiet to hear, but there is more sadness in the next four words than I have ever heard.

"I lost a daughter."

And when I hear that, I *so* want to go and hug Gram and hear that everything will be all right. I'm standing in the doorway and about to step forward when a large nurse walks—*bang!*—right into me, and shrieks with surprise. I'm knocked sideways, and the only way past her is into the corridor.

Lady's with me. The nurse is really freaking out: her hands touched me and everything.

"*Aaiiee!* I touch! I touch something, someone!"

There's a real commotion going on, and Lady and I run.

A minute later we're on the seafront, looking out over an indigo sea, and I'm feeling really, *really* confused.

It's not only that I have shouted at a hundred-year-old lady, and stormed out on my newfound dad like a petulant teenager from some TV show. It's also that—in all of this—I have ignored the fact that my own gran has been grieving secretly for nearly ten years. Gram's "I lost a daughter" keeps repeating in my head.

You can add that I am terrified that my invisibility seems to be permanent.

Plus, I am weak and exhausted, and I remember that I haven't eaten since last night. I haven't even thought about it, what with the worry and the excitement and the fear and the anger and about several billion other emotions that I have been experiencing in the last half day or so.

But yeah. Now that I *am* thinking about it, I am 100 percent starving, and thirsty too.

I turn to look back at Priory View and see my dad's hired Nissan Micra pull out of the driveway and speed away down the seafront with Gram in the passenger seat.

I know I have been too hasty. Without thinking, I raise my hand and wave.

Fat lot of good that does, what with me being invisible.

I see Dad's car retreating up the coast road.

I know I won't be able to do this—do anything—on my own. I look at the hand that I have lifted up. The polish I put on my nails is still there: on each hand, five little shiny discs that are almost—but not quite—invisible.

I turn back to the sea and plonk down on a slatted wooden bench.

I am going to be the Invisible Girl. You just cannot keep a secret like that. Gram's lies and deceit to keep me from the world of fame will have been pointless.

Because, unless I live my life as a total recluse, never going out, never going back to school, I will be known. Headlines. Documentaries. High-profile experiments. Medical research. Books.

I can see the headlines:

Dead Star's Long-Lost Daughter Is Medical Mystery

The Invisible Girl—Incredible Legacy of Tragic Singer

Have You Seen Felina's Girl?

Ethel Leatherhead or Tiger Pussycat "Boo" Mackay? Beatrice Leatherhead or Belinda Mackay? Miranda or Felina? Who cares who anyone is anyway? I'm not sure I even know myself.

I feel like nobody—which is odd. Odd, because I used to *think* that I felt like nobody.

Now I know I am.

CHAPTER EIGHTY-FOUR

Food, food, food. Wow, I'm hungry. My mind is spinning, anyway, and I'm feeling pretty lightheaded.

Options:

1. Go back into Priory View and hang around their kitchen. There's plenty of food there, but how would I get it? And assuming I could get hold of a sandwich or something, how would I eat it? Like I saw the first time I drank tea, stuff in my stomach stays visible for a little while until it is—what? Invisibilized? There are always nurses and carers here, there, and everywhere in Priory View. It's not a viable option.
2. There's a café down on the beach, but the same problems arise.
3. There's plenty of food back home, and it's really my only choice, so I cross the road and wait by the bus stop.

There's a bus that runs every half hour along the seafront all the way to Seaton Sluice. When it comes, the front doors don't open because there's no one else waiting to get on, and the driver can't see me. The central doors open and a man in a wheelchair is pushed out by his wife. There's just enough room for me to squeeze by them, holding Lady's collar.

But before the doors hiss shut again, one of the passengers calls out, "'Scuse me, driver! There's a dog just got on, on its own!"

And I see the driver open his little door and start to come up the aisle towards us.

I don't wait; instead I tug on Lady's collar and get off while the passengers and driver look on, smiling at the dog who can boldly get on and off a bus.

Half a minute later, I'm left waiting again, watching the bus in the distance.

To walk would take an hour or so. I'm exhausted and weak, but I have no choice. To make it easier on my feet, I go down the tarmac path onto the beach, where I start walking. It's the first boiling-hot day of the summer, and Lady runs in and out of the waves to cool down. Even the seagulls seem to be complaining about the heat.

I walk faster towards Culvercot and the church that overlooks the sea. No one notices the line of footprints that appear in the wet sand, or the two tiny semicircles of translucent fingernails that dance along above them.

What will Dad do now?

He promised he'd help me. Can I trust him?

To be honest, I don't really have much choice.

The afternoon heat seems to be increasing, and I can feel sweat droplets forming on my forehead.

If I can feel them, then that means someone could see them. I look down and there is the faintest sheen of sweat forming an outline. I have got to get out of the heat. I look up the beach and at the long flight of stone steps that leads to the church.

If I say a prayer at all it's one of those silent in-my-head types, and either the prayer is answered or I am just lucky: the church is open. Lady and I step inside the cool, dark interior—so cool that I give a little shiver at the contrast with the heat outside. I'm the only person in there. It smells of wood polish and incense, and I feel safe as I sit down on one of the back pews, the wood cold under my bottom. The heat and the swimming have worn Lady out, and she stretches out beneath a pew.

It's nice there in the shade. I think part of the tiredness that washes over me is because I can't properly close my eyes and shut out the brightness of daylight. *Maybe,* I think, *those countless little blinks that we do all day are a way of resting our eyes from the light?*

I've been in this church loads of times with Gram. She says she likes it because of the "liturgy," which I think is the words used in the service. It's all Old English, with "thee" and "thou"—just like people who never go to church always think it is. Gram also once said, approvingly, that no one ever plays the guitar with the hymns—which I think is a shame, but Gram doesn't.

As I sit, I slump forward, resting my head on my clasped hands, and I remember the words of something I used to say in church when I went with Gram. It's like a prayer, but it's not a prayer because you don't say "amen" at the end of it. Everyone says it together:

We believe in one God, the Father, the Almighty:
Maker of heaven and earth, and of all things visible
and invisible. . . .

"Just put it there, Linda—on that table. Thanks, pet."

I have been lost in thought and didn't even hear them come in, although the door is a heavy, studded one. I look round and there are two ladies who I sort of recognize but I don't know their names. Well, I know one because I heard it: the younger one is Linda.

Each is carrying a cardboard box, which she puts on a trestle table at the back, right behind me.

I'm staring at Linda because I *do* know her from somewhere. It's when she talks that it dawns on me.

"Ee, that's heavy, tharriz! I've gorra be careful not to dee me back in!"

The broad Geordie, the suntan: it's the lady from Geordie Bronze, and she's unpacking tins of soup, and bags of pasta, and loaves of bread.

"You better just leave it in the box, Linda. They've got to take it to the church hall anyway."

Back in the box it all goes, and I know what this is: it's stuff for the church's food bank, where people donate food for the poor.

I want to go after Linda and show her that I am invisible. Show her what happened after I used the tanning bed that she gave me. It's not like I'm proud or anything; it's just that if I'm going to have to get used to being invisible, she might be a good starting point. Perhaps?

But I'm too late. They've gone, the door shutting behind them with a padded thud, and I'm alone again in the silent church.

The boxes are on the table, lit by a shaft of light coming through one of the stained-glass windows, and I tell you: if this was a film, there'd be a choir of angels to accompany it, singing, "*Aah-aah-aah* . . ."

The bread is first to be opened. It's brown, nutty, and delicious. Most of the stuff in the boxes isn't much good to me: bags of flour and rice, raw eggs and vegetables (though I eat a carrot, which is OK), and tins that need an opener. There's a can of baked beans with a ring-pull top, so I open that and start to eat the beans with the bread. In the other box there's a bag of apples. I'm eating greedily, and spilling stuff, and I'm just about to take a huge bite of apple when the church door opens again.

I drop the apple and dodge behind the pew just in time to see the apple roll across the tiled floor towards Linda, who is carrying in another box. It's kind of like an instinctive reaction, this hiding. In reality there's no need to, as I'm invisible, but I'm glad I do because, looking down, I see there's a slop of un-invisibilized food hovering at stomach level.

Linda puts the box down and gawps, first at the apple, and then at the table. The other woman follows her in a few seconds later, holding two full bags.

"Ee, my God, looka that!" says Linda.

The other lady says nothing.

"It was rollin' towards me, the apple was. It just kind of dropped and rolled."

"Well, who's been at the food? We've only been to your car and back, Linda."

"Th' must still be here, Maureen."

"It'll be one of them choirboys," says Maureen. Then she raises her voice. "This food's for the poor people, you little sods!" she calls.

And it echoes around the building: "*Sods . . . sods . . . sods . . .*"

"Prob'ly hidin'," says Linda, and she starts marching up the aisle, looking left and right along the pews.

By now I've slid myself beneath the wooden pew and she doesn't see the strange blob of liquid slop in the shade.

"Was it you?" I hear her say, and my heart leaps.

But she's a few pews away, bent down.

"I've found the culprit, Maureen. There's a dog here!"

I hear Lady's tail thumping on the ground as she wags it.

"Ee, you cheeky monkey, what are you doin' here?"

Maureen says, "Who'd leave a dog in a church?"

And I stay there until Linda and Maureen decide to leave Lady where she is as she probably belongs to the organist or someone, and they leave a few minutes later, chuckling about a dog who would steal food from poor families and how they'll have a word with the Reverend Robinson.

I crawl out from under the pew, and I'm beat. I'm just

done. I'm exhausted from the running, and the hiding, and the lying, and the whole lot of it.

I pick up one of the little cushions that are used for kneeling on. I position it like a pillow, and I stretch out on the pew in the dark and try to sleep, but can't, because I can still see, despite closing my eyes. I find a hymn book and place it, open, over my face, and that shuts out most of the light.

Maybe, when I wake up, everything will be all right.

CHAPTER EIGHTY-FIVE

I hear the organ start.

The organist must have come in to practice. I take the book off my face and look around. The shafts of light coming through the stained-glass windows have shifted around the interior of the church.

I cannot tell what time it is, but it must be much later. The boxes of food have gone from the table at the back, so someone has been in, I know that. Lady is still asleep beneath the pew.

I walk slowly down the wide aisle of the church towards the altar at the front, and bits of the church services that I used to go to with Gram keep coming back to me.

I even know, without guessing, that the piece the organist is playing is Bach. This one is Bach's Toccata and Fugue in D Minor. I bet you'd know it if you heard it, honestly.

It's not like I feel religious or anything. I'm not having some huge revelation or being "filled with the holy spirit" like

Suki Kinghorn says she was after she went on some church camp and wouldn't shut up about her "new best friend," Jesus. (For a while the Knight twins teased her about her "invisible friend," which I thought was a bit mean, long before the idea of an invisible friend became more real than I would like.)

It's more like remembering. I gaze up at a huge carving hanging over the altar, of Jesus on the cross. It used to scare me when I was little. It's painted in colors, and there's blood on his hands and feet, and I remember the story of Jesus dying and coming back to life and I remember thinking, even when I was little, how unlikely that was.

Of course, that was all before I turned invisible, which I wouldn't have believed was possible when I was little either.

Is that me? Am I a living ghost?

I look down at myself: my invisible self, casting no shadow, like the vampires in films.

Can I live my life, my *whole life,* like this?

CHAPTER EIGHTY-SIX

Outside the church, it's light, but the temperature has dropped a bit with the advancing evening. There's no breeze, but at least I'm not going to sweat anymore. Out to sea, a huge thundercloud is building up, and the air is so thick that it even seems to muffle the sound of traffic on the seafront.

Behind me, through the thick door, the organist is still playing the Bach, which echoes in my head as I look up to the big clock on the side of the church. It's nearly nine, which is OK because . . .

Nine?

Nine o'clock?

As in, nine o'clock *tonight*?

I'm staring at the clock and listening to the muffled organ, and I see the minute hand clunk round to twelve. As it does, a thought stumbles forward to the front of my mind.

Boydy.

Light the Light.

Light the Light *tonight*.

He told me not to forget. I said, "Boydy, how could I forget?"

I forgot. He'll never forgive me if I'm not there. Never ever. How could I have been so selfish, stupid, unthinking?

Poor Boydy. He's put his heart and soul into this, he's spent money, he's risked ridicule, and now?

He *told* me it was going to be tonight. He's invited loads of people: journalists and TV crews especially. I tried to tell him that I didn't think it would be the sort of thing that people would turn up for—you know, "managing his expectations"—but, typical Boydy, he didn't want to know. All of which makes it even more important that I, at the very least, turn up.

Now I have let him down, and that's not what friends do. I can't even smile at my surprise at the realization that Boydy is now my friend: a proper friend, the kind you don't want to let down, because you know they won't let *you* down. I have been so wrapped up in my own problems that I've forgotten the thing he has been planning for months.

With no mobile phone, I can't call him to apologize, or tell him where I am, or to tell him this:

I'll be there.

If I run.

If I run from here to St. Mary's Lighthouse, I can get there by nine. What is it? Three miles? Four? I have never run that far, ever. But now I start, Lady trotting excitedly by my side, and the rhythmic action of putting one bare foot in front of the other is kind of hypnotic.

Soon I'm past the little amusement arcade and the tandoori restaurant in Culvercot, round the bend where there's the side road going down to the beach and the promenade.

Five minutes later, my breathing is deep, but steady.

"I'm coming, Boydy," I pant to myself.

Culvercot ends with a Welcome to Whitley Bay sign. The lighthouse is in the distance, white against the slowly darkening sky; there's the big white dome of the old Spanish City dance hall that's all boarded up; and I'm running past Waves swimming pool with its bossy attendants, and still Lady is sticking by my side. (She's usually pretty hopeless at "heel," but right now, she's like a dog in an obedience trial. Perhaps she thinks if she runs ahead, she won't be able to find me again.)

I've got it worked out. I don't want to steal Boydy's thunder. I'll wait until he's done the light thing. *That's* when I'll tell the people who are there. I'm assuming *someone* will turn up.

I'm running past people out for an evening walk. My breathing is heavy and rasping now. Noisy.

I just don't care anymore. I know people are turning in surprise at the sound of my feet slapping the paving stones, my panting, but if anything I'm getting faster because I know time is running out. My feet are agony now, especially my heel where I trod on the china dog, and I have to get onto the sand, so I go down the sandy path to the beach, where the running is slower but less painful.

We're nearly there. Five hundred yards more? Four hundred?

I picture Boydy to keep me going—his hurt face when he realizes I'm not going to be there for his big moment—and I scramble across the rocks to get onto the causeway to the island, slashing another cut in the bottom of my foot on a razor-clam shell, but still I keep running.

"Boydy!" I shout. "Wait!"

As if he could possibly hear me above the sound of the music that's playing on his home-rigged sound system. He's blasting out Felina. Of course he is. Because that's just what I need.

"Light the light
I need your love tonight.
I wanna see you, see you tonight. . . ."

The tide is retreating, but there is still water on either side of the causeway.

I'm close enough now to see them in the twilight. There's a group of people, but not many: maybe six or something. Is that everyone who has turned up?

Boydy is standing up some steps, elevated above them, and he's peering out along the causeway. He's looking to see if I'm coming, I'm sure of it.

The music ends suddenly, the way so many of Mum's songs do: a thrashing chord and a double drum beat—*boom-boom.*

Lady has evidently decided she isn't going to lose me, and she has run ahead towards the group,

"I'm here! I'm coming!" I scream through my exhausted breathing. My blood is pounding in my ears.

The small crowd turns to the source of the noise.

Then there's a light, and it's coming towards me. I turn in shock, and the car headlights are thundering at me along the causeway. It's Dad at the wheel, and Gram is next to him.

"DAD!" I shout, or at least I think I shout.

I don't really know. I know it's the last thing I hear.

He doesn't see me, obviously.

He feels the impact, though, as the car plows into me. All he sees is the splash as I bounce off the car and hit the water.

THE WHITLEY BAY NEWS GUARDIAN

Lighthouse Teen Still "Serious"

Doctors at North Tyneside General Hospital said last night that Ethel Leatherhead, the twelve-year-old girl involved in a freak motor accident on the lighthouse causeway in Whitley Bay on Thursday night, was still in a "serious" condition.

The driver of the car, Mr. Richard Malcolm, was Ethel's father. Her grandmother—Mr. Malcolm's former mother-in-law, Mrs. Beatrice Leatherhead—was a passenger in the car when it struck the teenager at 9:00 p.m. and knocked her into the sea.

Bystanders who helped with the dramatic rescue had gathered on St. Mary's Island for a "Light the Light" ceremony. A classmate of Ethel's—Elliot Boyd, thirteen, of Woolacombe Drive, Monkseaton—had been planning to effect an unofficial "relighting" of the decommissioned lighthouse.

Moments before the light was due to be switched on, they heard cries for help from Mr. Malcolm. Elliot Boyd waded into the waist-deep water where his classmate was lying facedown, apparently dead. Elliot, a qualified first-aider, dragged her lifeless body to safety, and he performed CPR until paramedics arrived fifteen minutes later.

It has not yet been established why Ethel was unclothed at the time of the accident.

A spokesman for North East Ambulance Service said, "Ethel is very lucky to be alive. She was, for all intents and purposes, dead when the ambulance reached her. She had no pulse and was not breathing."

She was rushed to the waiting ambulance, where paramedics performed emergency defibrillation—the administering of a controlled electric shock to stimulate the heart.

Det. Insp. Maxwell Ford of Northumbria Police said, "This was clearly a tragic accident and the police will not be pursuing charges against Mr. Malcolm. Our thoughts are with Ethel and her family."

North Tyneside Council, which owns St. Mary's Lighthouse, yesterday responded to public pressure and withdrew an earlier statement calling for action against Elliot Boyd for trespass.

"Without Elliot Boyd's quick and selfless actions, Ethel would almost certainly have died at the scene. In light of his heroism, we are taking no further action," said the mayor of North Tyneside, Cllr. Pat Peel.

The Reverend Henry Robinson, vicar of St. George's Church in Culvercot, where Ethel and her grandmother are members of the congregation, led an open-air vigil at the scene of the accident last night. It was attended by churchgoers and students of Whitley Bay Academy, which Ethel attends. He said, "Please pray for Ethel. She is a lovely girl with a wonderful smile, and we want her to make a full recovery."

CHAPTER EIGHTY-SEVEN

Things I notice when I open my eyes:

1. I'm not at home.

That's it. That's all I notice.

The light hurts, so I close my eyes again. (Closing my eyes makes it go dark again, but I don't notice this. Not at first.)

My head hurts. My chest hurts. Everything hurts.

I don't know how long it is until I open my eyes again, but when I do, this is what I notice:

1. I'm still not at home.
2. It's dark outside. I can see an orangey streetlight through a half-closed blind if I turn my eyes one way.
3. Looking the other way, I see there's a man sitting in a chair. His head is slumped forward.
4. The man is my dad.
5. I am visible again.

CHAPTER EIGHTY-EIGHT

I learn that Dad and Gram stayed with me at the hospital, never leaving my side, till I came round.

Fractured skull, two broken ribs, extensive bruising, cardiac arrest. That is, a heart attack.

I was dead when Boydy and Dad pulled me out of the water.

I was hit by the car, thrown into the water unconscious, drowned, and suffered a heart attack.

(In case you're wondering—and I know I would—I didn't have a "near death experience" and see what was happening as I floated above the scene, or feel drawn towards a bright light, or any of that stuff. I don't remember any of it.)

So I was pretty darn dead-as-a-doornail, brown-bread dead.

Now, though, I'm sitting up in bed.

Everything aches.

Gram and Dad stayed at the hospital until I "stabilized,"

taking turns to sit by my bed or sleep in the room that the hospital has for relatives of accident victims.

Gram cries a lot. She looks twenty years older. She keeps saying, “I’m sorry, Boo. I’m sorry. I’m so, so sorry.”

Dad says sorry a lot too, but he doesn’t cry. Instead he grips my hand—sometimes a bit too hard, but I don’t mind.

I think he’s saying sorry for running me over, which wasn’t really his fault.

Gram is saying sorry for my whole life.

The nurses come and go.

The doctors shine lights into my eyes, and murmur to each other, and ask me things like “What is your name?” to check my brain is OK.

No one has mentioned invisibility.

Good.

CHAPTER EIGHTY-NINE

A few days later, Boydy visits, and I end up in agony because he makes me laugh and I have broken ribs.

He brings me flowers! I have never been bought flowers before, ever, and it's nice.

"All right, Eff?" He has a solemn expression. "I nicked these for ya. Some fella down the corridor's died, so I figured he wouldn't miss 'em."

I stare at him.

He keeps a straight face, but not for long. "Kidding! Gave up me daily doughnut ration to buy you these."

That's what makes me laugh. He is poking fun at himself, at me, at everything, and once I start to laugh I try to stop myself because it hurts, but I can't, and I moan so hard one of the nurses comes scuttling in, tutting at Boydy, who has helped himself to a banana from a bowl of fruit at the end of my bed.

I'm in my own hospital room, not a ward, probably

because I've just come out of Intensive Care, and Dad has got up and left us alone.

Boydy sits on the bed, peels the banana, and takes a big bite.

"Glad you made it, Effow," he says with a full mouth. "If you'da snuffed it, there'da been a right ol' kerfuffle. Turns out, I'm a hero. Fanks for that!"

I feel myself starting to laugh again. "Don't!" I say.

"No, I mean it. People look at me a bit different. I'm not just the fat London loudmouth." He pauses and looks at me while he finishes the banana. "I know what they say, what they thought. I'm not stupid. But it's just me. It's who I am. Bit loud, a bit brash. I can't be anyone else. If you don't like it, tough."

"But I do like it."

He grins. "Yeah, well. You just got lousy taste, ain'tcha! You gonna eat those grapes?"

The nurse returns with a thermometer and a little cup of painkillers. While she takes my temperature, Boydy busies himself with the grapes, tossing them up and catching them in his mouth.

He finishes the grapes and takes something from his pocket: Jesmond Knight's mobile phone.

"He's back from the school trip tonight. This is wiped as clean as a baby's how's-yer-father."

"Hang on, Boydy. It's theft, isn't it? I mean, you've effectively stolen his phone."

Boydy grins. "Me? I think you mean 'we.' And besides, it's only theft if you intend to permanently deprive the owner of his property. This, I was just borrowing. Thought I'd shove it through his mail slot on the way home."

When the nurse leaves, Boydy pulls up the chair next to me and leans in close.

"So . . . did they find anything? The doctors? Anything weird? Any bits of you missing, or invisible?"

I shake my head.

"You haven't told them?"

Another shake. "Why would I? It's got nothing to do with the accident."

"But it's why your dad didn't see you. It's why it happened."

"And I became visible again when I died. Just like my tears, my puke, my blood. Once they left my body, they became visible. I guess the same happened when I was drowning: whatever was making me invisible stopped working. There's no proof of anything. All that's left is that last bit of the powder. You have still got it, haven't you?"

His silence says everything.

Eventually he murmurs, "It was in my trouser pocket. When I jumped into the water to get you, it all washed away."

"All of it?"

He nods.

I'm not even angry. If anything, I'm relieved.

Those people who know me the best—they know the truth.

Everyone else? Well, "extraordinary claims require extraordinary proof."

I reach, wincing, for my laptop and open it up. I'm about to show Boydy the video I took of my last venture into invisibility when I remember that I'm naked in it. I don't want to embarrass him, so I fast-forward to when I'm lying down on the tanning bed and things are not quite so obvious.

It's not a *bad* picture, exactly. It's in focus. It's just that the brilliance of the tanning bed's UV light creates a kind of blurry glow around me so that when I fade away, it's . . .

"Not all that convincing, is it?" Boydy says, looking glum. It could easily be a simple homemade special effect.

"It wouldn't persuade anyone." Then I smile. "But we know the truth."

CHAPTER NINETY

There are voices outside my room, and seconds later three girls come in, in school uniform: Kirsten Olen, Katie Pelling, and—of all people—Aramynta Fell.

The girls have been sent as a delegation from Mr. Parker's class to deliver a get-well card signed by all my classmates who are not on the adventure-center trip to the Lake District.

There aren't enough chairs in my room, so between them and Boydy they sort of share bed space and the two chairs that are there.

Kirsten and Katie behave as if everything is fine, and has always been fine.

And actually—that's OK by me.

But there's something bugging me about Aramynta. I can't put my finger on it. She's even being nice to Boydy.

She's behaving . . . suspiciously, I suppose. She definitely doesn't want to be there, and it is separate from the fact that she's always been at the very least frosty to me, if not completely hostile. There's something nagging at me, a memory trying to come to the surface, but I can't quite get to it.

We're talking about Mr. Parker, and Boydy's riot-causing Whitley's Got Talent performance, and Boydy's pretending to be all mysterious and saying he can't reveal the secret of his trick, when Katie says:

"You were close to it. You saw it, didn't you, Mynt?"

Mynt.

That's when it comes back to me. Jesmond's phone conversation in his bedroom, when he was arranging with Aramynta to claim the reward on Geoffrey.

I just blurt it out.

"Thanks for coming. But before you go: Aramynta? How much reward money did you collect from old Mrs. Abercrombie?"

And I know I've got her—not from what she says, but from the color she goes, which is the brightest pink I have ever seen on anyone.

"I . . . I . . . *What?*"

None of the others has any idea what I am talking about—not even Boydy. I tell them what I have guessed about Aramynta's role: delivering free newspapers and takeaway leaflets and identifying houses with pets that could easily be taken by Jesmond and Jarrow, to hold until a reward was offered. And if no reward was offered, it was an easy job just to return the dogs or cats they had taken.

I'm kind of making it up as I'm saying it, but I know I'm right.

Aramynta doesn't even try to deny it. She just stares at the floor.

"The twins are back tonight, aren't they?" I go on. "So unless you want me to go to the police—and I will, I promise—you will return the reward money to Mrs. Abercrombie."

"You . . . You have no proof," says Aramynta. But I can tell she's scared.

"Oh yes we do, don't we, Boydy?"

Boydy—who, till this point, has been watching me, astounded—snaps his mouth shut and springs to life. He reaches into his pocket and pulls out Jesmond Knight's distinctive red-and-white-striped phone with a football crest on it.

"Sure do," he says without missing a beat.

He stands up and addresses them like they are in a court, with his lawyer's voice. "Do you recognize this mobile telephone? Of course you do—it belongs to Jesmond Knight, does it not?"

"Does it not?" I have to bite my cheek to stop myself smiling. I can see where this is going. He's brilliant.

Aramynta nods.

Boydy turns the phone on and starts to dial a number.

"No passcode?" I ask.

He shrugs. "A careless crook is a caught crook, as my dad would say." Then he adds quietly, "And he should know. Anyway . . ." It's like he's pretending to talk to himself. "FaceTime seems to be working. Hello, Jarrow. How lovely to see and hear you!"

On the little screen of the phone is a stunned-looking Jarrow Knight. It looks like she's on the school coach. There's other people around her, but the only one I can pick out is Jesmond, who puts his face close to the phone's camera and snarls:

"Is that my phone, Boyd? You, my friend, are *dead*."

But Boydy just grins, super-confident.

"I don't think so, Jezza." He resumes his lawyer voice. "You see, on this very device, I found a good deal of evidence. Text records, call logs, the lot, all leading to the firm conclusion that several crimes have been committed—those of obtaining money by deception, and of holding an animal in contravention of the Domestic Animals Act of 1968. All of the evidence points to a prima facie case that the perpetrators of the said offenses are Mr. Jesmond Knight and his twin sister, Jarrow, of number forty Links Avenue, Whitley Bay."

He stops and points a dramatic finger at Aramynta. "And *you*, Miss Aramynta Fell, are an accomplice to the crime and will be prosecuted accordingly."

It's a bluff—a massive bluff—but it's enough.

Aramynta has turned white.

On the phone's screen, Jarrow is chewing her bottom lip furiously, and blinking hard.

We've got them.

Boydy turns back to the phone, which he's holding up selfie-style so that Jarrow and Jesmond can see the scene properly.

"Prosecuted, that is, unless all the money obtained by said deception is returned to the victims within a week." Boydy leans close to the phone. "Case closed. Sort it out, will ya?" He looks at his watch. "Mynt? Queenie Abercrombie can be first. You've got an hour until we call her to check it's been done. Got it? Go on, then."

Aramynta nods and practically runs from the room.

Boydy turns his face back to the phone, and he's dropped the posh voice. "I mean it, Jarrow, Jesmond. *All* the money returned, or everyone gets to know—starting with your dad. This phone will be posted through your mail slot tonight, but don't worry—I've backed up all the data. Bye-bye!" Without waiting for a response, he ends the call.

Katie and Kirsten have watched all this with mounting astonishment.

"What a jerk!" says Kirsten.

"Never liked her. Not really," adds Katie.

CHAPTER NINETY-ONE

After the girls leave, I ask Boydy, "That stuff about all the data you found on the phone?"

"Hmmm?"

"Were you just bluffing?"

"Not entirely. But, you know, when it comes to bluffing, Effow, I've learned from the best."

I've no idea what he means, but I will soon.

Three Weeks Later

CHAPTER NINETY-TWO

I'm out of the hospital, but I'm still aching all over and I have stitches in my scalp.

Dad has rented a house in Monkseaton. He wants me and Gram to move in.

To be honest, I think he wants *me* to move in and has asked Gram out of politeness, but I hope she does. It'd be fun.

In the end, I had to ask Gram to stop saying sorry.

She had been doing *exactly* what Mum asked her to do. For my sake, she endured ten years living as Beatrice Leatherhead instead of her real name, Belinda Mackay. She worried every day that someone might recognize her, or make the connection between her and "Felina."

She persuaded Great-Gran to go along with the deception, on the promise that she would tell me the truth when I was "old enough." But by then she was so far into her lies that she couldn't extract herself.

I grew up as Ethel Leatherhead, and that is who I am. I

did *not* grow up as "Boo" Mackay (or Malcolm? Who knows?), daughter of the tragic princess of pop, Miranda "Felina" Mackay—and that suits me fine.

Who wants to be *that* visible?

And if Gram hadn't lied, what would be different?

My mum still would not be here. That wouldn't have changed.

My dad would still have had his "lost years," as he calls them, and would still have come back.

I might have grown up in London, but do you know what? I went there on a school trip once and it's not all it's cracked up to be. There's no beach, no seagulls, no lighthouse.

And there'd be no Boydy, a proper friend who makes me laugh every day.

I'm going round there later. He invited me with this text:

Mr. Elliot Boyd invites
Ms. Ethel Leatherhead
To an evening of supper and revelation
18 July, 7:00 p.m.

Supper "and revelation"?

What the totally heck?

CHAPTER NINETY-THREE

I'm at Boydy's at seven, and when he answers the door, he's changed out of his school uniform (which is strange for him) and he's in a clean white shirt, although he's wearing summer shorts. He looks shiny, like he's had a bath.

When I go into his front room, I burst out laughing because there are two candles lit on the dining table, even though it's still light.

"Boydy! What are the candles for?" I laugh and then wince because laughing still hurts a bit.

"Oh, them? Nothing. I, erm . . . I think my mum left them there from some client or something from before, that'll be it."

"Where is your mum? I'll go and say hello."

"Oh, she's erm . . . out."

He's acting shifty, or nervous. Perhaps he's edgy about the revelation, whatever that's going to be. I would expect Boydy and me to get down to playing some music, or the Xbox, or watching TV, but instead he has opened up the French windows onto the terrace (which—now that I've written it—sounds *much* grander than it really is, as it's actually a little paved area of the tiny backyard).

He brings me a juice with ice, and takes a deep breath.

"You're not the only one with secrets, you know, Eff?"

He plays with his hands for a bit.

I wait patiently. I can tell this isn't easy for him.

That's when he says that his dad, the big-shot London lawyer, is currently serving a seven-year prison sentence in Durham Jail for fraud.

"Wow," I say, which sounds a bit odd as it comes out, but it's what I feel.

"That's not all, though." He's not looking at me while he says this, and the next bit he just blurts out.

His mum has bipolar disorder, which he explains is a mental condition that means you are sometimes crazily energetic to the point of being manic, and sometimes horribly exhausted and depressed. Sometimes she can't work, and once she was even admitted to the hospital.

"When was that?" I ask, but I think I already know the answer.

"When I started hanging out with you. My aunty came came up from London for a bit, but she didn't want to be here. I needed someone who would just . . . I dunno. Not be horrible to me. With Mum gone, you were about the only one."

I sip my juice in silence. I don't know what to say.

Eventually, he breaks the silence.

"Does it matter?" he says.

I must look blank.

"Does it matter that my dad's a crook and my mum's a . . ." He thinks for a moment. "That my mum's mentally unstable?"

"Matter? Of course it matters! I mean, they're both pretty big deals."

"No, I mean . . . does it matter to you?"

And that's when I get it.

"No, Boydy. It doesn't mean I like you less. We all have rivers to cross, but we all have the materials to build bridges."

He curls his lip at me, scornfully.

"It's something my gran says," I explain.

"Blimey. I thought you'd gone all serious on me."

Then he talks. About his mum's illness (which started years ago), his dad's desperation when his law company started to lose money, and the small deception that grew into a big fraud, and his dad's trial, which happened just as his mum was admitted to the hospital.

"He's a nice guy," says Boydy of his dad. "You'd like him. He . . . He made some bad choices, though."

"And now you're in charge?" I say.

"Well, when Mum's bad I've gotta be, really. Right now, she's fine. She's visiting my dad. Now—are you hungry? It's a new recipe I'm trying."

That's when I realize the reason he's such a good cook. It's because he has to make stuff for himself when his mum's not around.

I feel like I'm kind of seeing him in a whole new light. He's odd and jittery, though, all the way through supper, which he insists we eat at the table instead of from plates on our knees, which is our usual way. It's some beef thing, which is lovely, and I keep going, "Mmmm, yummy" and stuff, but he's still distracted.

Eventually, he says, "Effel?"

"Boydy?"

"There's something I've been meaning to say."

"Yes?"

I'm on my guard now, because I thought all the revelations were over. What's he going to say? Oh, hang on. Surely not. *Surely not?*

I hold my hand up and say, "Boydy. Stop there. I hope you're not going to 'ask me out' or anything like that?"

There's a long pause, during which Boydy just stares at me. His shoulders have drooped and he looks a little sad.

"Don't be crazy," he says eventually. "I wasn't going to ask you anything like that at all. I mean, we're best mates, yeah? I like being your friend, and it would be a shame to spoil it, wouldn't it? I mean, to risk our friendship by . . . by . . . No, I wasn't going to ask you that. *Tsk,* honestly, Effel. What do you take me for?"

Well, that's pretty emphatic. Phew.

"What were you going to ask me, then?"

"Oh, erm . . ." He thinks for a minute. He's lost his train of thought. "Would you like sorbet?"

"That was it?"

"It's lemon. All the flavor, half the calories."

He's a good friend, Boydy.

But that's all we are. Just friends.

Four Weeks Later

CHAPTER NINETY-FOUR

Boydy's dad, it turns out, was not a stand-up-in-court sort of lawyer. More like a sit-behind-a-computer-all-day sort of lawyer, doing stuff like taxes and something called "digital forensic accounting," which I can't even begin to understand.

His prison isn't a metal-bars-and-hard-labor sort of prison either. It's called a Category C Prison, and he's allowed visits, and a computer and the Internet and stuff.

What it means, though, is that as a favor to Boydy he is investigating the payment I made to a bank in China—Hong Kong, actually—for Dr. Chang His Skin So Clear.

Boydy told him that I made the payment (on Gram's card) and didn't receive any goods, so we didn't have to explain the whole invisibility thing. Mr. Boyd—Pete—says there are two likely outcomes of an initial investigation.

The first is that it is a small company changing banks, moving accounts, but keeping the same physical and IP addresses. These, he says, are fairly easy to track down.

The other is that it is a much bigger corporation, doing lots of different types of transactions between countries, and opening and closing bank accounts in different banks all the time with multiple fake addresses, and somehow not leaving a trace in the electronic world—to keep two, three, four steps ahead of people like him. They are often impossible to track down, especially without a large team and—in this case—fluent Mandarin and/or Cantonese. Pete has neither.

If it is the first—and Pete says he is optimistic—then there's a chance we can obtain some more of the strange concoction.

Also, he is friends with a fellow prisoner in his cell block who knows both Mandarin and Cantonese and who says he will help.

What then?

Who knows?

CHAPTER NINETY-FIVE

It's nearly the end of term, and I wish I could say that something awful has happened to Jesmond and Jarrow, but nothing has. They have, however, been *very* quiet. There have been no more posters on the lampposts. Word has circulated about that particular scam, and any popularity they had seems to have evaporated.

Mrs. Abercrombie got her reward money back.

As for the others? Aramynta tells me they did, as well, and I'm going to have to trust her.

I suppose that's a good result.

I haven't told anyone yet about the Felina-is-my-mum thing, though I don't want it to be a big secret.

I'm still wondering what to do about my name. Ethel Leatherhead is not my real name; it's Tiger Pussycat "Boo" Mackay.

Although what's real and what's not has been questionable lately.

And my skin? Much better, thank you.

Much better.

Five Weeks Later

CHAPTER NINETY-SIX

It's my birthday tomorrow, my thirteenth.

It hasn't rained for weeks now. The Links is getting yellow and dry, and the cloudless evening sky is a flat, endless, deep violet.

We *would* do this tomorrow evening on my actual birthday, but Dad has to fly back to New Zealand to sort out some stuff, so we've brought it forward a day.

Is it a birthday party? Not really. I didn't want it to be—it's more important than that.

Besides, it would be the strangest thirteenth birthday party guest list, all of us gathered on the big flat rock underneath the lighthouse.

There's:

- Me, obviously.
- Gram.
- Lady.

- Boydy and his mum AND his dad, who is out of jail on a day license, which is when you are allowed out of jail to see your family. (He's nice. Basically, an older, fatter version of Boydy and not at all criminal-looking. Boydy's mum is smiley and shy.)
- Mrs. Abercrombie and Geoffrey. (I know, but I kind of had to invite her because I wanted Gram to have a friend there—and anyway, she's much nicer to me now that Geoffrey has stopped growling at me. She'd be even nicer if she knew it was thanks to me that she got her reward money back.)
- Reverend Henry Robinson.
- Kirsten Olen (who I have now told about Mum/Felina, but not about the invisible stuff. Not yet).
- The same guy from the *Whitley Guardian* who was at Great-Gran's hundredth. (Boydy's local-hero status is about to be further enhanced and he's going to become even more bumptious, but I don't mind so much now.)
- And—of all people—Mr. Parker, and a jolly lady called "Nicky" who he introduced as his partner. (I had not had Mr. Parker down as the sort to have a girlfriend. Mr. Parker, it turns out, is a secret lighthouse enthusiast. He told Boydy that he could borrow the school's mixing desk and amplifiers, and even went into school

during the holidays to collect them. I thought that was quite a big deal, but Mr. Parker called it "a mere trifle for a fellow pharophile.")

Nothing, and no one, it is turning out, is what they first appear.

Boydy is pacing up and down, looking all nervous. He had a haircut last week, and has shaved off the fluff that was on his chin, which looks much better and in fact there's not much of a double chin under the fluff after all. He's also got himself some new clothes. It's nice: it's like he has dressed up for the occasion. Not sure about the patterned shirt, to be honest, but at least his new stuff fits him. I found him a lighthouse keeper's cap on eBay (Who knew there were such things? Not me), which he loves.

There is another guest yet to arrive. Dad has gone to get Great-Gran from Priory View. Normally all the residents are in bed by nine, and they were very reluctant to let her go.

"Let her go?" I heard Dad say on the phone to them. "Are you keeping her prisoner or something, or is she a paying guest?"

That did it.

Only, they're late. Which wouldn't normally be much of a problem, but the causeway will be beneath water in about twenty minutes and we'll be stuck on St. Mary's Island overnight.

We're all anxiously peering along the causeway and up to the parking lot, hoping to see headlights coming towards us in the twilight.

Dad wouldn't miss this, would he?

I'm wearing Mum's T-shirt, the one that still smells of her a bit. I know it might change the smell, but somehow I don't mind. Not tonight.

"There they are!" calls Boydy, pointing to a pair of headlights coming towards us, and I breathe a small sigh of relief.

Next to Dad is Great-Gran, a tiny figure in the passenger seat. When the car pulls to a halt at the bottom of the steps, near the flat rock, I can see someone else as well, a man, sitting in the back seat.

"Who's that?" I ask Gram, but she has no idea.

We already have a wheelchair waiting, and I push it to the car to help Great-Gran out.

"Stanley?" I say when I get nearer and see who the old man in the back is.

"Yeah," chuckles Dad. "Your great-gran didn't want to come without her boyfriend, did you, Mrs. Freeman?"

Great-Gran smiles broadly and nods as she eases herself into the wheelchair; then she smiles her watery smile at me and says, "Hello, hinny."

Dad takes over the wheelchair while I go round and help Stanley out. He's frail, but steady on his feet.

"Hello, Boo," he says in a reedy old-man's voice. "I've heard all about you. It's very nice to see you."

(It's only afterwards that I wonder what he meant by that. Was it a reference to my invisibility? Had Great-Gran told him? I'm surprised to discover that I don't really mind either way.)

"Let us pray," says Reverend Robinson.

And as we all clasp our hands and start to mumble the Lord's Prayer, I keep my eyes open and look around at the gathering.

"Our Father, which art in heaven . . ."

Old Stanley stands behind Great-Gran's wheelchair and adjusts her woolen shawl for her. Great-Gran hasn't closed her eyes, but instead is focusing on a point far out to sea. Her lips move as she mouths the familiar words.

Mrs. Abercrombie has put Geoffrey down on the ground and he's much happier, sniffing around a rock pool with Lady.

Kirsten is in charge of the music, and she stands behind the school's mixing desk.

Everyone says "Amen," and there's a pause while a pair of seagulls answer loudly overhead.

"Are we ready?" asks Boydy.

"Hang on, hang on!" I say.

From my pocket I bring out a packet of Haribos, and open it, tipping them onto my hand. I give them out, one for each person.

"Some of you will remember that these were my mum's favorite," I say, and everyone has a sad smile as they start chewing.

Dad has to take his nicotine gum out first.

I nod over at Kirsten, who slides up a fader. Mum's song blasts out, rich and loud:

"You light up my life when I see you
And all I want is to be with you. . . .
You light the light in me—
Come on, baby, Light the light!"

When Mum starts singing "Light the Light," Boydy flicks the switch on the extension cord snaking up the lighthouse, and the light of a million candles drenches the flat rock, beaming down from the glass-encircled top thirty-eight yards above us.

It lights up the whole beach.

It lights up the sea.

It lights up the whole world, it feels like.

Stanley cheers, and claps, and shouts, "Bravo!"

And everyone else follows his lead.

Gram reaches down into her canvas bag and hands me the carved brass vase with the lid that I saw in her cupboard the day I went rummaging. It feels like a lifetime ago, and—in a way—it was.

I take a sniff of the T-shirt I'm wearing, then pry off the lid of the urn.

As Mum's song continues to play, and people suck their sweets, I hold up the urn to let the dusty contents spill out and they are immediately carried away on the wind, out to sea. One or two ashes have fallen by the rocks, and a wave soon swishes over them. In a few seconds not a single bit remains in the air or on the ground.

I look around. Everyone is crying. Not loud, not sobbing, but Gram is wiping her eyes, and even Dad has this funny expression, like he's struggling not to cry. Boydy's mouth has that upside-down smile that I have seen before.

Lady has lain down on the rock and is looking out to sea.

I say "Everyone is crying"—well, everyone but me.

Me? I'm grinning!

Everything is right; everything is perfect.

Dad has come up behind me and he squeezes my shoulders, and Gram's holding my hand.

"Bye, Mum!" I say, and I wave out to sea with my other hand.

That's when I decide that I'm going to be Ethel. Ethel Leatherhead. Family nickname: "Boo."

That's who I am.

No one has noticed that the causeway is now completely underwater. It's going to be an interesting night.

The End

ABOUT THE AUTHOR

Ross Welford's debut, *Time Traveling with a Hamster,* was called "smart, engaging, and heartwarming" in a starred review from *Booklist* and appeared on virtually every major award list in the UK. A former business journalist and television producer, Ross lives in London with his wife, children, border collie, and tropical fish. Follow him on Twitter at @rosswelford.